GODS ascendent

ALSO BY T. G. AYER

Young Adult Paranormal

THE VALKYRIE SERIES

Dead Radiance

Dead Radiance Audio

Dead Embers

Dead Embers Audio

Dead Chaos

Dead Chaos Audio

Dead Wrath

Dead Silence

Joshua - Dead Radiance

Joshua II - Dead Embers

Joshua III - Dead Chaos

Joshua IV - Dead Wrath

Joshua V - Dead Silence

THE HAND OF KALI SERIES

Fire & Shadow

Blood & Gold

Time & Fate

Fury & Virtue

Spirit & Soul

~

Adult Urban Fantasy

THE DARKWORLD SKINWALKER SERIES

Skin Deep

Lost Soul

Last Chance

Blood Promise

Scorched Fury

Fate's Edge

Grave Debt

Oath Bound

THE DARKWORLD SOULTRACKER SERIES

Blood Magic

Demon Kin

Blood Curse

Demon Soul

Blood Moon

Demon Bones

Blood Born

THE DARKWORLD IRIN CHRONICLES SERIES

Retribution

Requiem

Resonance

Revelation

THE DARKWORLD ORIGINS

Pyros (Logan)

Ailuros (Kailin)

~

THE DARK SIGHT SERIES

Dark Sight

Cursed Sight

Vissarion

Shadow Sight

Dark Prophecy

Cursed Prophecy

Shadow Prophecy

~

THE APSARA CHRONICLES

Immortal Bound

Gods Ascendent

Dominion Falling

Vengeance Born

Last Legion

~

A SEASON OF ASH AND BONE

Heartfyre

~

Adult Sci-Fi

HANDS ASSASSIN

Death Dealer

Death Mark

Death Strike

Hand's Assassins Series

~

NEW ADULT CONTEMPORARY THRILLER W/A TONI VALLAN

Beautiful Collision

Beautiful Conviction

~

PSYCHOLOGICAL HORROR W/A TONI VALLAN

Dark Shadows

Splinter

GODS ASCENDENT

THE APSARA CHRONICLES BOOK 2

This is a work of fiction. Names, characters, places or incidents are either the product of the author's imagination or are used fictitiously, and any resemblance to actual persons living or dead, business establishments, events or locales is entirely coincidental.

Cover art by Eduardo Priego

ISBN-10: 0995112630

ISBN-13: 978-0995112636

GODS ASCENDENT

USA TODAY BESTSELLING AUTHOR

T.G. AYER

CHAPTER 1

Vee ducked, glad when the bullet that had been aimed at her heart whizzed over her shoulder instead. Life seemed to keep throwing things at Vee, and she had to wonder when the day would come when she would not be able to survive it.

Not that she wasn't up for the challenge. It was just there was only so much a girl could take.

Vee grunted, pain flaring in her wing as the bullet tore through the fragile dragonfly skin, leaving a ragged hole behind. She glanced up at the wound, scowling at the ripped membrane, which—despite the injury—still shimmered, incandescent even in the murky light.

Vee sucked in a breath and sank low, shaking her head at her carelessness. She ought to be aware of the dangers by now, ought to know that despite the power of her ethereal appendages, they were still as fragile as a butterfly's wing.

Even without hellhounds and owl-shifters to watch her back.

A twinge of worry ripped through Vee's gut. But she couldn't afford to be distracted by thoughts of her missing bodyguard. Besides, she could protect herself well enough.

So said the guns and knives strapped to her upper thighs, the blades in her boots and the chakra tied to a loop at her waist, not to mention the trishula, hidden by godly glamor and currently hanging from a strap off her shoulder. She'd dressed in as close to all-black combat gear as she was inclined to get; jeans, turtleneck, warm multi-pocketed jacket and beanie to hide her hair. Her only concession to style? Refusing to wear combat boots and instead running after demons in a pair of medium-heeled, sexy knee-high leather boots.

No-one gets between Vee and her boots.

Fashion aside, Vee was well-equipped to protect herself. Or so she'd believed. She was now tempted by Mac's offer of bulletproof clothing, just so that she could minimize the risk. Nivaan had been pushing the issue as well—him being all protective of her was very sweet, but he'd better not push it. Still, considering what she came across on a daily basis, protective gear would be a welcome bonus.

Only problem? As far as she knew, bulletproof clothing didn't come in wing size.

Now, she folded her wings as close to her body as she could; she had to protect them as much as possible if she had any hope of using them should the time come.

How incongruous. A badass, demon-killing apsara with fragile diaphanous wings? It just didn't fit. That was like giving Lara Croft a feather instead of a knife.

Vee shifted her gaze around the warehouse, then peered between the two crates in front of her, trying to get a look at her assailant. The place was one gigantic room, housing thousands of boxes, crates, and small shipping containers. Lots of places to hide.

Two months had passed since her entire life had changed. Dreams had come true, her greater fears had been realized, and she'd been granted boons from the gods.

Boons, and gods. When related to Vee herself, she had to

wonder if such blessings would be a precursor to more trials and tribulations in the future. Good things never just fell into Vee's lap. They usually came accompanied by bad news, trouble, or a bucket load of crap.

And the gods? Gods were known to be a fickle lot—back when they used to exist, of course. Vee wanted to laugh. She'd never expected that she'd ever have to face a real god. Gods had faded from existence centuries ago, and most people had ceased believing. Vee included.

Now, she believed.

Wings were a damned good reason to believe.

So were chakras and trishulas.

Vee had just ducked behind a large box when it exploded, sending her flying backward. Shards of wood turned into a barrage of deadly missiles as they flew through the air. Vee landed hard on her back, narrowly missing a squadron of jagged stakes. The trishula clinked as it hit the floor and Vee felt the wings at her back crumpling beneath her weight. She knew by now not to be too concerned with smashing or folding the fragile appendages; they seemed impervious to that kind of damage.

Bullet-holes were another thing altogether.

Her wing now throbbed where the bullet had ripped it apart, aggravated from falling onto the injured appendage, and as she rolled over and scrambled for cover behind the nearest support column—a massive square concrete pole—Vee struggled for breath.

She forced herself to calm down, her mind going to her grandmother, Radha, channeling some of the matriarch's sense of peace. As Vee exhaled, she felt a veil of calm envelop her, and her thoughts cleared, the fog of pain evaporating, her mind quickening.

Vee reached for the chakra strapped to her waist. As soon as her fingers grazed the carved metal it began to shimmer, the gold letting off an intense glow. Vee frowned, aware the light would call attention to her hiding-place behind the pole. She drew a glamor over the weapon, the way Syama had taught her, summoning the power of the elements to camouflage the chakra's heavenly luminescence.

Vee had been passionately learning how to cast a glamor, pleasantly surprised to find the skill within her range of powers. The ability hadn't yet reached optimum efficiency though, so she worked with the assumption of a fifty percent chance of failure to hide herself.

Vee blinked. And now she hit an all-time low. The glamor wasn't working. She considered a second try, but she didn't have the time to mess around.

Instead, she took a breath, lifted her chin and yelled, "Stop. Give up. You know you've got nowhere to run." Her words echoed around the warehouse, disappearing into the rafters high above.

"Keep telling yourself that," Vee's assailant replied, his tone a deep, gravelly baritone. "You're injured. I can tell you're in pain." He took a long, loud and lusty breath and then let out a howling laugh. The sound was manic and held a note of utter joy within it.

Shit.

Vee scrambled for ideas. The bhayakara demon she fought was one who lived on pain, who created disharmony and grief in order to feed off the agony his victims experience. She'd never known such a thing was possible until Karan had called a few hours ago.

He'd given her a rundown on a possible pain demon loose on the streets of New York. She'd taken the case, passed the details on to her superior, Anthony Rossi, and had gone directly to the location. Which had turned out to be a warehouse filled with boxes, some of which contained bad imitations of life-sized Greek and Roman statues.

She grimaced as she ducked behind the pillar to avoid being

hit in the face by a chunk of curved white buttocks. Near Vee's foot was a lone breast, pale white with the nipple chopped off. Hard to tell if it had once belonged to a girl or a guy.

Vee shook her head. Focus.

Bhayakara were tricky demons, surreptitiously feeding on human pain and terror, deliberately causing that fear over a period of time. They were intelligent, diligent, and persistent.

And when they were desperate they became dangerous, and often careless.

Vee had gotten lucky that this particular demon hadn't fed in a while. He'd been desperate for a dose of energy-giving terror and had left a strong aural image at the home of his most recent victim. The woman had barely been alive, sucked dry of her emotions, but Vee had seen enough of his aura trail to follow him right to the warehouse.

She ducked down, thinking hard. A row of twenty-foot containers shielded her, though probably not for long. She raised her wings and tested them, glad to see that they appeared to be fully functional despite the gaping hole in the top of her right wing. The sight of it filled her with fury, and she dusted them out and softened her stance.

Bouncing on her knees, Vee flapped her wings and surged into the air, twisting and turning as the bhayakara followed her with a hail of gunfire. The demon was of the kind that seemed to like bigger weapons to compensate for his own inherent weaknesses.

He lived on the physical pain of others, but Vee suspected that he'd not tolerate pain well when inflicted upon himself. She banked left in a sharp turn and swooped down behind him, wincing as bullets slammed into concrete behind her, creating large gashes in ceilings and support columns and staircases.

He was far too indiscriminate, clearly blind to the fact that his behavior was likely to bring the building down onto his own head. Idiot.

Vee smiled though. She could use that against him. She sank between the crates, then scurried along the floor, hiding within the shadows. Gunshots echoed overhead, blasting away the corner of the crate in front of her. He'd created a large gap between her current hiding place and the next stack of palleted boxes.

Vee remained still and waited. Sure enough, he continued to riddle the crates ahead of her with bullet-holes. Vee smiled, watching as he drew closer and came into view, first a muscled shoulder and then a bulked-up torso, as he took small steps in a tight circle.

Trigger-happy asshole.

CHAPTER 2

"I can feel your pain."

His words were slurred, and Vee wasn't sure if it was the structure of his vocal chords or if he always sounded that drunk.

"Stop wasting your time, woman. You either come willing or die trying to escape."

Not a chance, buddy.

Vee pulled her chakra away from her back where she'd been holding it to hide its glow from the demon. She didn't care if he saw it now. It would be too late for him anyway.

She raised the chakra and sent it spinning toward him. The weapon made an odd sound, a sort of low thrum that reminded Vee of a helicopter's blades as they rotated before takeoff.

The sort of sound that made a person want to duck.

Not our fearless demon, though.

He turned in the direction of the oncoming chakra, a frown twisting his chunky black eyebrows together. His lips lifted and his wide mouth glittered with dagger-sharp teeth.

The deathly fine edge of the curved blade barely skimmed the top of the demon's head as he crouched to avoid the beheading.

Then he got to his feet, grinning as he turned to face Vee, his lips turning up in a self-satisfied smirk.

"Thought you were smart, huh, little human?" he rasped, his nose ring glittering in the light. A demon with body-piercings.

How original.

Vee leaned against the concrete column beside her and smiled pleasantly at him. Her wings still throbbed but she revealed none of her discomfort to her quarry.

He frowned, probably annoyed with her lack of response. "What? Nothing to say when you fail?"

Vee shrugged. "Nothing to say because I didn't fail."

He lifted a brow. "You must be confused, little human."

"Nope. Not confused at all."

Vee kept smiling as the chakra returned on its journey back to her, even as it closed in on the grinning demon.

He frowned as the low humming of the spinning weapon drew closer, the almost hollow sound echoing around the warehouse. He began to pivot, and the movement—along with his turning neck—only made it easier for the blade of the chakra to do its work.

The weapon sliced through muscle, sinew, and bone with such ease that for a moment Vee felt bad. Until the demon's human glamor flickered and dissolved, revealing his true form.

Vee's attention was drawn to the demon as his body shuddered from the impact. She watched as his skin pulsed as though something lived beneath it, the pustules covering his body glistening as if about to burst. His eyes bulged as the blade made its way through his spine and severed his head from his body.

She raised her hand and caught the gleaming weapon in her fingers, grimacing at the feel of the metal slick with demon blood. But her attention was only partially on the gore covering her palms. Vee found that she was tempted to look away as the head began to tilt and fall from the bhayakara's neck. But she forced herself to watch. She was the executioner, and she had to hold herself accountable. It would be so easy to turn into a vigilante, seeking vengeance and wreaking havoc.

She refused to be that, whether it meant she would turn into a tool wielded by the gods, or if it meant she'd be a crazy paranoid creature on a path to vengeance.

So she made herself watch as the head turned over and over, the demon's lifeless eyes staring at her as if he were still living, intent on getting his own brand of revenge.

His head hit the concrete floor with a hollow thunk and Vee winced, half expecting the skull to crack, for it to burst like an egg smashing into the ground. Instead, it merely rolled along the floor and came to a stop against a concrete support pole.

Vee shifted her attention back to the body which still stood in the same position, as if he were a little stunned and confused as to what had happened. Then he lurched forward, his knees giving way as he fell. He hit the ground and would have landed face-first had he still been in possession of his head.

As it was, the impact with the ground sent a gush of blood out of the gory opening at the bhayakara's neck. Vee sidestepped just in time, avoiding the splash of blue-black blood.

Weapon in hand, she decided it was time to get gone. She didn't want to be around for the next stage of this particular demon's death-song. Unfortunately, even as she hurried away across the floor of the warehouse, the smell of sulfur and ammonia still managed to follow her.

She held her breath and strode off, eyes ahead, searching the rafters, scanning the aisles of stacked boxes as she weaved between the supporting pillars. Vee rounded another pillar, and paused, glad she could no longer smell the demon.

And she never saw him coming.

When Vee thought about it later, she had to admit that she'd had no reason to believe anyone else was in the shipping warehouse other than herself and the bhayakara.

The arrogant demon had been careless. Now he was dead.

And, it seemed likely that if Vee didn't get to her senses fast enough, she'd be just as dead.

Something large, musclebound, and strangely cold hit her broadside and sent her flying into the concrete support pillar that she'd just passed. She slammed hard into it, feeling the bones in her spine crack loudly, feeling the staff of the trishula cut into her ribs, feeling the surge of pain as her injured wing was jarred behind her.

The pillar stopped Vee's escape, allowing her no clear way out.

She slid to the ground, blinking hard to get a good view of her attacker. She'd already been able to ascertain a few things: tall, swarthy, cold-blooded. A man and yet not anything like a man.

Vee lifted her gaze and met the cold silver eyes of a pey demon.

Fudge.

Vee swallowed and backed up, sliding a little to the left of the concrete pillar. Her eyes were wide as she stared into the creature's cold gaze. She was so very dead. Pey demons were nothing to joke about. Meeting one face-to-face rarely resulted in anything but death.

And her hellhound-slash-warrior-slash-bodyguard was nowhere to be found. Vee so needed a fairy godmother right now.

Vee gritted her teeth. It had been her own choice to head inside the warehouse after the demon without backup. Speaking of backup, shouldn't they have arrived by now?

The pey let out a soft growl, lifting his horned head into the air.

Shit.

Vee recognized that movement, wishing her glamor was good enough to use to extricate herself from the danger she now stared in the face.

The pey demons was calling out to someone. Partner or mate,

Vee didn't want to find out for herself. She had to do something. Fast.

At her side, the trishula still cut into her ribs, its awkward angle making its position more than painful. Vee moved her hand up her thigh, aware that the demon's red eyes were tracking her fingers as she slid it toward the weapon. She lifted her other hand, reaching for her chakra, successfully distracting the creature long enough for her to grab the triple-bladed spear and give it a firm shake.

The movement allowed the magically endowed spear to take its full form. The golden blade lengthened, and even as it grew longer, Vee was spinning it around, holding it at her shoulder like a javelin.

During the last two months, Vee had been schooled in the use of the weapon Lord Shiva had bestowed upon her, had spent hours practicing hard in the hopes that someday—when the time came—she'd be able to use it either to protect herself, or to save someone else, and to honor the god who'd seen fit to give such a priceless treasure to her.

She hadn't exactly imagined the scenario being that of defending her life against a pey, of all creatures. They weren't even supposed to be out of whatever hell it was that they had been banished to.

Vee was about to send the trishula hurtling through the air, hoping to impale the oncoming demon, when a noise to her right drew her attention for a fleeting second. Another demon lingered there, soot-black hair in disarray, a bloody smile on her face, her demon teeth gleaming.

Double shit.

CHAPTER 3

A pey was bad enough. But when faced with his better half, things went to hell in a handbasket fast.

The peymakilir, likely the mate of the demon salivating over Vee, growled low and rasping. The sound was enough to distract Vee from her aim.

As if they had planned their course of action, both demons ran at Vee. Instinct ruled her limbs as she lowered the trishula so the end sat at her hip, its point aimed at the pey. His mate, however, Vee had little defense against. Her chakra was on the other side of her body, lodged between her hip and the pillar, her satchel she'd left at home, having decided at the time that this job didn't need a bag of stuff that went kablooey.

Bad move.

She felt for the knives strapped to her thigh, grabbed one and released it straight at the demonwife. The blade hit the creature in her chest with a loud thunk, but she still kept coming. In a second smooth move, Vee grabbed blade number two, noted that the pey was a yard from her and still on his way to impalement, and let the knife loose.

The second blade hit the peymakilir in the throat, but she still kept coming.

Vee's heartbeat ratcheted up as she considered herself, for all intents and purposes, doomed.

She inhaled sharply, convinced she was dead, and then saw a multitude of red laser lines splayed across the pillars around her. The cavalry was here, but possibly a little too late for Vee.

She exhaled and felt the impact of the pey against the three points of the trishula. To her right, the peymakilir hurled herself at Vee. Even as Vee twisted herself around and attempted to throw her spitted demon onto his mate, she was prepared, bracing for impact.

It had all happened way too fast for her to do the smart thing. Despite all her FBI training, despite her apsara training, acting on instinct had been her only option.

An explosion ripped the air and Vee ducked her head.

Someone had thought it would be a good idea to blast the head off the peymakilir before she sank her teeth into Vee's throat.

Again, a move born out of instinct.

Vee felt a moment of relief at not being alone in lack of smarts. Had Vee been in that agent's place, a rifle would have been sufficient. A bullet to the brain, and then move fast, perform the rites and toss the body into the nearest fire.

Vee sighed and twisted back upright, allowing the trident to drop to the ground and release the pey. He was barely alive, with a triple blade to the gut insufficient to put him out of his misery.

His mate, on the other hand, was definitely dead.

Vee got to her feet slowly and tugged the trident out of the pey's body. She wanted to tell the agents who had surrounded her that they were wasting their time taking the bodies back to the lab in the hopes of researching the biology of these creatures.

Rossi had recently mentioned that they'd wanted to study the demons in the hopes that the R&D division could look into the development of ammunition to help Vee's team defend themselves against the demon horde that seemed to steadily become larger and harder to fight.

But Vee knew what would happen to the two demons within a few hours after death. The pey and his mate would not die as the bhayakara demon had—in a puddle of ammonia and sulfurous muck. No. The pey couple would disintegrate, their bodies rapidly drying until a mere movement would disturb the pile of ash they would become. Ash so pure that nothing—not even DNA—would remain for testing purposes.

It was sad and amusing at the same time.

Black-clad agents milled around as Vee got to her feet using the trishula to support her weight. Vee sniffed herself and wrinkled her nose. She needed a bath. Badly.

But, with Assistant Director Rossi's head bobbing in the distance as he made his way toward her, she knew she had no place to run. Something splattered the floor at Vee's left ankle, and she glanced down. The chakra was dripping demon sludge.

Just fabulous.

The trishula had ceased its magical glow and now shivered, as if it somehow sensed the presence of so many people. Vee held it up and waited as it shrunk in size, allowing her to attach it to the sling at her shoulder.

Rossi approached—wrapped warmly in a dark wool-lined coat—and Vee was relieved to find Brent Cadiz with him. At least Brent would be on her side. She straightened and turned to face the two men as they approached, appreciating the wary glance they gave her.

Rossi looked a little stunned. "I'm not even sure what to say," he said staring at the sludge puddle and then at the dead pey. He seemed to be avoiding the pile of remains that amounted to the female demon.

The pey moaned, trying to turn toward Vee. The keening

sound ended on a high note that had the closest agents—including Vee—slapping their hands over their ears.

"What the hell?" Brent squeaked and stepped away fast, clutching his laptop close to his chest. "That thing is still breathing."

"Yep," Vee said, smirking, her amusement helping to keep the pain from her throbbing wing at bay.

"He looks…angry."

Vee stared at Brent, her face void of expression. "Wouldn't you be angry if your wife's brains were splattered around the warehouse, right after she'd been stabbed in the chest and throat by two flying daggers?"

Brent grunted in response, then took another step away from the moaning demon. "Perhaps we ought to put it out of its misery."

Rossi looked over at the techie. "I'm a little concerned, Cadiz. Such a disregard for life could be dangerous."

"That thing…" Brent turned to look over at the body of the peymakilir, "…isn't human."

"Doesn't mean it's not alive," Vee replied.

"But you're the one who just killed them," the techie said, eyes wide, though a little suspicion had begun to crease his brow.

"I don't kill all of them, Brent. Besides, that's a moot point. If you guys hadn't come, I would have had to kill them anyway."

"See? Dispensable." Brent smiled smugly, then folded his arms as he leaned toward the pillar behind him. He missed and stumbled then scrambled to right himself. Vee hid a smile as he straightened and tugged at the lapels of his coat.

Vee sighed. "Not dispensable. Dangerous. They were threatening my life. It was either me or them."

"Don't look to me like it was you or them. Looked more like it was you or her…it." Brent pointed at the remains of the female demon.

Rossi grunted and silenced whatever it was Brent had been

wanting to say. "What's your assessment here, Agent Shankar. You've got two very different, unrelated species in one location."

Vee nodded. "I suspect they may not be related. I have a feeling that the lead was solid. It led me here to find the bhayakara. He's the one you saw over on the other side."

Brent frowned and glanced over his shoulder in the general direction of the demon's liquid remains. "You mean the puddle of yellow slush?" Vee nodded. "Right," he replied, looking a little uncomfortable now.

"So what about these two?" Rossi jerked a chin at the dead—and dying—demons before them. "After Slushy over there? Or something more sinister?"

Vee shrugged. "Perhaps they were lying in wait for him? Who knows. He didn't seem too much of a threat, so I'm wondering if he could have been an informant of some kind." Vee glanced down at the bodies of the two pey demons lying at her feet.

"Or?" Rossi probed, seeming to easily read her train of thought.

Vee sighed. "Or it could be that they were tracking *me*."

Brent's eyes widened. "I'll get onto traffic cams in the area." Before anyone could respond—or add to his task list—the techie was gone, hunkering down a safe distance from all present demons and setting up his small workstation. Before long he was tapping away at the keyboard, paying no attention to anything around him.

Rossi cleared his throat. "So anything you want to tell me about these demons who are on your tail?" he asked softly, his eyes still on Brent.

Vee shook her head even though Rossi couldn't see her face or movement. "No clue. I'll have to put out a few feelers to see what I can dig up. The odd thing was they didn't seem desperate. They almost appeared to be calm, as if the kill was routine, as if they'd been through the tag team thing before and it had been easy for them in the past."

"They were comfortable with each other?"

"With this type of demon, they are more than likely a mated pair."

"Can you give me a debrief?" Rossi's eyes sparkled with interest. Vee had enjoyed working with him. His open-mindedness had been a huge help when she'd started out working for his off-the-books FBI squad. Now he'd begun to take strange demons, and tales of deific beings and god-given boons in his stride.

Vee nodded. "I'll email it once I get back home." She made a face again at the amount of demon blood and gore she had on her person.

With a short nod, Rossi turned and then stopped. He glanced over his shoulder at Vee. "Go home, Shankar. You need a bath."

His words generated a round of good-natured chuckles from the agents within hearing distance, and she shook her head, trying and failing to glare angrily at them. She turned on her heel and headed across the warehouse, deciding to scan the place one more time.

As she circled a stack of containers across the way from where the demonic couple had ambushed her, she caught sight of a new aura, a strange pale yellow that hadn't been there before. Vee had passed on this route when she'd moved away from the bhayakara demon and hadn't seen any sign of this aural signature.

The voyeur had to have arrived after she'd killed the bhayakara.

Someone had been watching Vee.

She stepped closer to the aura and stared at the floor. The remains of a cigar littered the bare concrete. Vee reached into her pocket for a tweezer and a plastic bag. She proceeded to retrieve all the pieces of the cigar as well as some of the ash that had been left behind. She labeled the item then continued on her way, the bag dangling from her fingers.

As she closed in on the place where the two other demons

had been killed, Vee realized that the person who'd been watching had not been in a hurry to leave. He'd waited for her, likely up until the point when he'd seen her kill the first demon.

Vee crouched again. Ashy footprints marked a small narrow spot behind two crates a mere twenty feet from where Vee had sat after she'd fallen against the pillar. He'd ground the cigar into the floor with his shoe, leaving a smear of tar and charcoal on the bare concrete. Didn't seem to be the careful type.

Her quarry was long gone now, not likely that he'd stick around to get himself caught.

Rising to her feet, Vee thought about the two pey demons. *Now, who exactly was following who? Had he set you up, or were you two trying to set me up?*

Vee shook her head.

She'd provide Rossi with the full report on the incident before she went to bed that night. Or was it morning already?

For now, all she knew was she had to get home soon, before the blood dried into her jeans and she'd have to throw them out. As Vee turned to walk out of the warehouse, she frowned. Getting clean was her top priority. But she also had to pay a visit to Karan before he got too impatient.

He'd been the one to send her on this wild demon chase to begin with. He ought to be informed of her brush with death. And also be told that someone else was watching her. Other than him, of course.

Given the lack of the voyeur's interference, Vee considered the possibility that perhaps it had been Karan himself who had been observing her. But she shrugged the suspicion away. That would make absolutely no sense. Karan was a puzzle. He was mysterious, and well connected. But there was something else about him—like his ability to freeze time, of course—that made her wary of him. The last thing Vee needed was to rock the boat in terms of their working relationship.

She still wasn't entirely sure how she'd landed this gig, but she wasn't about to look a gift horse in the mouth.

Vee strode out of the building and headed into the bright moonlight with one thing in mind, and one thing only.

A hot bath, and a jasmine and cocoa butter bath bomb.

Okay, so maybe that was two things.

CHAPTER 4

Without Syama to transport her from place to place with her magical teleportation ability, Vee was forced to use the mundane method of walking and taking public transport home.

She would have done so tonight if Rossi hadn't arranged a car for her to take her home. The man was far too observant, and Vee had to remind herself that he was a trained agent.

She slid into the back of the car and gave the driver her address, then fell into an almost morbid silence as he drove off. Vee checked he phone, in case Nivaan had left her a message, she missed the guy too damned much.

She smiled at the memory. Of Nivaan and his adorable niece Sona. Vee had tried hard not to think too much of Nivaan, more so because the man's mere existence made her weak at the knees. She was no wilting wallflower, no fainting Miss. And yet when Nivaan was around all she wanted to do was to faint in his arms so that he would sweep her up and take her away with him.

Vee grinned at her strange imaginings. The object of those fantasies would burst into uncontrollable laughter should she ever admit to having them. Vee considered telling him—and making a fool of herself in the process—just so that she could hear that laugh.

She shook her head and hid a smile. Who would have thought that Vee Shankar would ever fall for a guy?

She sighed as the cab zipped through the city streets. Reality only hit her when she was alone, without the stress of catching and or killing demons to distract her.

Vee stared out at the city streets as they flitted by, but all she saw was her grandmother's face.

Radhima.

She'd been so young at heart, so filled with the love of life that she'd often drawn Vee out of her own self-pity. Now she was dead as a result of something Vee had done.

Maybe that deed had been done when Vee had been a kid. So what? It had still been her fault. She'd been the one to open the vortex, to kill the demon Kasipu, to cast her father into an uncertain hell. She'd been the one to bring the wrath of the demon's brother down on her family, and in the end, cause the death of her beloved grandmother.

A pained sigh echoed within the vehicle and Vee glanced up to check if the driver was annoyed or upset about something. But the man's eyes were focused on the street ahead, and he didn't even twitch when he caught Vee staring at him in the rear-view mirror.

Frowning, Vee turned her attention back to the view of the city. At night the lights were so beautiful, the shadows and darkness hiding the bleak sadness of what lay within the abandoned alleys, and beneath the overpasses. The homeless had never been anything but a consistent issue for the city, both financially, and in a humanitarian light.

But ever since the demons had begun to seep through into the city, the homeless population had burgeoned. Demons preyed on them, decimating their numbers, but those same demons eventually joined their number, more so when they discovered that our world was not the land of milk and amrita they'd believed it to be.

This time it was Vee who sighed, and when the voice spoke in her ear, she almost jumped out of her skin.

"You know, I always thought you were a responsible, level-headed child." Radhima shook her head and studied Vee's face. "I expected more from you."

Vee snorted. The apparition had haunted her ever since her grandmother's death. Vee knew she was generating this ghost, probably born out of her own desperate need to see her grandmother again.

"What?" said the ghost, her eyes narrowing. "Now you won't talk to me?"

Vee glared at the apparition. "Not here. You're going to make people think I'm crazy."

The ghost snorted. "For a smart young woman, you're terribly dense."

"What's that supposed to mean?" Vee snapped, forgetting that the driver was directly in front of her. A glance up confirmed that the man was now paying attention to her, his scowl saying he was probably wondering if he should take the turn for Bellevue instead.

When Vee glanced back at the apparition, she found Radhima's eyes staring down at Vee's phone. Vee rolled her eyes and let out a long-suffering sigh. As she picked up the phone and pretended to take a call, she had to admit that her imaginary grandmother was pretty smart.

Vee gritted her teeth.

The ghost is a figment of my imagination, for god's sake. Even I'm *beginning to believe my hysterical ravings.*

Phone to her ear, she said, "What do you want?" She felt ridiculous. It was too bizarre to be talking to something she'd dreamed up. What the hell was happening to her?

Maybe Bellevue isn't such a bad idea.

Radhima's voice was calm. "I want to help you."

"This isn't real," Vee snapped, glancing up at the driver. The man had turned his attention back to the road, although he flicked his gaze back to her every few seconds, as if watching for the slightest hint of crazy.

"It is real. I don't know why it's so hard for you to accept."

Vee sighed. "You're gone. You can't come back. This is just... because I want you back with us, because I can't accept it. It doesn't mean anything. Just...the grieving process. Which I apparently suck at." Vee swallowed the hard knot in her throat, tears threatening to spill over any second.

The ghost leaned toward Vee, and her heart stilled. She could feel the warmth emanating from Radhima's—or rather the apparition's—arm. Vee's eyes widened as she stared at the spot which the ghost had touched, and then looked back up at her grandmother's eyes.

"How can I prove it to you?" she asked Vee softly.

Vee shook her head. This was getting insane. "You can't prove anything to me. Don't you get that? I need to work this through at my own pace. I don't need you...talking to me all the time." A glance up at the driver showed the man's sad, empathetic expression. Vee felt awful for misleading him, for making him believe she'd been dumped or abandoned by someone important in her life.

Better than letting him find out you're talking to your grandmother's ghost.

Radhima shifted slightly, so she was facing Vee directly. "Do you need more proof? This whole thing is getting a bit tiring. I thought I'd have gotten through to you by now."

"You can't get through to me. I'm trying to heal and this..." Vee waved her hand around the back of the car, "...this is all just making it worse."

"I know dear, but it's not meant to make you feel worse. If you will just listen to me, then I can make you understand."

"There is nothing to understand. You're gone. I'm dealing with it. Don't make it worse than it already is." Then Vee paused and glared at the ghost. She found herself wondering for the briefest moment if this ghost was haunting her mother too. She frowned. "You'd better leave Mom alone. She doesn't need you making things worse for her. She's got way too much on her mind."

The apparition sighed and sat back. "They say the worst pain is when a mother loses a child. I can agree but from a completely different perspective." She turned to stare at Vee. "It must be easy when death takes you away, far from this plane so you can't see your loved ones, be around them and not be able to touch them or talk to them."

"This is crazy," Vee whispered. Something was niggling at her now. This ghost was a figment of her own imagination but what she was saying...they were things Vee had never considered. Was it possible....

No. She shook her head but before she could speak Radhima lifted her hand. "No. Don't say it. Not yet. If you really want me to leave, if you really truly don't believe I am real, then perhaps there is nothing I can do or say to change that. But at least take the time to think about it."

Vee opened her mouth to respond, then shut it without uttering a word. What could she possibly say to the apparition that would even make sense? Then she let out a soft breath. "Fine."

"Good." The ghost grinned, looking far too pleased with herself.

Vee pursed her lips and lifted a brow. "Don't get too excited. I only said I'll think about it."

Vee's warning didn't seem to have an effect on the apparition, who clapped her hands happily and began to fade away. Then, suddenly the image of the old woman strengthened as she returned, her expression intent.

"Oh, and don't forget one thing… You're not so special that you'd go crazy just from the death of a loved one. You lived through and survived your father's death. Why would you lose your marbles over me? You're too strong for that. If you weren't, I'd doubt the gods would have seen fit to choose you as their emissary on this plane."

With those words the ghost evaporated, leaving Vee alone in the back of the car with a driver who was again staring at her suspiciously. He was right to be concerned about her mental state.

Vee sighed and clicked her phone off.

Just fabulous. She was now actually beginning to consider that her imaginary grandmother could be real. Maybe she really was going nuts. Insanity would certainly make more sense than ghosts.

Vee started as Radhima's voice echoed in her ear. "And gods and demons? How much sense do *they* make?"

CHAPTER 5

Walking into the house, Vee tiptoed across the hallway and hurried up the stairs as quietly as possible. She'd almost made it to the landing when a voice stopped her in her tracks.

"Where have you been?"

Vee turned on her heel and looked down at her dad who was standing at the foot of the stairs holding a cup of tea in his hand. He was frowning at her, studying her filthy clothing, his nose crinkled as if she'd been rolling in cow poop all day. He wouldn't be far off.

She sighed. "On a case."

He tilted his head. "You have bhayakara goo on your shoes and clothes, and you seem to have a little bit of pey blood on your face. Not to mention a smidge of brain matter in your hair."

Vee's hand lifted to her head, worried now about getting the muck out of her hair as soon as possible. "Ugh. I have to wash it off."

She was turning to race up the stairs when her dad said, "Stop."

The tone was so stern that she had little choice but to obey.

The only movement she made was to look over her shoulder and watch as he set his mug down and jogged up the stairs toward her. As he came, he retrieved a little plastic bag from his pocket. Dropping the contents onto his palm, he chose the tweezer and slipped the spatula back into his pocket. Then he reached out with the tweezer and picked something out of her hair.

"When did you come over to the dark side?" Vee asked.

Raj Shankar had seemed resistant from the start, making it difficult for everyone to explain that they'd advanced the mode of paranormal hunting and were now also working with the FBI. Not to mention researching weaponry and magic.

He'd demanded that Vee give up all the nonsense, insisted that she do research instead. Everyone had tiptoed around him, including her mother who had moved into the house to take care of her newly-alive husband. Her other husband had moved out, much to Vee's disappointment. She'd known Mac would leave eventually and yet she'd hoped he'd change his mind.

Perhaps if her grandmother had been there, things would have been different. She'd have set them all right. But in the end, Mac had moved out, promising Vee that she would always be welcome in his home. And Vee had been left to tend to her oddly subdued mother, and a father who didn't seem to be all there.

Now, Raj chuckled. "If you can't beat 'em..."

Vee scowled as he repeated the process, taking a sample of the blood on her cheek, and finding another splotch caught in the hem of her pants.

Although she wanted to brush him off and race to her bathroom for that much-desired bath, she endured his inspection and remained still until he was done.

"There." He stood back and lifted the plastic bags toward Vee. "You'll likely need those."

"Thanks, Dad," Vee said, taking the samples. She wasn't sure if she should say anything and the awkward silence hung over them for a long moment.

She was about to say something—which would have just been small talk—when her dad cleared his throat. "Right. My tea is getting cold. And you stink." He turned on his heel and skipped down the stairs to retrieve his mug. "Would you like me to make you a cup?"

Vee smiled and shook her head. "Thanks. But I'm going to be a while."

"I see," he gave a small smile. "You've turned into your mother."

Vee scowled and must have looked incredibly angry at the thought because her dad lifted a hand. "I meant that she used to take ages in the bathroom too, primping in front of the mirror, making sure her hair was just so."

Vee raised her eyebrows. "Now *that* I find hard to believe," she scoffed.

He shook his head, a fond smile caving his lips. "Oh yes, she did. Not that she needed it though. Your mother was so beautiful when she was younger."

"Dad. She's not old. And neither are you." Vee smiled, studying his face, finding herself memorizing his features again, as if something was telling her she'd better immortalize every plane and curve because he could be taken from her any minute. In the days after they'd brought him home, Vee had woken in cold sweats, finding herself hurrying to his room to confirm that he was actually there, that she hadn't imagined the whole thing.

Now she smiled at him, wanting to assure him that he had a long time yet to enjoy life with them. Life with Vee, the way it should have always been.

He shrugged. "Sometimes experience makes you age more than you can ever imagine normal life would."

Vee's heart tightened. He'd taken the conversation down a path she wasn't prepared to go. And he seemed to recognize that as he took a sip of his tea and nodded at Vee.

"Off you go now. You're stinking up the house." Without

another word, he turned and headed off toward the kitchen and out of Vee's line of sight.

Vee smirked and hurried up the rest of the stairs and along the hall to her room. Inside, she removed her weapons and left them in a pile on the bathroom floor. Then she sat on the chair beside her bed and began to take off her boots. She was unlacing them when she let out a sobbing breath.

The conversation with the ghost in the back of the car had come rushing back to Vee. No matter how much she denied it, she had to admit that the apparition had made sense. But she didn't want to think about it. She didn't want to spend another moment ruminating on things that were so difficult to deal with.

What if she hadn't been imagining it? If all along she'd been ignoring her grandmother's attempts at contacting her. Vee shook her head. No. That makes no sense.

Keep telling yourself that.

Vee threw her boots across the room, not caring when they hit the bathroom door which swung open on impact, barely even paying attention as they skidded along the tiled bathroom floor and came to a stop beside the toilet.

The shoes seemed to have a mind of their own. They probably knew how filthy they were.

Maybe the boots will start talking to me too. That would totally make sense.

Letting out a soft groan, she forced herself to admit—however much she wished it would not be true—that she just had a bad case of denial.

Vee undressed and bagged the clothing then left it on the chair by the door with the samples sitting on top of it within a cooler. She'd take it to her lab later in the morning. She planned on giving them a thorough once-over and hoped they would survive the inspection.

She found it strange that the biological remains of the peymakilir hadn't turned into ash as yet. Vee had stared hard at the pieces of brain matter that her dad had extracted from her hair. They were in perfect condition. Nowhere near ash, even though they should be white dust by now.

Vee gave the boots one last glare, then forced herself to clean her weapons. She spent a few minutes wiping them down with disinfectant and then polishing them with a few drops of neem oil which always seemed to keep them clean and tarnish free.

When she was done she headed to the bedroom on bare feet and padded to the far wall. A discrete amount of pressure on a specific spot had a panel pop open, and she placed the weapons onto their designated shelves. The secret cupboard had been Mac's idea. He'd insisted that it would make no sense for Vee to use the weapons room downstairs when her weapons were best stored within her reach.

In case of an emergency.

They all knew what it felt like to have someone taken from their home, from right under their noses. So, Mac and Vee had taken all the precautions necessary to make the house more secure.

Once the weapons were stored, Vee almost ran into her bathroom, scrubbing both her body and her hair under the hot shower spray. After getting clean, she filled her tub and popped a bath bomb into the clear water. The scent of jasmine and cocoa butter filled the bathroom, and Vee inhaled deeply before sliding inside the welcome embrace of the hot water.

Her muscles ached, from the fighting, from the tension. She'd lost track of the number of reasons her body ached these days. Only when the water had cooled somewhat, did Vee rise from the bath and dry off.

Her bed awaited her.

CHAPTER 6

The next day, Vee headed out to Central Park. Karan's text had given her directions to the pond and wooden bench near a coffee vendor called Perk You Up.

Her wings still throbbed, but she'd been surprised on waking up to discover that the hole within the iridescent gauzy membrane had closed. A large discoloration and what looked a lot like a bruise still covered the wing, but it appeared well on its way to near-perfect recovery. The rest of her injuries merely smarted, and she'd had no trouble slinging her messenger bag around her torso. She'd figured she was better off traveling ready for action—whatever that action might be.

On the way, she considered the text from Akil and what it meant.

Syama is okay. Bringing her home asap. Expect trouble.

Akil was cryptic on a normal day. But sending texts like this was downright rude. The kid needed to have a little more training on humans and social interaction. The owl-shifter had literally flown into Vee's life one day and had never left. He'd saved her life and ended up convincing her that he was here to stay. Add that to the fact that he'd been the courier who had delivered her chakra and her conch to her, and she knew she'd never banish him from her life.

He was family.

The way Syama was family.

Vee inhaled sharply and pressed those emotions deeper down inside her as she walked the curving path toward the pond. The wind was brisk and breezy, throwing Vee's hair around her head. She retrieved a tan beanie from her pocket and slipped it onto her head. She was still a little on the exhausted side after last night's escapade, and she was feeling a little fragile in the wake of the apparition's claim of being real.

It was just another day of craziness in the world of Vee Shankar.

She strolled past mothers pushing babies in strollers, and fathers throwing balls to their kids. The pond seemed a little crowded too as a large group of kids huddled at the edges, each eagerly attempting to set their little boats afloat without drowning them. Little waves bounced the multitude of colored boats around, the water churned by the persistent wind.

The wind seemed to be good for something else too.

Up on the hill, dozens of red-cheeked children jostled for position, holding tightly onto their rolled-up strings, tugging at the lines holding their kites aloft. A myriad of colored kites danced high above them, and Vee paused to stare up at the spectacle.

With no snow in the last week, the day was perfect for families—if a little cold. Perfect to remind Vee of her own shattered family, devastated by grief, shocked and in disarray as the dead came back to life and lives were forced to change to adjust.

She blinked away tears of self-pity and focused on the bigger picture. Her life was no longer hers. She had a large role to play, responsible to the gods now, and not just to the mundane works of a mere human being.

Whatever they had seen in her, she had to make every effort to earn it.

Vee headed for the wooden bench beside the coffee cart and settled on it shifting the messenger back around so she wouldn't get stabbed by a pointy sheath or gun-barrel. She relaxed, content to just watch the children play, the kites battling for space against the blue sky, the little boats bobbing on the surface of the little lake, no doubt many destined for destruction in head-on collisions or tantrums.

A shadow loomed over Vee, and she tilted her head up, the hand tucked inside her pocket holding a Taser ready.

"You will not need protection against me, I assure you," Karan said softly before settling down beside her.

"Yeah. So said every serial killer in history."

Karan let out a soft laugh and met Vee's gaze. His piercingly dark eyes gleaming with amusement.

Today he wore a white suit with the narrow Nehru collar that he seemed to prefer. His hair was long and touching his shoulders, the wind tossing his locks around his face as though he were a model on a photo shoot.

Looking at him now made it so easy for Vee to believe the man was harmless. Yes, she trusted him more now then she had when she'd first begun to work with him, but she still remained wary, watchful, constantly looking for a sign or a tell that would confirm that something was up with him. Her gut was never wrong, and it had been screaming at her since they'd met.

But not for the normal reasons.

Vee didn't believe that Karan was a danger to her. Their relationship was mutually beneficial. Perhaps what worried her was his persona. Karan was attractive, oozing sex appeal, and she'd often wondered if he turned it on just to tempt her. But she was immune. He was not her type.

The man was intriguing, but dangerous. He was influential and knew things, dangerous things that people would kill for, would kill him for having. And he was passing much of that information onto Vee.

Add that to the fact that the man possessed the power to stop time and you had a ticking bomb ready and waiting to go off.

Vee was intrigued, yes. But she was all too aware that he was dangerous. And ruthless.

When you wrestled with a snake, you had to remember to stay far away from the fangs.

Still, wrestling aside, Vee was not too embarrassed to admit to herself that she felt used by the man. As if she was a puppet and all he had to do was tug on her strings, and she'd dance to his tune.

Karan wriggled on the seat then shifted to look at Vee. "Coffee? I believe Mauro over there makes amazing beignets." He spoke with a casual smile that would have anyone believe that Vee and he were friends meeting up or a couple on a date.

Vee shook her head. The thought of fried dough covered in sugar made her stomach turn. "Thanks, but I'd rather not. I've been a little queasy since my run-in with demon blood and guts a few hours ago." She gave a small shudder and wrinkled her nose. "I can still smell them on me. And I'm about to get up close and personal with samples of demon blood and guts soon too." Vee made a strange sound inside her throat and Karan cast her a concerned glance. She swallowed hard, aware that she'd sounded like she was about to throw up.

"Are you not feeling well?"

Vee lifted an eyebrow. "Everything I just said about blood and guts? That didn't give you any hints?"

Karan's mouth lifted in a small smile. "I admit I was unsure. You are of course an Apsara warrior. The thought that you would be ill at the sight of blood had not occurred to me." The look he gave her implied her reputation had fallen a smidge in his estimation.

Vee shook her head, cleared her throat and said, "Apsara

warrior for all of five seconds. Without the necessary training, in case you missed that part." Vee tilted her head to study Karan's face. "Is that why you picked me. You knew who I was?"

Karan shrugged. "What is it that you agency people say? I'm not at liberty to discuss it?" He smirked.

Vee huffed. She was beginning to lose patience with the man. Or whatever he was. "I have work. I'm assuming you want a rundown of what happened last night?"

Karan sat back and folded his arms. He didn't respond, but Vee knew him enough to know that she'd better be giving him the details fast before he lost his patience. Karan was not the type of man who appreciated it when things didn't go his way.

"You were right." He tapped his head and flourished an invisible hat as he took credit for his information. Vee rolled her eyes and continued, "The murder scene out in Queens turned out not to be murder. Just a case of extreme pain extraction."

Karan—who had folded his arms again— ran a finger over his lips. "So, it *was* a bhayakara. I had suspected so."

Vee turned to face him, folding a knee onto the bend. "So you knew I was going to come up against a bhayakara, and you didn't bother to give me the heads up? I could have died." Vee kept her tone even, but her ire had risen at the thought that he could have sent her in armed with a little more information than 'a demon sucking people dry and leaving them for dead.'

Karan cast her an impatient glance. "I didn't know. I suspected. I didn't want you going in prepared for what I may or may not have suspected would be waiting for you. Besides, you went in wary and expecting anything. I wouldn't have thought you'd have wanted it any other way."

Vee let out a breath and bit onto her lower lip to stop herself from yelling at the man. After taking a long calming breath, Vee looked up at Karan and continued, "I tracked him to the warehouse, and I killed him. Satisfied?"

Karan smiled and nodded. He leaned forward and slapped his

hands onto his thighs. "Just as I expected. You always come through. That's why you're my favorite."

Vee made a rude sound. "Well, just to be clear, things didn't go as you'd expected."

Karan paused. "You just said you managed to track him down and eliminate him."

Eliminate. Such a sanitized word.

CHAPTER 7

"I eliminated him, yes. But the other two demons who happened upon me? Who almost relieved me of my warrior Apsara head? I was unfortunately only able to *eliminate*," Vee fashioned air quotes in the air as she spoke the word eliminate, "one of them."

"Other two demons?" Karan was now at the edge of the park bench, turning to face Vee, his olive skin darkening.

She nodded, sitting back again with a sigh. She was so tired. Was this what her best years were supposed to feel like? Constant, never-ending direness? "Pey demons. A mated pair from what I saw."

"Were they together?" Karan paused as my eyebrows rose. He gave a short shake of his head and said, "I mean with the bhayakara?"

Vee shrugged. "I didn't stop to chat. A little in a hurry to prevent the whole-being-ravaged-by-a-pey thing." Vee let out a long breath and shook her head. "Sorry. Tired."

Karan nodded in silence, appearing not to have been affected by her shortness. He spent a few seconds staring off at little floating boats as the sound of laughter and yelling from the children around the pond rose and fell on the chilly morning air, a starkly mundane backdrop to the horror of the New York demon underworld.

"Let me try and figure out what that means. I didn't have any Intel on this particular demon working in a group. Do you think this could have been a coincidence?"

Vee shook her head, frowning as she thought back to the attack of the hellish couple, how they'd moved in utter silence, approached without her even hearing them. "They knew what they were doing. They were coordinated, moved as though each step had been planned. They were either there for the bhayakara or for me."

Karan was already nodding, his train of thought meeting Vee's with little effort. "I will look into it and let you know." He got to his feet and turned, as if to bid Vee goodbye.

Scowling, Vee surged to her feet. "That's all you have to say? I come within an inch of losing my head for good, three times in ten minutes might I add, and all you have to say is you'll look into it?"

Karan shifted his gaze to Vee, his eyes now glowing a feline gold. Blood rushed to her head as she registered a sudden silence in the park. She swallowed hard as she turned to scan the area around her. The kids around the pond were frozen in place, hands pointed, mouths open. A little boy, faces scrunched, stared at the scoop of ice cream that was falling from his cone, bound for his feet. Up the hill, a man had thrown a Frisbee, and his cocker spaniel had frozen in mid-jump and was hovering in mid-air, jaw open wide, teeth glinting.

Behind the park bench a little boy had climbed a tree and was balancing on the branch, one foot in the air. His face was filled with laughter, although a small hint of consternation shadowed his expression.

Vee turned to the coffee cart, and her heart stilled. A woman carrying a baby was walking past the cart while the last customer was in the process of turning away from Mauro, a cup of steaming coffee in each hand.

The mother was smiling and whispering to the pink-swaddled infant who was staring up at her, a wide grin on the baby's face. She remained unaware of the danger.

Vee turned to stare at Karan, unsure if she should be yelling at him for being so careless or if she should really be wondering if he'd known the danger the mother and child had been about to face.

"What are you doing," Vee whispered, afraid that if she spoke too loudly, the frozen time might shatter and people would get hurt.

Karan, who had been watching the boy in the tree, turned to look at Vee. "The world is so full of unknowns that even when you believe that you see everything around you, you know nothing at all, you are blind."

"I don't understand what you mean. *Or* what it is you hope to achieve. All I see is someone playing games with the lives of innocent people." Vee dragged in a rattling breath as her gaze flickered back to the mother and child. "I've debriefed you. I was hoping you'd have something constructive to tell me other than to play games with the lives of innocents." Vee waved her hand at the frozen park, catching sight of the kites overhead. Though mostly still, there was a hint of movement, a flicker of a tail here, an undulation of a wing there.

Vee's attention snapped back to Karan—he was surveying the park as if drinking up a stunning view. Heat had built up inside her head so much that she felt her skull was about to explode. Stress, fatigue, and the gods only knew what else, built up the pressure inside her brain. She was about to yell at him to stop this insanity when he shifted his gaze back to her.

"There has been another murder. But this one is different. It could be connected. I cannot say with any degree of certainty either way. What I do know is that a killer is on the loose, and lives are at stake." His eyes narrowed as he stared at Vee. "*Your* life could be at stake. Do not be careless."

Vee had opened her mouth to respond but found herself closing it slowly. Then she took a breath. "Scene of the murder?"

Karan jerked a chin to Vee's phone. "Already sent. You should get a message soon." He sighed, and the sound died in the vacuum that surrounded them. "I chose you. Forget my reasons. Consider the choice as having been a task to select the person best suited for the role. Perhaps you have an advantage, and perhaps we need that advantage. But believe me, nobody is exploiting you. At least not for reasons that you yourself would not wholeheartedly agree with.

"This world…this plane…it's no longer the place we once loved. Kaliyug is here, and the demon horde has broken free from their chains. I'm helping you, however I can, using whatever means I have at my disposal. I'm sharing information with you, bits and pieces, snippets of whispers on the grapevine that filter to me. I pass what I can verify on to you. I refuse to willingly put you in harm's way.

"You are far too valuable in this game. The portal grows with every day, every hour that passes. We cannot be precious or sensitive about our tasks, about what we find ourselves having to do to keep this world safe. The Demon Horde grows stronger every day. And make no mistake, there are entities out there who are just waiting in the shadows for an opportunity to take control of this plane away from the gods. I do what I must. You do what you must."

Vee wasn't sure what to say. His monologue had been lengthy, and she'd been unsure of whether she ought to be asking questions or if she should have gone to help get the woman and her child safely away. She'd remained frozen on the spot, as if she too were caught up in Karan's web.

He inclined his head, his expression saying that he wasn't in the least bit offended that she'd had no decent response to his words. He turned and walked toward the cart and calmly removed the two paper cups from the man's hands. He set the cups onto the serving counter of the cart and turned on his heel.

A bird called in the distance and the sound of the wind skimming Vee's ears almost drowned out the creak of a nearby branch.

Karan walked across the path, avoiding a jogger whose skin glistened with sweat, and a pair of teenagers whose eyes were focused only on their devices. Vee frowned as she watched him, holding her breath as time began to run again, slowly as if the brakes weren't strong enough to hold and they were giving a little at a time.

Vee shook her head, unable to believe the risks Karan had gone to simply to make a point.

She'd meant to go after him as he walked past her and headed up toward the tree. But she stopped as he paused beneath the branch, then stepped back a foot, as if gauging the distance from the branch to the ground.

The niggle became a tugging on Vee's brain.

Then Karan moved into position below the branch and curved his arms. Just in time. The world righted itself, kids yelled and laughed, and kites bobbed on the icy wind.

"What the..." the perplexed customer said behind me.

"Hey, watch it," growled the mother, a lioness protecting her cub.

A dog woofed and a man said. "Good boy, Roscoe, good dog."

A branch creaked louder until the crack echoed around them when it broke.

A boy fell from the tree, letting out a shriek.

He landed in Karan's arms, staring around him in shock. Karan set the kid on his feet almost instantly. Then he tugged at the hem of his coat, righted himself and strode off down the pathway.

Before Vee could call out to him, her phone buzzed to alert

her that she'd just received a message. She retrieved her cell phone from her pocket and studied the contents of the email. Then she glanced up and scanned the crowd for Karan's retreating form.

Her lab work was going to have to wait. She had a crime scene to visit.

Won't Monroe be happy.

As Vee left the park, her mind already focused on the new murder, something Karan had said hit her. He'd said, "That's why you're my favorite."

Favorite what?

There were only two options that made sense. She was either Karan's favorite FBI agent on call twenty-four-seven, or she was his favorite heavenly warrior.

What in all the gods' names had he meant by that?

Were there more Apsaras out there?

CHAPTER 8

Karan paced the narrow portion of carpet that bore no pattern. It was an odd habit. One that had not gone unremarked on by his companions. He'd never been comfortable with walking on something created by the hands of another.

The intricate beauty of hand-woven rugs always reminded him that a human being had slaved over that piece, weaving the threads, assessing the pattern with a level of scrutiny that only a conscious being could afford. He'd be willing to bet that though a computer—in this modern age—would recreate such a piece with perfect accuracy, that it would still lack what a human would give to the art.

It had something to do with spirit. Karan believed that everything a creative person touched, a sculptor, an artist, a dress designer, they all created out of a passion that was inherent to them, almost like a song sung to their own individual tune. No two people could create something that mirrored the other to perfection. Even the greatest forgers had a specific style unique to them. So unique in fact, that specialist could identify those particular habits and recognize the artwork as a reproduction by a particular forger with a mere glance.

Karan had been fascinated by art and the art world. Though he'd been sent to perform an arduous task, his eye had wandered —he'd never admit it—to the art of humanity. Often, he'd wonder if art was the essence of the spirit. Artists toil to bring their work to life. Often not merely for money or for accolades, simply to bring out that inherent need or desire within themselves that seeks the light, that desires freedom.

Some people would consider an artist a selfish person, in that their service is to their art as opposed to a business or for the greater good. But Karan had never seen it that way. The goddess Laxmi, mother of light, was also the goddess of music, art, and dance. Was it any wonder that those talents were the abilities the goddess of light, the goddess of personal wealth, sought out?

He heaved a great sigh and stopped his pacing. He knew what had gotten him so restless. His meeting with the Apsara Vaishnavi in Central Park had not gone as he had hoped.

He had slipped up, said something to her that had made her wonder. He had come to New York with one task—to help guide the apsara toward her destiny. But knowing she was in danger made him feel edgy. He wished he had an army at his command which he could charge with her protection. But he could not make a move. He could not alert those few who would wish to harm her.

They had been through this all before. Such a long time ago that it had begun to seem like a myth. A story of their past that they were beginning to forget. This world was not made for the gods, and yet here they remained until they could enter their own realm again. The time would come, Karan was sure if it. But he had little idea as to when that will be.

A knock on the door drew his attention and a demon was ushered inside.

"Carl," Karan called out. "What do you have for me?"

Carl was Karan's contact deep within the demon army. Unbeknownst to the gods—not to mention humanity—the Demon Horde was amassing far faster than expected.

"I have some information on a sub-sect of the New York Demonic Horde Assembly—the peys," the man said as he handed over a file. "They haven't officially broken away, but they are performing as an independent battalion."

"What kind of risk do they pose to our mission?" Karan asked, suspicious now in light of the covert attack on Vee by a pair of pey demons.

Carl tilted his head, his startling fuchsia eyes gleaming. "I'm not sure if they do at all. They seem to be functional and self-dependent. As a whole, they aren't a danger to either the Demonic Horde or to our goals. The reason I'm mentioning it to you is that this particular sect is mother goddess worshippers. I know from my contacts that their priests have repeatedly attempted to summon the goddess. I don't know they have ever been successful but that is of a concern to you, I believe?"

That was not a piece of news that Karan wanted to hear. Had they succeeded in receiving Parvathi's attention, things could definitely go sideways for the gods. Should Parvathi align herself with the demons, there was no turning back from that. But Karan needed to get a little more information on if she'd ever had any dealings with them before he pointed suspicion in her direction.

Karan nodded and began to pace again. Carl was a mild-mannered man, not overly eager. As a mole he'd turned out well, a demon with a human wife and two halfling children, merely seeking to ensure the safety of his family in the greater scheme of things. Karan supported his wife and children while Carl went undercover for him.

Until now, Carl had been his sole source of information from within the Horde. Even Cassandra hadn't budged on information. He suspected he'd need to pay the scorpion goddess another visit sometime soon, but he put that in the back of his mind.

"So, what can I go on that is concrete?"

"That murder in Manhattan, I just heard more about it come through. It's a horrific scene. The police are fearing the worst."

"And the Horde Assembly?

"They don't deem it important."

"And this sub-cult?"

"They are all smiling happy people at the moment. Things seem to be going according to Ishanie's plans."

Karan nodded. He didn't want to hear that something else had happened that he'd need to send Vaishnavi to investigate. Despite her abilities, she was making herself all too vulnerable by putting herself in harm's way.

He'd seen the images in her mind, the ones of the man who was following her. She hadn't told him as much though. Perhaps she didn't believe the events to be connected. Or perhaps she felt as though she wanted to deal with the problem herself. Or perhaps she didn't want to believe that someone was after her. The Apsara was an unusual creature, strong, powerful, knowledgeable, and yet she held herself back with such intensity that it worried Karan. If she lost her focus, he'd have to think of something else to do to help her.

Karan looked over at Carl who'd removed a small device from his pocket and was busy tapping at the screen. "Carl. Can you get Nate to bring the car around? I want to meet my agent at the scene of the crime."

"Very well, sir."

The man left the room, and Karan gritted his teeth. She won't be happy to see him, but he needed to ensure she was informed of the possible danger to her life.

Karan only hoped that it would not be too late. Things were far from what they appeared to be right now.

And Karan had a distinct suspicion it was going to get far worse.

CHAPTER 9

Vee headed out of Central Park, sending the details Karan had emailed to her on to Brent. She'd requested a warrant ASAP, to which he'd replied with 'On it,' which Vee knew meant he'd have the paperwork sorted and emailed to the relevant parties within the hour.

He'd followed with a second message that annoyed her, and yet did not surprise her.

The traffic cams in the vicinity of the warehouse hadn't picked up a thing. Probably because the demons had been smart enough to jump from location to location.

Vee stepped toward the curb and flagged down a cab. Her mind remained focused on Karan, his freezing of time, his passionate response to her criticism, the calm way that he'd passed on the next case to her, not to mention his little hint that she may not be the only Apsara around.

She snorted as she thought about the number of other things about the man that both frustrated and fascinated her. A cab finally slowed and drew to a stop for her. She pulled open the door only to be dosed with a blast of comfortingly warm air with a side of ear-shatteringly loud rap music.

Vee winced as she slid inside, pulling her bag off her body. She had placed the satchel on the floor at her feet and was about to tell the guy to turn it down when he turned and greeted her with a broad smile that made his eyes twinkle. Her cab driver was a cheerful old Japanese man, and she didn't have the heart to yell at him. More so when she saw the photos of what must have been his brood of grandkids, all hanging from the top of the windshield like bunting.

She smiled back and raised her voice to give him the address, then settled back, pulling the beanie off her head and stuffing it onto her bag. As soon as she was able to block out the angry lyrics of the current song, her thoughts pulled straight to Karan again.

She realized that she really ought to stop questioning him. She had long since accepted that she'd never be able to fully trust him. Full disclosure was not something he was capable of. He drip-fed her information, both about current cases and about himself and why he'd chosen Vee. Not to mention the issue of where he was getting his information from.

But the one thing that stuck with Vee though—the thought swirling within her head, threatening to make her dizzy—was his implication that there were others like her.

Other Apsaras.

Vee's mother, though a daughter from a strong Apsara line, had not been gifted with the kind of powers Vee possessed. Devi's ability was of a calming, more empathetic type, nothing in the vein of Vee's destructive abilities.

Not to mention the wings.

Vee's own existence implied that it was possible there were others out there, and the idea that she was not alone lifted her spirits. Until she realized that it was possible that Karan had just meant she was the FBI agent he was most partial to.

She wished she was able to figure the man out.

"You know, when a goat is staring you straight in the eye, you can do one of three things, yell loudly and frighten it away, stare it down and get head-butted for your troubles, or turn and run—"

"Which would result in being head-butted in the ass," Vee murmured softly, her voice drowned out by the rap music to which her cabdriver bobbed his head. She smiled and glanced over at Radha—or rather her ghost, since Vee still wasn't entirely sure she was real. "Yeah. Heard that one before, Ma."

Radha smiled and nodded her approval. Today the ghost wore a deep red silk sari, a bright red dot on her forehead. Vee shook her head and said, "You do know that nobody has ever had any clue as to what that means. Every time you quoted it people would roll their eyes and smile."

The apparition grinned, her white teeth gleaming as a ray of sunshine caught them as the driver took a right at the intersection.

Radha looked over at Vee. "Sometimes people like to tell themselves that a thing is too hard to do, to be, to understand. It's usually because they already know the answer but won't allow themselves to admit it."

Vee stared at the old woman, both marveling at how she glowed in the sunlight, and annoyed at her non-answer. She shook her head. "What is that?" she asked, her attention suddenly drawn back to the red bindi on Radhima's forehead.

"What is what, dear? You are going to have to be a little more specific than that." The apparition's answer was serene.

Vee raised her finger and began to point it at Radhima's forehead. Belatedly, she realized where she was and held her hand low on her lap, though her finger still pointed at the ghost's face. "That. What's it doing on your forehead."

"Oh," Radhima answered giving a soft laugh. "My bindi." She inhaled slowly and shifted to look Vee in the eye.

In that moment, Vee felt the warmth radiating from her grandmother, although a part of her mind swore that it was only the sunshine streaming through the window and heating up the back of the already warm car.

It occurred to Vee that each time she held these conversations with this figment of her imagination, Vee herself seemed to fall into a sort of natural acceptance that the vision was real. She should stop doing that, or else she'd confirm to herself that she was nuts.

"My mother once told me something in the days before I was married. She said that a woman's laughter is like the sound of birdsong. That a woman's love is like peace for the soul, and that a woman's life is her only true possession, one that can never be taken from her. The world may see a woman as an extension of her husband. They may take her visible claim on her marriage," Radhima pointed at the bright spot of red on her forehead, "*from* her when he leaves this plane. But nobody can control the one true fact that a woman is the embodiment of life. Unless we choose to stoop to utter barbarism, nobody can take that life power from her. Do you know what the red bindi is a representation of?"

Vee was startled by the sudden question. She'd been lulled by Radhima's voice, by her beautiful words, and the inquiry jolted her from what she discovered had been a place of peace. Vee cleared her throat. "A representation of marriage. Something about the goddess Laxmi. Fertility? Being the light of the household?" Vee shrugged, running out of responses.

"And who do you think created those rules. The gods? Would a god have decreed such a thing?" The old woman shook her head. "Those who choose to negate a woman's claim on her husband's estate, those who wish to destroy the power she'd once held as his consort, they are ones who sought to instill that barbaric ritual."

"But you wore the bindi all through your marriage. And you allowed them to remove it when Babaji died?" The longer Vee spoke, the more uncertain she felt. Radhima was turning everything Vee had known about her past on its head.

Radhima smiled and stared out of the window for a moment. When she looked back at Vee, her eyes glistened with unshed tears. "There was a good reason behind my mother's advice. She was giving me the tools to live a life as a strong woman…a strong woman who had to pretend to the world her entire life."

Vee frowned and sat back. She wanted to laugh it off, make a joke and change the topic. Her grandmother's words made her uncomfortable, and she sensed the natural social urge to protect herself from the truth. But that was cowardly. She'd be disrespecting Radhima by making light of her pain.

Vee said the only thing that she could think of. "Do you want to talk about it?" Vee felt tears burn her eyes and she swallowed against the tightening in her throat.

The old woman smiled and shook her head. "That is not the conversation we are having now, child." She inhaled slowly and looked up at the sky. "I understood much later in life what my mother had meant. You see, nobody owns the birdsong. Perhaps the bird is caged, but its music is free to dance on the wind, to make people smile. Our birdsong is the song of our hearts, our creativity, our literal voice, our art. Even caged, we can still make ourselves heard."

Vee's ears were ringing. The reality of what her grandmother was saying was hitting her hard. She had to force herself to breathe, to listen as Radhima continued, "A woman's love? It can only be had when her partner has traveled the right journey, conquering ego, uplifting selflessness, giving freedom. A woman's life? It's the one thing nobody can take from you."

The back of the cab was steeped in silence for a few moments until Vee said, "What about a woman's body…her physical self?"

"Physical life?" Radhima tilted her head to study Vee. "Physical form, yes? That can be beaten down. But not your inner essence. That's yours no matter what happens to your physical self. Even through great trauma, one's inner essence remains within us. We just have to find our way back. I won't say the journey is ever easy, but we do what we must to go home," she said, patting below her sternum—at the point of the solar plexus chakra.

The cab rolled to a stop and Vee peered out at the address, reaching for her bag. Her eyes widened at the sight of the red carpet and the gold plaque set into gray stone beside the entrance. She raised her eyebrows and turned to share her surprise with her grandmother when she realized that she was alone.

Radhima was gone. Vee sat back, stunned, deflated. She'd been speaking to the ghost—apparition—for all this time and she'd totally forgotten that the old woman wasn't even real. And yet she'd felt real. And Vee wasn't thinking about the warmth that had emanated from her body from time to time.

No. It had been more than that.

"You're a fortunate young woman," a high, crackly voice said from the front of the cab.

Vee snapped her attention to the driver—who had twisted around in his seat and was facing her— and frowned at his words. She didn't feel particularly fortunate right now. Still, she shook her head, confused as she waited for him to elaborate. "Good spirits don't often visit us, you know. If she's coming to you and she's been kind and loving, then you know she's here for a reason other than to do you harm." The old man smiled and winked. As if that was going to make her feel better.

Vee tilted forward, still frowning. "You saw her."

He nodded. "When you live a long life like I have, you tend to see a lot of strange things."

You can say that again.

Vee glanced back at the empty space beside her. "I thought I was imagining her," she murmured.

The driver shrugged. "If that was the case, I'd say that imagination of yours is very strong."

The things Vee's grandmother had said had been illuminating. And yet it made her realize something. Vee now had information she could take to her mother. A fact about Radhima's life that she'd never been told. A piece of the past that Radha's daughter no doubt knew.

A tiny part of Vee's mind asked what she would do if it turned out that Mom knew nothing about her mother's marital discontent.

Vee suppressed a sigh. She had no choice but to speak to her mother now. After what the apparent apparition had just revealed, Vee owed it to herself and to her ghostly gran, to confirm once and for all if she was real.

Though the cab-driver's confirmation should have been enough, she still needed her mother's response to what Radhima had revealed.

Because if Vee's figment-of-imagination grandmother was really Radhima come back to the land of the living, Vee was going to have an epic meltdown.

CHAPTER 10

As Vee entered the hotel room—or suite if she wanted to be specific—she grimaced. Her nostrils were assailed with the scent of blood. The apartment itself was cloyingly hot—despite the cold outside—the sun had just passed its zenith and was at the perfect angle to light up the room. The brightness only highlighted the white-on-white decor within the plush suite.

Vee dug inside her messenger bag for a pair of bootees and latex gloves. She slipped the coverings onto her shoes and then—as she strode further into the room—drew the latex gloves on.

Crime scene techs and police officers milled around the front living room, hands, and shoes also protected. A few shifted their attention to her as she entered, their spines stiff as if ready to tell her to get lost. She waved a gloved hand and drew her jacket aside, revealing the FBI badge and gun on her belt.

The sight of the badge turned a few expressions sour, but not everyone appeared to be entirely hating her. She had a few people on the local force who respected her enough to at least greet her with a modicum of civility. She greeted the room and kept walking past a feature table that lay on its side, a large brass bowl toppled over with white roses and carnations strewn across a patch of wet carpet. Thick cream pile covered the floor, and white and gold marble end-tables were scattered around the large space. All the furniture was white leather or expensive fake fur or hand-woven wool.

Its pristine condition was destroyed by the streak of blood on the far wall, and a large oval shaped bloodstain on the carpet near the windows. A pair of double doors opened to Vee's left, and from the low hum of voices, she figured that was the location of the murder. Vee walked over to the inner doorway, and entered right into a middle of an argument, their huddle blocking the view of the victim on the gigantic bed beyond them.

The three cops embroiled in some sort of turf argument all turned to look at Vee who stood serenely on the threshold. Detective Andrea Monroe stood closest to Vee, and for once she didn't ignore her. The two other detectives didn't appear to know Vee. Which could work in Vee's favor.

Or not.

Monroe strode toward Vee and held out a latex-gloved hand. Vee raised an eyebrow and looked at her hand, then took it and gave it a short shake. Whatever the woman was up to, Vee decided she'd enjoy the semblance of professional courtesy Monroe was currently affording her.

"Agent Shankar, glad you could make it." Monroe smiled, though the expression didn't seem to meet her eyes.

And Vee had a strong feeling that the detective's bad attitude was not directed at Vee herself. Monroe turned to the waiting men and strode off without a word. Assuming Monroe had meant for her to follow, Vee hurried after her.

She scanned the room as she went. Large, at least ten times the standard size of a double bedroom, cream wool carpeted the floor, deep mahogany furniture completing the plush expensive decor. Floor-to-ceiling drapery graced the right-hand wall— which consisted of one giant window— and was currently flung wide open. Allowing the sun to stream inside. Had Vee been in charge she would have shut the curtains, especially knowing what heat did to biological evidence. Surely Monroe knew that.

She came to a stop in front of the two detectives. Both had already begun speaking, but Vee lifted a hand, cutting them off. "Can we get those drapes closed, please? Before the biological evidence degrades?"

Monroe raised her hands in the air and then dropped them. "That's exactly what I've been trying to tell them, but they refuse to listen."

Vee shifted her attention to the two men. "And why exactly is that?"

"This is *our* jurisdiction," said the first detective, poking his thumbs into his belt loops. He wore a pale pink shirt, unbuttoned to reveal a tanned chest covered in a thick layer of chest hair, a fat gold chain gleaming around his neck. His hair was cut short, military style, and his shoulders were muscled. He wore dark chinos and cowboy boots, which he hadn't bothered to protect.

His partner on the other hand—dark-suited and elegant—was so pretty Vee had to force her jaw to close. Startlingly blue eyes, thick hair cut long on top to grace his chin, short and sensible at the back. High cheekbones, full lips, firm chin, all making Vee peg him as Middle Eastern, Persian or something East Asian. He stood there, watching her watch him, his stance wide, his eyes devoid of emotion.

Neither man introduced themselves.

"Jurisdiction or not, you clearly do not understand the concept of preserving the evidence." Vee reached into her messenger bag and withdrew two more pairs of bootees. Handing them over she said, "I'm sure that should you win the argument over jurisdiction—which you likely won't because Monroe is Special Victims and you guys just want to make things difficult—you will ultimately want to catch the killer. To do so, you will require evidence. Viable evidence. The sun coming in through those windows is turning this place into an oven."

Out of the corner of her eye, Vee could see Monroe opening her mouth.

Vee didn't allow the detective to speak. "I'm absolutely confident that my associate Detective Monroe here knows procedure. So, can I assume that it is you two detectives who saw fit to ignore protocol?" Hands now on her hips, Vee looked over at Man Chest, who stared at her, features schooled—so he was good at this—and then turned to look at Pretty Boy who let out a soft hiss of breath.

Out of the corner of her eye, she caught movement as Monroe waved at a tech to close the drapes. Within a few seconds, the drapes drew shut and the room was filled with bright light from an expensive chandelier that probably cost as much as it had to decorate the whole suite itself

Vee knew that she'd made an impression when she'd entered. And not a good one. The men shared a glance that spoke volumes, their lips turning up in a pair of matching smirks. "Something amusing you, detectives?" Vee asked. She was beginning to lose her patience with their insolent stares.

Neither of the men were interested in her words. They were both staring at the front of her shirt where her boobs were currently stretching the buttons because of her hands-on-the-hips stance. She usually had her jacket buttoned, but with the stifling heat within the apartment, she'd instinctively and unconsciously released the buttons at some point.

Vee wasn't prudish by any means, but the outright rudeness and disrespect of these two men had her head burning up. Time to flip the two assholes.

"She's here because she got a call. And I don't mean just-a-call." Monroe thrust a thumb in Vee's direction. "When *she* gets a call, you know it's from high up in the food-chain. Sorry guys. I would have loved to fight you on this—and win—but if I know one thing, that package of tits and ass already has a warrant to take over this case. You two may as well skulk back to your precinct and cry on your captain's shoulder."

Vee tried hard not to smile as she shared a glance with Monroe. "Ass too?"

Monroe nodded, then jerked her chin at Pretty Boy.

Vee lifted her eyebrows, pursing her lips in disgust as she looked back at them. "Are you two still here?"

Man Chest took a step forward, sticking his face close to Vee's. She merely smiled and said, "You do know that's not a threat, right?"

His eyebrows scrunched.

"You. Shoving your face in mine. Showing me how strong you are. Threatening me with your height and your physique and your manliness." Vee moved her hand, cupping her fingers in position. "Show me more of your power, detective. Because I'll be happy to show you mine."

Just as Vee glanced pointedly at her hand, Monroe let out a decidedly unladylike bark of laughter. "Gianni, she's got you by the cojones. Literally."

CHAPTER 11

Monroe curtailed her laughter, likely taking the dead woman into consideration, and Vee wasn't amused to find Man Chest's—or Gianni's—partner grinning widely.

Meanwhile, Gianni stepped away from Vee's cupped hand and readjusted his pants. As if that would change anything.

Vee moved around the men and ignored them as she turned to study the bed. Likely the biggest bed she'd ever seen, it was covered in a silk duvet that had once been a delicate cream color. Matching silk sheets and pillowcases bore a randomly patterned combination of dull red and cream.

A setting more for romance than murder.

Vee shifted to the bedside, studying the victim's body, which was a strangely gray, almost ashen color—a sure sign of an extreme lack of blood. The victim lay with her torso hanging over the edge of the bed. Vee crouched down beside the victim and inspected the woman's throat. It had been clawed open in one swift move, after which it appeared the woman's blood had been extracted. Vee didn't need to access her aural reading skills to know that.

"Victim's name?" Vee asked without looking over her shoulder.

"Victim checked in under the name Susie Ling. New York driver's license. Looks like she was a gossip columnist for a local rag. We're following up on the address on the license."

Behind Monroe, Pretty Boy was saying, "So what does the FBI want with a New York serial killer case? He hasn't crossed state lines anyway."

Vee shifted and looked over her shoulder at him, to find him staring—very pointedly—at her ass. She rose to her feet and turned to face him. "I didn't get your name?"

"Detective Hasif." He extended a hand, revealing very well-manicured fingernails.

Vee gave his fingers a dirty look and met his eyes. "Okay, *Detective* Hasif. Firstly, how is it that you are so sure this case doesn't cross state lines? And secondly, what makes you think that the FBI only deals with crimes that cross state lines."

Hasif lifted one finger, his eyes flicking to Vee's cleavage for a few moments before he spoke. "Because we've been tracking this case for the last four months and nothing indicates that the killer strays too far from this particular area."

"And you came to that conclusion how?" Vee asked.

"Sorry, *Agent* Shankar. That's privileged information." He smirked.

The man was getting on Vee's nerves. For all his beauty, he was just as much a misogynist as his distasteful partner. Vee paused. That was a bit of a prejudiced thought. The man was an asshole, but having a beautiful face never once guaranteed the owner a beautiful personality or heart.

Vee let out a long breath. "My warrant says it's not."

"I haven't seen a warrant, Shankar." Gianni had finally decided to jump into the battle, although Vee noticed that the man remained on the other side of his partner, as far away from her as possible.

"If you check your emails you will," she said with a sweet smile. Or what she hoped was a sweet smile. Inside herself, the smile she gave them was nothing short of demonic.

There was a long pause before Monroe took a step closer. "Gentlemen. This is a closed crime scene. I'm leaving too, so I'll be happy to escort you out."

The two men stared at each other, weighing their options. Gianni snorted and snagged his cell phone from his pocket. A few swipes later, he looked up and gave Vee a filthy glare, his lip curling in a snarl. "She's telling the truth. I got a copy of the warrant forty minutes ago."

Vee didn't say a word. She wasn't above crowing—particularly with these two louts—but she wanted the men out of the room as soon as possible. The heat would not only damage the integrity of the biological samples, not to mention it would also be affecting the strength and clarity of the auras she intended to read.

The two detectives spent a minute hesitating until Vee sighed and turned away from them. As she stared at the victim, Vee said, "Do you need help finding the exit, boys? Monroe offered, but I need her advice on something, so we'll get someone else to help."

Hasif sputtered. "She's staying?" Looking over at him, Vee lifted an eyebrow and gave a sharp nod. She hadn't looked at Monroe once, and now hoped the detective would play along. "This is *our* jurisdiction. You can't toss us out of here and then allow *Monroe* to stay." His voice held an almost whiny quality that set her nerves on edge.

Vee forced herself to concentrate, then walked around the bed to inspect the feet of the woman who was currently splayed across the mattress, her guts ripped open. The fact that they were having a power struggle while this poor woman's body cooled was distasteful.

She glanced up at the two men. "I've worked with Monroe on Special Victims cases before. And if she looks at my tits and ass, she doesn't make it as obvious as the two of you. Even if I had the power to keep you two on, I wouldn't because you have disrespected me from the moment I walked into the room."

Vee paused to draw her camera from her pocket and take two photos, one of the woman's neck which revealed strange bruises, and the other of the wound in her neck that confirmed Vee's suspicion of the killer's species.

She still hadn't heard them leave. "Oh, and this is a closed investigation. I've already subpoenaed all your files on the case going back however long you've had this killer on your radar."

Both men's mouths opened, and Gianni's jaw clenched as he launched himself at her. "Not a step closer, Gianni." Monroe jerked her head at the door to the room. "If you know what's best for you, you'll leave now. You don't want to take her on. She's got balls the size of Texas."

"That much is clear." Gianna spat the words and Vee glanced up at him. "Crime scene fellas. Please endeavor to keep your biological substances—sputum included—to yourselves. I'd ask for a mask for you but since you're leaving..."

Monroe ushered the two men outside, but Vee was no longer paying attention. The whole discussion and argument with them had been tiring. She encountered men like them all the time, the ones who believed women were mere possessions, who thought women to be beneath them, who refused to accept a female in charge of them.

Good thing they were gone then.

The outer door slammed closed, and seconds later Monroe returned, coming to Vee's side. "Why'd you keep me on?" When Vee said nothing, Monroe huffed. "Even if it was just to stick it to those two dick-heads, I'm happy."

Vee shook her head. "It wasn't." Then she paused and grinned. "Well, it was, kinda. But I do need you."

Vee looked around at the crime scene techs. Monroe answered before Vee could ask the question. "They're ours."

"Good. Then they'll know where to send the evidence samples."

Monroe nodded, well used to Vee's requests that half the evidence be sent on to Vee's own lab at Shankar Industries so she could work on them herself—that was, of course, only when she hadn't been able to obtain her own.

Vee gave a short nod and turned away to study the body. "I'm going to need some space and privacy."

One of the forensics techs—most likely new—gasped. "We can't leave the crime scene unattended. Not until everything is bagged and tagged."

Vee turned and waved them off. "Don't worry. I just need space for a few minutes. You'll have me in your sights the entire time."

Though still hesitant and sending her suspicious looks, the forensics techs got to their feet and walked over to the door. One stopped on the threshold. "This far enough?"

Vee smiled. "Plenty. And I promise I won't take too much of your time." For a moment, Vee felt like an animal in a circus, about to do some amazing trick to impress the audience.

Monroe stood a few feet back having settled into the pattern she and Vee had used over the last few months. Monroe now took up position about ten yards away, giving Vee enough space to work, to study the body and everything else that had happened. This was the part Vee dreaded.

The part where she watched a murder happen in real time.

The auras of the two cops, both a combination of dark green and brown, made a straight path to the position in which Vee had found them when she'd arrived. Neither of the men had been here before Monroe, so she'd been the one to secure the scene. Monroe's aura showed her entering and studying the body from a million angles.

As Vee stared at the aural patterns, she focused on those of the woman and one other person who, to Vee, appeared to be the intruder. The green-and-black aural image described a person of at least six-foot-five and of a large physique. Darker, almost red-black streaks within the image made her stomach tighten.

Karan had been right. This was a demon attack. But even knowing what the perpetrator was, didn't ease Vee's concern. It was what had really happened to the victim that Vee had to watch. And knowing already that it was going to be bad made her want to turn and run off.

Big bad FBI agent huh?

CHAPTER 12

Reading crime scenes had never been easy.

In fact, it had always been tough, not that Vee had been doing this gig for so long. But watching a person's death—however fractal the aural patterns could make the scene—had always made the experience painful. Over time, she'd learned to keep her emotions in check, to control her expression and be professional.

The problem was, Vee was the type of person who disliked horror movies—she'd have to watch most of it with half-closed lids and shut her eyes whenever she thought something awful was about to happen.

And she was also the person who would bawl her eyes out when watching a sad scene on TV.

Her emotional reactions were at total odds with her job, and she knew it all too well.

So, standing by and watching a person get ripped apart—even when the images were a lot like watching people on an infrared camera affected by bad static—was always painful and frustrating. It made Vee feel helpless, made her feel as though she needed to go find the killer right then and administer the same treatment to him.

Now she took a deep breath and forced herself to concentrate, to put her emotions aside and focus.

Vee stared at the body, her vision blurring for the briefest second. Soon the room shifted in color and was filled with patterns of auras all meshed into each other. Fresh aural imprints were intertwined with those from earlier in the day, and Vee had to spend a few moments sifting through them.

One at a time, she studied an imprint then removed it from her vision. If she had to describe it in a physical way, it would be as if she'd lightened or erased a single person's aura the way you'd adjust images in photo-manipulation software.

The only problem was that Vee had to work backward, sifting through the intertwined strands, studying them and then lifting them away from her vision. She could still see them all, but somehow her brain had decided that she could switch that particular aura off until she was done studying the scene.

She sifted through and ticked off the forensic people, then the policemen, Monroe and then Gianni and Hasif. Her vision was now less filled with auras, and she was able to concentrate better. She chose then to look at earlier in the day and remove those who were not suspects.

The cleaning crew of three had come in mid-morning, and from what Vee saw the company needed a good raise. The three women were very thorough.

At check-in time, the victim arrived alone, and had been brought up to the suite. Her aura was cool, revealing her confidence and unworried mood. She was levelheaded, not the kind of person prone to bursting out into song or profanity. She toured the rooms, guided by the porter.

Not much later, she ordered a meal using the bedroom phone then changed into what Vee assumed were more comfortable clothing. The aura suggested soft, loose-fitting pants and an oversized tee. Then she headed to the lounge and curled up to watch TV until her food arrived. While she ate, the demon appeared. He'd materialized near the windows and had hidden behind the long drapes, his position beyond Susie's field of vision.

Vee frowned, unsure now of how the man had gained access as her vision confirmed that the door to the hotel suite had remained locked. A sinking feeling filled her stomach, and Vee swallowed hard against it. The magical entrance meant only one thing. Karan had been right about the nature of the killer.

He'd watched and waited until Susie finished her meal and headed for the bathroom where she drew a bath and undressed, removing something—perhaps a necklace—from around her neck, dropping it onto the countertop.

The gold aura glinted again as the chain shifted; the victim had placed it too close to the edge of the counter. The chain moved again, unspooling as it was pulled over the edge and dropped inside something that sat beside the sink. Vee made a note to check that with Monroe.

She focused on the demon now, whose aura shifted, edged with blues and whites which implied he'd pulled a glamor over his form, perhaps to make himself invisible.

The intruder took a glance at those corners, then slipped inside the bathroom to stand beside the door as the victim readied herself for a night in. From the strength and size of the aura, Vee had to guess that it could belong to either a gigantic wrestler with a fever, or one of a powerful demon species.

Vee waited as she watched the aura of the killer. He'd entered the bathroom, the gigantic space larger than some homes, with separate cubicles for two toilets and a double sink and counter almost two yards long. Much of the bathroom was carpeted, and from the bloodstains on white pile near the tub, Vee suspected his attack was imminent. The bedroom had begun to darken, providing plenty of shadows and dark corners within which to lurk.

Susie's aura shifted between colors which Vee guessed was her mood relaxing from the soak in the tub. To interpret the finer details of a person's aura, Vee would have to spend a large amount of time with that person, to study their possible moods and make guesses as to the colors and how they related to the person's mood and emotions. For now, she could only assume, but she was making educated guesses nonetheless.

When Susie was done, she rose from the water and wrapped herself within a towel. She stepped from the bath and began to dry her body before pulling on a bathrobe. She faced the mirror, and was brushing out her wet hair when the demon's aura shivered and changed, her aura darkened as she caught sight of his reflection in the mirror before her.

The demon attacked, encircling her neck with his arm. She struggled, flailing and grabbing aimlessly at him but she had no power against him whatsoever.

A flare of darker astral lines caught Vee's attention as Susie grabbed onto the faucet—the only thing she could hold onto. The demon had pulled hard, and Susie's desperate grip broke, ripping open a fingernail as well. The bleeding at the wound, though minor, had caused the glowing. Evidence that the forensics people had missed. Though it was likely that they hadn't gotten to the bathroom yet to look for evidence.

The demon dragged her back a few feet from the stain on the carpet—which Vee could see beyond her vision of the shifting auras.

Susie's struggles continued, and she managed to grab hold of the demon's ear, pulling hard. Vee made a note to have forensics check beneath Susie's fingernails for DNA—demon DNA of course, but Vee still needed to confirm.

The demon's aura changed suddenly, his imprint darkening with rage or pain or both. Much of Vee's observations were left up to interpretation, and she supposed that the demon's fluctuation in aural color could also have meant arousal or fear, but in the context of what she was witnessing, her gut told her it wasn't.

Reacting to Susie's attack, the demon punched her in the head and swung her around. She flailed like a rag doll and hit the carpeted floor. But there was a strength in her that Vee admired, and she watched as the woman tried to get back onto her feet.

Vee wasn't sure what Susie had thought she could do against the attacking demon, but the woman must have been desperate to get away, to fend him off.

It was hopeless.

As Susie rose to her knees, preparing to boost herself to her feet, the demon swung a hand at her neck. And spilled her blood onto the floor.

The aura of the lifeblood shimmered with white fractal patterns as it gushed, as Susie grabbed her throat. Blood seeped from her wound, dripping past her fingers and falling onto the carpet and matched up perfectly with the large stain.

The demon wasn't wasting time. He grabbed for an ankle and dragged Susie into the bedroom, stopping only when he reached the bed. Fluctuations in Susie's aural patterns implied a range of emotions that Vee assumed ran from terror, anger, shame, and helplessness.

Still, the woman didn't just lie there waiting to die. She got to her feet, managing to stand despite the blood loss. But her attempt to flee failed as the demon smashed his fist onto the back of her head and she sank to the ground weakened by the blow. He didn't give her time to move, just grabbed her and tossed her onto the bed where she moaned and tried to roll over. His blatant disregard for her made Vee wonder if he believed she was not worth the effort.

The demon lunged for Susie who scrambled backward on the bed, but the demon was on her in half a second, moving so fast

Vee suspected he'd done a partial jump. As he swiped at her, Vee confirmed his species.

A pey.

To encounter a second pey demon within the same twelve-hour period was highly unusual.

Worse yet, here he was murdering a woman in a high-profile neighborhood. It was almost as if he was acting without forethought, without planning.

Vee focused on his movements as he attacked the victim, shredding her abdomen and moving over her to feed at her neck. Fueled perhaps by adrenaline, the woman bucked against him hard and tried to move away. The movement brought her to the edge of the bed, but the demon was still in control, feeding on her until her strength began to wane. Vee swallowed as she watched Susie's aural patterns fluctuate and fade at the point of her death.

Vee had stiffened as the demon got to his feet and stalked into the front room. Her focus had been on the aural patterns in the bedroom during the attack, so when the demon exited the room to be confronted by another person, it was a surprise.

Vee would have come across the aura of the newcomer eventually, but to now see that there was another victim in this crime was a shock. She'd suspected as much considering the attack had happened in the bathroom, and the woman had been dead on the bed within seconds, no time for the demon to take her out to the living room and attack her there—especially to justify the blood in the living room. Despite Susie's best attempts at escape, she'd been overpowered with no hope of surviving.

Now, Vee watched as the demon stared down the visitor who was much smaller in size than Susie, appearing to be another slight-built woman or a teenager.

The person backed away, bumped into something, probably the central feature table that Vee had seen when she'd entered. This was how it was knocked over.

The demon lunged at the victim, swiping hard at the neck area, likely using his long, curved claws. The trajectory of the swipe sent blood spurting in a wide arc resulting in the spatter patterns on the wall and picture window behind the victim.

Still, it appeared that the attacker hadn't killed the victim. Vee was about to forward through the aural pattern when she paused. Something was strange about the person's aura, a strong glow of fractal patterns in the abdominal area. Vee concentrated on the looping swirls of color but already had a suspicion about the glow as she honed in on the shimmering pale blue and gold lines.

The second victim was a woman, and she was carrying a child.

CHAPTER 13

Vee's stomach churned.

The demon paused, hovering over the woman and Vee had to wonder if he'd also realized that the woman was pregnant. His attack stopped, and he knelt before the victim whose aura implied pure terror.

Her hands lay over her abdomen, and Vee felt almost ill when she recalled that the pey had attacked Susie with a blow to the gut first. Had he done the same with this unknown victim, she'd have lost her child instantly.

But the pey seemed to have ceased his attack, waving at her to get to her feet. She obeyed, seeming to not have the same ability to resist as Susie had, which again implied that the woman was much younger or probably just not as strong as Susie.

It also explained what had given Susie such strength to fight back; she'd known the other woman was coming to see her. Vee had noticed that the second woman had entered the apartment alone, probably with a second key from the front desk. Which could mean Susie had had an arrangement with the hotel for a key for a second guest.

The demon closed in on the woman and wrapped his arms around her. Then both the aural patterns vanished.

In the second before the demon jumped the victim away, Vee caught the golden glint of something at the woman's neck. It was possible that she too had worn some sort of gold jewelry, which from its aural patterns had a high chance of being made of the same metal as the one she'd seen Susie drop onto the bathroom counter.

Vee took a shuddering breath and straightened. Looking up, she found herself standing in the living room a foot from the second bloodstain.

Monroe was talking to a couple of cops nearby and from what Vee could tell the outer room had been emptied as she'd worked. She hadn't realized that she'd moved into the living area and was grateful that Monroe had seen fit to preempt Vee's need for privacy and had evacuated the outer suite.

Monroe looked over at Vee, who jerked her head at the detective then walked back into the interior room.

Vee beckoned Monroe to the bathroom even as the other woman asked, "What can you tell?"

Vee sighed and waved a hand at the bathtub. "She ate a meal, then had a soak in the tub. The attacker entered the bathroom and surprised her. She fought him, and he reacted with a blow to her neck. Causing the bloodstain here."

Monroe nodded. "That's more or less what I thought. There was water at the bottom of the tub, along with granules from what looked like bath-salts, or a bath bomb."

"Yeah, the bloodstain and the drag marks are pretty self-explanatory. She fought him though. He came up behind her, and she would have seen him in the mirror before he struck."

Monroe frowned. "How can you tell that she was at the wash-basin?" Her expression had begun to fill with suspicion.

Vee shrugged. "There is a blood droplet from a broken fingernail behind the faucet. You may want to get a sample."

Monroe nodded, although the detective didn't look pleased. "Yeah, the techs haven't come in here yet. But a broken fingernail isn't something they should have missed."

"Not a fingernail. It's a drop of blood."

"And you noticed this how?"

"I considered various possible scenarios and checked the bathroom accordingly." Vee gave a shrug and took a few steps back. "I'd guess he grabbed her from behind and she'd have kicked. Explains the bruises on her knees and toes—kicking out and hitting the cupboards."

Monroe's eyes were dark as she stared around the room, and then focused on the double washbasin.

Vee continued, "At that point, I'd guess she would have reacted with greater desperation. Probably reached out to grab him, scratch him, pull his hair. Anything to stop him."

"And how the hell can you tell such a thing?" The detective's brow furrowed as she scowled at Vee.

"I can't tell. I'm thinking of possible scenarios. It's possible she did nothing, but would that explain the bruising on her knees and feet, the bruising on her fingers and the broken nails. We should consider that a possibility. Not investigating all the possible scenarios and outcomes is reckless and lazy."

Vee wanted to bite her tongue as soon as the words left her mouth. Monroe was a touchy woman, easily offended. And she had never been happy with Vee's involvement. Vee didn't need to alienate the woman by being insensitive. But when she looked over at Monroe's reflection in the mirror, she found that despite the detective's cold frown and stiff spine, the woman was nodding slowly as she scanned the room.

"I'll have the team double-check her fingernails. That's a standard thing anyway, but I'll chase the results." She looked up at Vee. "If we're still helping you out."

Vee pursed her lips. "Yeah. Just don't let those two find out."

Monroe nodded then retrieved her little notebook from inside her jacket pocket and began to scribble on it.

Vee glanced around for where she'd seen the golden chain fall, spotting a pair of hotel-issue slippers beside the counter. "Oh, and there is a piece of jewelry inside one of those slippers beside the washbasin."

The detective paused in her scribbling and glanced over in the direction in which Vee was looking. "Don't tell me…you considered all possible scenarios?" she asked, her expression bland.

Vee resisted the urge to roll her eyes, and instead turned and headed back into the bedroom. "Here he left her on the floor probably thinking she was done. But maybe she tries to move… to stand. He's likely done. This is taking too long. He grabs her and pushed her onto the bed—"

"Grabs her shoulders which is evident by the bruising on her shoulders," Monroe said with a nod.

"She lands and then he guts her. She's still desperate to get away and tries to pull herself to the edge of the bed. But he finishes her off."

"Yeah, that much I can see too. But my question is what the hell happened to all the blood. There isn't enough here to warrant the kind of attack you are talking about."

Vee lifted her hand, intending to dig into her bag for her evidence kits, but a small plastic bag was placed into her palm. She cast Monroe a grateful smile and held onto it as she crouched down beside the body and used the enclosed tweezer to remove the evidence.

The girl's fingers were rigid despite the warmth of the apartment. Reaching out, Vee grabbed a hold of what looked like a long strand of dark hair. She drew the tweezer away, depositing the strand of black hair into the plastic bag. Vee scribbled the codes for her lab sample and then handed the bag to Monroe who was closest. Vee kept going, removing another strand of hair from beneath the victim's body.

At last, Vee studied the body itself, lifting the sheet to inspect Susie in case of rape, not required considering what Vee had already seen, but she had to go through the motions of being a good investigative officer exploring all options. "The forensics team will do a rape kit, but she doesn't appear to have been sexually assaulted," Vee murmured, more to herself than anything. She got to her feet and stared down at the woman.

When she sighed, Monroe asked, "All done?" Vee nodded. "What you got?"

"I'm still not sure how the killer gained entry, but the victim had no other visitors until the killer arrived. She called for room service. The killer was already here, waiting for his moment to strike." Vee mimicked the move in the specific spot that the killer had stood before he'd hit the victim.

"And the dine and dash?" Monroe cocked her head at the ravaged neck of the victim.

Vee made a face. "Looks a lot as though he bled her somehow." Though Vee faked ignorance of the somehow, she knew all too well. The pit of her stomach burned at the thought, and she knew she had to get a report into Rossi ASAP.

Vee glanced at the detective who held up a hand. "I'm sure autopsy is going to confirm all those injuries exactly as you've described, but the forensics techs are going to ask what the perp did with the blood. Did he drain her elsewhere then return with the body or are we dealing with a vampire?" Monroe's loud snort showed how little she believed in the supernatural. The woman liked her facts hard and visible.

Vee shrugged. "Whatever he did, you're right. There's a lot of blood unaccounted for." Vee turned and looked at the picture window. "He was done here, so he left the room. Possibly he was looking for something."

Vee moved out of the bedroom and traced the demon's steps, stopping only when she got to the bloodstain on the carpet.

"We have a second victim."

"This stain's not Susie's?" Monroe's spine stiffened as she studied the blood.

Vee shook her head. "There isn't anything to explain why he would have brought Susie out here." Vee paused and waved a hand at the inner room. "When during his attack would he have had the time? Or the reason?"

"So someone else entered the suite and was attacked here." Vee nodded as Monroe walked around the toppled end table to study the spatter on the window. "So, we have two murder victims."

"No."

"What do you mean?" Monroe scowled.

"We have one murder victim and one abduction victim."

"Now how did you manage a conclusion like that?"

"Not enough blood spatter to indicate murder. And she's not here. It's possible he took her elsewhere to kill her, but that makes no sense, especially since he'd already begun his attack." Vee motioned at the bloodstained carpet.

"The woman in there didn't have enough blood to match the spatter and stains either."

"Good point. I just think that the lack of a body implies he took her. And it's likely that she'd been special enough to take *her* body away and not Susie's. There's something different about the second woman." Vee was trying to find a way to come to that conclusion out loud without making the detective suspicious.

"What do you mean?"

"I think he may have changed his mind about killing her. He'd inflicted the first injury, but then he stopped and allowed her to live. Even took her away alive. There's something that he wants from her."

"You think he's a sex fiend or something? Get his rocks off on raping a dying woman? Blood fetish maybe?"

Vee shook her head. "Susie wasn't raped. I don't think this is a sex-related crime. Something else is going on here." As Vee thought about it, she wondered if they could obtain enough evidence to test for pregnancy. She looked at Monroe. "I have a gut feeling but don't laugh." Vee felt bad about playing Monroe, but there was no other way to explain her reasoning to the detective.

"You want me to pinkie swear?" The woman snorted. "Tell me what you got."

Vee shrugged and pointed to the bloodstain. "Let's see how much blood we can sample for an HCG test."

Monroe's eyes winded. "You think she's pregnant."

"I think she is. But it would be nice to get some proof."

"How in the holy heck did you deduce something like that?"

"Just a hunch. I'm trying to understand why he'd take her. What could she have had that he'd let her live? Pregnancy is a strong possibility."

"That would imply they want the baby for something. Could it be possible that he was here for the baby in the first place and Susie was just collateral damage?"

"Possible." Vee's response was non-committal as she didn't want to interfere too much with the detective's own deductions. Vee's own deductions were based on the hesitation the demon had experienced. She knew the abduction had been impulse-driven. But she wasn't able to reveal that without blowing Monroe's mind. "For now, let's assume there is a pregnant woman missing. I'd also like to have the DNA compared for familial relationships. And get me what you have on Susie's background and history."

"Think they're related?" Monroe nodded as she scribbled on her notepad.

Vee gave the detective an apologetic smile. "Gut feeling."

Monroe looked up and grinned. "So far that gut of yours has proven correct. Let's hope your track record can maintain its GPA."

Vee rolled her eyes and received a snort from Monroe.

Strange that the woman had actually begun to warm up to Vee. Monroe had always been testy and sharp, and Vee had often thought the detective had passionately disliked her.

"So, can I assume that you want our precinct to handle the case?" asked Monroe as she tucked her notebook back inside her jacket pocket.

Vee considered it for a moment. "Let's leave it as unofficial for now. I don't think the FBI has the power to pass judgment on a complicated jurisdictional battle—even if we supported your claim. You might want to verify with the chief. Either way, until I gather sufficient intel, I'll mark this one as a joint effort."

"Then you are going to eventually take it from us?" Now Monroe's tone had turned cool.

Vee shook her head. "No. Even if we do technically, I'd still like for you to remain on board. I just hope that your jurisdictional battle doesn't rule for the assholes. It probably won't but the way things go, assholes may know assholes who may know assholes." Vee shrugged.

Monroe grinned then suppressed her expression. The techs had returned and were back to being busy. "So, how do we find the abduction victim? We don't even know who she is?"

"I'd start with finding out everything we possibly can about Susie, then check on all the people she's interacted with in the last few months, track their movements, get in touch, see who's been missing or who's been acting weird," Vee spoke without thinking, then realized that Monroe had been thinking out loud.

The detective grunted, and Vee glanced back to see anger and irritation flicker across her eyes.

Great. Way to go on destroying what little professionalism we had.

The whole afternoon had passed—evidenced by the weaker light outside, and by the low insistent throbbing in Vee's wing where the wound was slowly healing. Deciding it was time she reported into her boss anyway, Vee turned to Monroe. "Keep me posted?"

Monroe nodded, pulling her cell phone from her pocket. She turned away to make her call.

Vee left without another word, pausing at the door to rip off the bootees and gloves and shove them into a waiting rubbish bag.

She had a few things she needed to get done today, and the day was already over. Funny she could get magical weapons from the gods and not extra hours in the day.

Be careful what you wish for.

CHAPTER 14

Inside the elevator, Vee placed a call to her boss.

"So, was it a solid lead?" was his first question.

"Yes, sir."

"What species are we talking?"

"Pey. Same as this morning."

"Coincidence?"

"Likely not. But this one is a little different. I'm sending some images through. Monroe's got a bunch of evidence on hand. I've requested priority access, and she's assured me I'll have them, but Brent can do his thing already."

"Debrief?" asked Rossi.

"Victim is a female, single from what I gathered. Booked into the hotel yesterday at 4.37pm. Ordered a meal at 5.03pm then relaxed. Meal arrived 6.12 pm. Intruder arrived during the meal at around 6.30pm. He watched and waited until the victim took a bath at 7.10pm. Intruder entered the bathroom at 7.40pm and proceeded to attack her. She put up a fight, so I think we'll get DNA from her fingernails. Time of death 7.59pm. Body was unusually devoid of blood, so the Pey suits the MO."

"Good. I'll wait for your report then?"

"That's not all, sir."

"Oh?"

"There was another victim."

"He killed two people?" Rossi's voice rose. "But the report was one body discovered."

"That's because he didn't kill the second woman. He took her with him."

"So we have a missing person too."

"Yes. And it gets worse. The woman is pregnant."

"I see. I'll have the team put an APB out on her. Do you have a description?"

"Short in stature, slight build. Pregnant."

"That's all you got?"

"Unfortunately, yes. For the moment. Monroe's doing a background on Susie and everyone she associates with."

"Good. So, Monroe is still on the team?"

"As long as the turf war is resolved and falls on her side. We can't afford evidence going missing, and I wouldn't put it past those two detectives to mess with the evidence just to show us a point." The elevator dinged as she reached the first floor.

"Right. Keep me posted."

Rossi assured Vee that he would pull a few strings to ensure the case fell into Monroe's lap—if it happened that the crime scene landed in Gianni and Hasif's jurisdiction.

Vee rang off and tucked her phone back into her pocket as she headed outside.

The last thing she needed was to cross paths with those two creeps again.

Vee smiled at the doorman and headed to the edge of the sidewalk. She waved a cab down and sighed with relief that one was actually coming her way on the first try.

What she didn't expect was for the cab to speed up as he made a beeline for her. Instinct told her to use her wings, but she knew she couldn't do that without jeopardizing everything, not only what she was but also the existence of the supernatural worlds.

But she didn't need to make any decisions.

Someone slammed right into her, so hard that she and her attacker/savior went rolling over and over onto the sidewalk. As they went, Vee heard the cab's tires screech as he tried to redirect his aim and follow Vee where she now lay on the ground, a little dazed.

Out of the corner of her eye, she saw the cab swerve, attempting to avoid a delivery truck that was parked in front of the hotel. The cab-driver failed and slammed into the rear fender of the truck, the loud pop of the airbag filling the street.

Vee grunted and looked up, curious who she had to thank for her life.

Her stomach swirled as she stared into Gianni's eyes. He was smiling as he lay there on top of Vee, pressing against her chest and stomach and compressing her lungs, not to mention forcing her back against the irregular-shaped contents of her satchel on which she'd landed.

She lifted her head and shoved at his shoulders. "I need to breathe."

The push got him to roll off her chest, and Vee sat up and took a deep breath, flinching as her cheek smarted. Just one more injury to add to her current list.

"That's the thanks I get?" He stood, his cheeks red as he tugged at the waistband of his pants.

Vee shook her head. "I'll thank you when I get to breathe. You were pressing all the air out of my lungs," she snapped.

Vee boosted herself to her feet, shifting her messenger bag to her side. Around her, people were rushing about, someone yelled for the ambulance, while another voice called for the cops.

"Don't go anywhere. I'll check on the driver and be back in a second," Gianni instructed. Moments later he yelled, "Where the fuck did he go?"

Vee frowned and walked closer to the damaged vehicle, and watched Gianni as he stared around the street, his skin blotchy with anger. She couldn't tell him that with the driver's seat empty, the chances were high her attacker had been a demon and would have merely vanished from the seat. Or turned himself invisible to then crawl out from the open door.

"Asshole thinks he can run down a lawman?" The detective stalked about like a frenzied rooster until another cop walked up to him and spoke into his ear.

Gianni nodded to the man then stalked away from the cab and came to stand by Vee's side. She'd been tempted to leave, annoyed that he'd left her standing on the sidewalk as if she needed to remain out of harm's way like a helpless female.

Same helpless female who'd almost been run down by a deranged cab-driver and who'd been saved by the very man who'd appeared to be concerned for her safety.

Vee gritted her teeth and waited for Gianni to reach her side, she folded her arms.

"Know anyone who'd have wanted to kill you?" Gianni asked looking Vee up and down.

She raised an eyebrow. "Know anyone who'd have wanted to kill *you*?"

Gianni paused. "Yeah. Good point. Then again, I guess an FBI agent would probably have more people out to kill him. Or her," he tacked on giving her a wary look, as though she'd have been offended by his reference to the FBI agent as male.

She rolled her eyes. "Did you get anything?" Vee asked, following the act of someone who'd almost gotten run over. "How could you lose him?" Vee asked, feeling a little guilty. But the question needed to be asked or else he'd wonder.

Gianna glared at Vee. But she recognized his flushed coloring as anger and embarrassment for having lost the guy. "Not sure how he got away. I wonder if they had it on autopilot."

Vee nodded. "Could be. Especially if there was no sign of a

driver." Vee agreed with him in the hopes that it would help end the conversation faster. But she doubted the auto-pilot reasoning more because of how fast the cab had tried to swerve from an impact with the truck. Autopilot would not have cared what was in the way. And even remote-jacking wouldn't have encouraged avoiding the truck. Only a living being would want to avoid killing himself.

And, just because the demon could have jumped before the crash didn't mean he wouldn't have instinctively swerved. Not all demons were that skilled and it was likely she'd been attacked by an amateur.

Vee jerked her chin at the cab, indicating she wanted to have a look. Gianni looked like he was about to say Vee couldn't look at the car, but then caught himself. Perhaps he suddenly realized who he was speaking to.

He waved her onward, following close behind as she headed to the car.

She bent over and scanned the interior through the broken passenger window. Her vision shifted briefly as she studied the auras within the cab. And sure enough, Vee recognized the combination of shimmering lines and ragged patterns that made up the aura of a rakshasa demon. She hated being right sometimes, especially when it raised the possibility that the two demons who had attacked her this morning may not have been there looking for the bhayakara demon. They could have been after Vee herself.

Vee focused her thoughts and straightened, then inspected the exterior and circled the cab more to get a better idea of speed and impact. She didn't need the information, rather was merely going through the motions in order to not look suspicious.

Still, at the end of the day, she had to find out who was it that wanted to kill her.

It could be anyone ranging from a cop on the force, all the way to the demonic underbelly of New York City. Perhaps a visit with Cressida Lane was called for. Not that Vee wanted to, considering the woman gave her the creeps.

Gianni was speaking, and Vee had to force herself to pay attention. "Don't worry. We'll find the bastard who did this. We'll check all the footage from the traffic cams around the block. I think we should get you a couple security guys. Keep an eye on you in case something else happens?"

Vee smiled. "Now tell me how that will look, Gianni? An FBI agent with a security detail of local law enforcement?" Vee shook her head, suspicious now that perhaps Gianni had orchestrated the whole thing, in order to justify having Vee watched twenty-four-seven. What better way to get info on her activities than to be the one to 'keep an eye' on her safety? "Don't worry Gianni. I'll have the FBI look after my safety, thanks. My boss will be onto it the moment I tell him."

"Better do it quick 'cos I've already called it in."

Vee gritted her teeth and walked a few yards away. What were these guys up to? Were they taking advantage of the incident and hoping to put her ability to do the job in question with the threat of her safety being an issue? Were they hoping a security detail would hamper her investigation? Or hoping to ingratiate themselves with her, save her life, give her a security team, and maybe she'd allow them access to the crime scene?

Or had it really been a demonic attempt on her life and all Gianni and his team were doing was protecting her?

Vee retrieved her phone from her pocket and rang Rossi who sounded surprised that she'd called him again so soon.

She proceeded to give him a rundown of her near-death experience.

"Do you really believe that your life could be in danger?" he asked, his tone filled with concern.

"I don't know sir. I don't see how. But I don't doubt that it is odd that the cab-driver happened to be a demon—species I am not particularly familiar with—who disappeared before anyone could question him." Vee kept her voice low as she watched Gianni approach her.

"Demonic? They can disappear right?" asked Rossi.

"Yes, sir. That's possible. But I don't believe a cab would be the kind of transportation they would use."

Gianni now stood at her side, and Vee had to remind herself to give less away as she spoke.

"Right. I'll get Brent onto the traffic and security cams to get us more details."

"Thank you, sir, but I believe that would be a dead end."

Rossi paused. "Very well. Do you need security?"

"Not at this time, sir."

Rossi chuckled. "Why did I suspect that would be your answer?" Vee laughed and Rossi rang off seconds later.

She turned to Gianni. "See," she waved her phone at him, "My boss is organizing an FBI security detail for me."

Gianni looked a little disappointed, making Vee more suspicious now.

Vee smiled. "Thanks, Gianni. You saved my hide. I'll keep you posted on my security detail."

"Happy to save that hide, Shankar," Gianni said giving Vee a lascivious look up and down. "And just let us know if there is anything we can do."

"Thanks. I will."

Like hell, I will.

CHAPTER 15

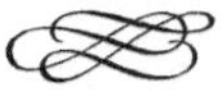

Vee was hurrying down the sidewalk away from the hotel, when a black SUV pulled up. Her phone pinged with a message from Karan to say the SUV was his.

As she jumped in the back seat, she glanced over her shoulder and watched Gianni staring at her. She pretended not to notice and slide inside beside Karan who looked concerned.

"Don't tell me you already know?"

Karan nodded. "We have our own intelligence grapevine."

Vee grunted then said, "Better change your plates."

"What?"

"The plates for the SUV. Gianni over there will be running them as we speak. Hopefully your identity is hidden, or he's going to know who you are."

Karan gave a cool nod. "What happened?"

"A cab came at me, clearly aiming to run me down. Gianni managed to throw me out of harm's way. Cab crashed, but before anyone could go over to check, the driver—who also happened to be a demon—had disappeared." Vee stared over at Karan waiting to see if his face would give something away. But nothing.

Instead, he sighed, studying her bruised cheek. "I do not like that your life is in danger."

"And somehow you believe that it was not in danger in the past?"

Karan stared at her. "You're not taking this seriously. I have had word that the Demon Horde Assembly is troubled by an uneasy political climate, which only increased the problems that result from infighting and struggles for control. The pey demons have split from the Assembly and are attempting to establish the strength of their own Core." Karan sighed then shifted in the seat and was staring at Vee. "And now someone out there wants you dead?"

Vee wasn't sure how to respond so she remained silent. She'd never seen Karan this worked up before.

He sighed again and looked away. "You're important. More important than you know."

"So you think I need to get myself protection? That I need to hide myself away?"

"I know you can take care of yourself, but that doesn't mean you need to be reckless."

"Trust me, I am far from reckless. Not too long ago, we dealt with demonic home invasions. Whoever these assholes are, they don't scare me."

Karan nodded and tapped his finger on the side of the leather folder that sat in his lap. "I hope you are right. We need you alive."

Vee suppressed the desire to tell the man that she was capable of looking after herself. But instead, she forced herself to nod. Of course, he needed her to be alive.

To do his investigative work, that's why.

KARAN DROPPED Vee off at her home, assuring her that he'd glamored the vehicle for a large part of the trip so they would have lost anyone attempting to tail them.

Vee smiled in acceptance, aware still that such maneuvers would not stop anyone who'd decided to surveil her properly. She headed inside, watching the street just in case. After shutting the door, she studied the street again, accepting her nerves were on edge now and she may as well double-check.

Just as a precaution.

As she watched, she messaged Rossi, bringing him up to speed on Karan's update on the Demon Horde Assembly's internal upheaval. Rossi responded confirming he'd put the team on high alert.

At least *he* was taking it seriously.

The house was silent, and Vee took the opportunity to hide in her room for the rest of the evening. Even food wasn't something she was interested in, especially after having spent her afternoon at the suffocatingly warm hotel room.

An hour of training, a shower and then bed.

Just what the doctor would order.

At the thought of the doctor, Vee's mind drifted to Nivaan. He'd been in Europe for the last month on mahabidala business, and his absence had pointedly confirmed to Vee how much she cared about him. Long distance relationships sucked.

Good thing he'd be home tomorrow.

Vee fell asleep thinking about Nivaan's cheeky smile.

CHAPTER 16

Denial can only last so long.

The next morning, Vee awakened after a restless sleep. She'd played the whole scene over and over in her head, wondering if she could have missed some small detail.

Someone had tried to kill her. She had to accept that and move on to step two: find out who they were and hopefully avoid a third attempt.

Third, because she was pretty sure the attack of the killer pey couple had also been a hit. Thankfully, so far Vee had managed to evade those attempts. Now she was left with wondering who they worked for and why they wanted her dead.

Vee forced herself into her training gear and headed down to the gym. After an hour of various weapons exercises—including the trishula—Vee figured it was time she stopped avoiding the inevitable.

She had to go see her Mom.

~

A STRANGE FEELING coiled in Vee's gut as she stepped off the elevator. She'd been thinking about Karan and the last words he'd spoken before he'd dropped her off at home last night. His parting comment was something to the effect of a warning for Vee to take care of herself.

She was well aware that she was an important asset to him, but she still couldn't understand why. What did Karan hope to gain from feeding Vee information regarding demonic crimes against the people of New York? Even Rossi had mentioned recently that although the enigmatic snitch was valuable and was helping their team fight supernatural crime, he too couldn't understand where they were headed.

Though Vee had suggested cutting him loose, Rossi had disagreed, insisting they needed to see this through. Even if they were being used, they were cleaning up the demonic rogue element within the city. That in itself was enough of a reason to play nice with Karan.

But Karan wasn't the only person whose strange behavior remained on Vee's mind.

Radhima's ghost, or rather Radhima herself, was present for a reason as well. As much as Vee wanted to keep ignoring the fact, she knew it was both unhealthy and irresponsible. Add to that she could be hurting her grandmother's feelings by ignoring what was right in front of her own eyes.

Now she hurried through the hall toward her mother's office, feeling a slight twinge in her knee as well as her shoulder. Though Gianni had been kind enough to save her from death, he'd inflicted a few unnecessary injuries on her instead. Nothing that needed medication though. Not yet.

Vee ventured into her mother's front office where Kesha—her personal assistant—stood, arms akimbo, staring down at a collection of plas readers that were spread across her desk. Devi and her team, which included Vee, had long ago gone the green route in that the entire building was run off solar power generated from the solar panels and blinds installed on every window in the building.

They were completely off the grid with only backup generators at the ready in case of a power failure. In addition, Devi had insisted they move away from paper, so staff no longer printed documents out on destroyed trees. Devi had been impressed by the plas reader tech, and now every staff member used plas readers to send files that in the past would have been printed on paper, whether for visual aid, or as a discussion or sharing point in meetings, or just to keep in a tray, the plas sheets had become such a commonality in the building and at home that seeing a sheet of paper sometimes offended Vee.

Kesha's dense black curls hid her face as she studied the plas screens, but before Vee could call out to her, she looked up. With a welcome smile, she waved Vee inside.

Devi stood in front of her plasma screen, pausing and rewinding a video. She shut it off quickly as Vee walked deeper into the room. But not quickly enough. Vee had seen enough of the recording to know that her mother's mind was still focused on the golem that had entered Vee's lab and had attempted to kill her.

The lab surveillance had caught the entire thing on tape and Devi seemed to be studying for clues to...what? Vee would have to ask her at some point.

But Vee had come for an entirely different reason. She went to her mother, and they embraced. Vee kissed her mother's cheek and smiled. Since the night that everything had changed in their lives, since her dad had been returned to them in exchange for Radhima's life, since Mac had moved out of their home, since Vee had been bestowed with the trishula—not to mention having her wings reveal themselves—her relationship with her mother had changed.

A subtle difference—a tiny bit more affection, a kiss on the cheek, a touch on the arm, Devi straightening Vee's hair—little things that had raised Vee's awareness that she actually did have a mother capable of affection.

Vee smiled and then drew back. "You look tired, Mom."

Devi smiled almost absently. "You look damaged, child." She frowned as she studied Vee's face, then traced a finger along the bruise on her daughter's cheek. Vee smirked. "Wish I could say you should see the other guy."

"What happened?"

"In the battle between Vee and the sidewalk, the sidewalk won."

"You fell?" Her mother's tone implied that she found that hard to believe.

Vee sighed. It wouldn't pay to play games with her mother about what had happened. The woman had her ways and would find out eventually and then she'd nag Vee to death about not being told earlier. It was a lose-lose situation.

"Someone tried to run me over. A creeper detective shoved me to safety."

Devi's jaw dropped. "Please tell me they caught the asshole?"

Vee shook her head. "He's the one that got away in this instance."

"How the hell is that possible?"

"Cab was empty when the cops went over to check it out. Was only seconds after I was hit."

"What are you saying? Demon attack?"

Vee nodded. "Yeah. Auras confirmed it. Besides, how else would the driver's seat be empty within seconds of impact? The airbag would have hindered a quick escape. And even if you consider the vehicle being on autopilot, the seat held enough aural presence to confirm a demon did sit in it. Plus, the driver swerved to avoid hitting a parked truck."

"Not something an autopilot would do," Devi murmured.

"Still, it makes no sense. If you're a demon and you want to kill me, won't you use your super easy appearing-disappearing ability? A hit and jump would be more likely."

"Someone trying to scare you?"

"Possible. But it would mean that someone has demons on their payroll."

Vee rolled her eyes. Exactly what part of 'the demons are out to kill me' didn't surprise her?

CHAPTER 17

Devi sighed and waved a hand at the double sofa seating arrangement in the corner of her office. Vee sank into the soft cushion and sighed with relief as she leaned her head onto the backrest.

"Sore?"

"Somewhat."

"What drugs?" Devi asked.

"Nope. Not taken any yet."

Devi brought Vee a glass of pomegranate juice, to which Vee responded with a wrinkle of her nose.

"You know I despise that stuff," she said, making a face at the drink.

"Drink it. It's good for you."

"Sometimes I think mothers were invented to torment."

"Ditto."

Vee rolled her eyes, accepted the drink, and sipped. She swallowed and set the glass on the coffee table, careful to ensure she used one of the many coasters her mother had set around the room. The woman was totally OCD about watermarks on her furniture.

"So, I need to speak with you about something."

"I knew this wasn't a social visit," Devi said, bringing her own glass with her and drinking. She took a seat beside Vee and set her drink on the coffee table before turning her attention her daughter.

"What is it?"

"It's about Radhima."

Devi's mouth tightened, and her eyes glistened. The mention of her mother was enough to bring her back to the reality that the matriarch was gone.

"Are you finding it hard to cope, honey? Need to talk?"

Vee shook her head. "No. I mean yes." Vee paused and took a breath. "I'm coping, but I need to ask you a sensitive question."

"Okay," Devi said carefully, her lip curving in an amused smile.

Vee cleared her throat. "So...I'm not sure how to approach this exactly but here goes." Vee sat up and shifted to face her mother. "Was Radhima unhappy in her marriage?"

Devi's face paled as she stared at Vee. It only took a second for her to shake her head. "Not that I know of. Why do you ask?"

Vee had never known she'd be able to tell off the bat when her mother was lying to her. But, Devi had this tiny little eye-twitch thing she did when she was being evasive or outright lying.

When had Vee gotten so good at reading her mother?

Vee let out a soft controlled breath. "Mom, you don't have to lie to me, okay? I can take the truth. If they were unhappy, or if he was abusing her in any way, I can take it. I didn't know Babaji, so you're not going to be destroying any of my loving preconceived notions about the man."

Devi's eyes widened for a moment, and she played for time, reaching for her glass, sipping and wiping a droplet of condensation from the side of it carefully.

Then she sighed. "I think something happened that she wouldn't speak of."

"Liar," said a voice beside Vee. Though the word was harsh, the tone was somewhat amused. Vee had to force herself not to turn and give Radhima's ghost a warning glare.

She wasn't sure she could talk to her mother about the issue if the ghost was sitting there listening to every word she said. A voice in Vee's head reminded her that at least she'd made Vee aware she was there. She could just as easily not have manifested physically, and instead remained a silent voyeur—which would be all the more uncomfortable.

So she chose to ignore her grandmother and focus on her mother. "I don't believe that, Mom. I know she told you at some point."

Devi tilted her head and stared suspiciously at Vee. "So how do you know this?"

"It doesn't matter," Vee waved her hand, then paused as she considered her reasons for not telling her mother the truth. It seemed strange that she was dealing with her own mother as if she were interrogating a suspect. She let out a sigh. "Okay. You do need to know the truth. Radhima told me."

"What?" Devi's jaw dropped as she stared at her daughter, amusement catching the corners of her eyes.

"I'm not joking, Mom."

Devi's amusement fled then and then she sighed and got to her feet. She went to stand at the picture window, the light from beyond her revealing only her profile to Vee.

Her sigh was long and painful, her shoulders hunching over as she stared into a past filled with what Vee could only suspect were terrible memories.

"It's not what you think. He didn't beat her. At least not with his hands."

Vee's stomach tightened as her mother's words drove a shard of horror into her heart.

"His words were his weapons, the insults, the demeaning way he spoke to her as if she wasn't worth a damn, as if she had no rights, deserved nothing. I used to listen to him when he'd speak to her. He always used this almost-kind voice, as if he were disciplining a young child. 'I'm only doing what's good for you'."

Devi let out a pained laugh that sounded a lot like a sob. Taking a shuddering breath, she continued, "She had no authority over anything. Not even my upbringing. My aunts—his sisters—were allowed more control over what I wore, where I went, and what my daily choices were. We'd always had that disconnect, and I think as a child I blamed her for not standing up to him."

"Did he do that to you too?"

Devi nodded, her spine stiff. "To him, we were woman, chattels, things to control, to barter. And because I refused to bow to his will, he disowned me."

"Oh. I had no idea."

Devi shook her head and turned to look at Vee. "We never told anyone what happened. Mom and I left him and went into hiding with the Guild."

"The guild?" Guild possibly meant there were many more apsaras out there than Vee had thought. Now Karan's words made much more sense.

Her mother's voice drew Vee's attention back. "Yes. The Apsara guild. They're an organization that looks after Apsaras in need."

"I don't get it," said Vee, folding her arms around her waist. "For such a powerful supernatural race we seem to be pretty powerless. We need a guild to take care of things, to make the higher level decisions?"

Devi shook her head. "That's where you're wrong."

"About what? Being powerless," Vee smirked. "I can't jump, I can't fly—well not high enough that I'd be impressed."

Devi sighed. "I mean that you are wrong about being supernatural—not that you're right about the Guild either." Devi ran her hands up and down her thighs, as if she didn't know what to do with them and had to keep them moving. "Our familial line does not belong to the supernatural race. It's a technicality, but the apsaras were heavenly winged warriors. The emphasis on *heavenly*."

Vee frowned. "So what? We're not supernatural, we're divine?"

"Something like that. The race of the apsaras as we know it was one descended from the Sage Narada and the General of the Kings Guard, Tilottama. That's a blend of human, although an ascended spiritual human, and a divine creature.

"But because of the anomaly that meant not all descendants would receive the ability of the apsara, it meant that the powers were diluted and sometimes didn't rear its head for generations. We lost our standing as a divine race. For years, the Guild sought to ensure we gathered and trained all the apsaras we could find who had any significant form of power. Latent and mild talents were also put to use. Latent and mild talents like mine." Devi had the power to calm a person down, like a sponge, absorbing the stress and fear only to replace it with peace and tranquillity. Though she'd never talked openly about her powers in the past, since Vee's dad had returned to them, she'd begun to mellow where her apsara ability came into play. Now she nodded, "Ma's powers were much stronger, but she bound herself willingly."

"She got her powers bound?" Vee couldn't stop her outrage from filtering into her voice.

Devi shook her head. "No. The fear she experienced through her life, the sense of self-preservation she possessed, told her to hide her power. But *your* power, on the other hand, is explosive in comparison. You, your very existence is confirmation of who and what the apsara line truly is. Had our race continued to merely possess mild levels of power, you could have classed us as telepaths or telekinetics. Powers along those lines. But there isn't anything supernatural about us."

"So we get off on a technicality," Vee muttered, still unsure how to process her mother's revelations.

Devi gave Vee a quizzical look. "Until you," she said softly. "You spelled change."

CHAPTER 18

"I still don't understand what is so special about me. I don't mean me Vee, but me special apsara."

"Did you miss the part of the warriors of heaven?" Vee frowned at her mother's words. "The apsaras were the royal guard. They protected Lord Shiva in his abode, and wherever else he went. They weren't limited in their powers either. Everything you have and more."

"The books imply there was a battle, after which the apsaras were ousted, and the gods began to disappear," said Vee.

Devi nodded. "It's more complicated than that, but that's the gist of it."

Vee stiffened. "Okay, wait. I thought you weren't an apsara?"

Devi nodded. "I'm not truly one, but your grandmother was. My father found out about her heritage. I think Mom blamed herself for being careless. You're not really meant to keep your identity from those you love. Just as the sage and the Apsara who began our line were very much in love, every Apsara hopes to have the same with their partner.

"But Mom knew from early on that he wouldn't be receptive. But after I was born, the guild needed confirmation that I didn't carry the gene. She'd assured them that I didn't, but they insisted that they needed to test me for themselves. She should have arranged to see them out of the house, but she hadn't counted on how suspicious he was. He'd set up secret security cameras and microphones around the house to watch her every move, and he'd heard everything she and the guild discussed.

"They told her that it was still possible that I'd come into my wings when I came of age and warned her to keep me safe either way because I carried the gene. They also asked if she still refused it bring her husband into the guild core, saying that all around support was important.

"He used that against her when he confronted her about it. Insisted she show him her wings." Devi let out a hiccupping sob, and Vee felt sick. She knew what her mom was about to tell her.

"She showed him. In her terror they just revealed themselves. And he…he ripped them right off her shoulders."

"She stayed with him after that?"

Vee's ears were ringing, and she barely heard her mother's response. "Yes. She stayed. The guild wanted to take her away, but she told them it wasn't possible. He'd threatened to kill her if she ever left, but he also took steps to ensure people would not trust her. He had a psychiatrist friend declare her unfit to be alone with her child and brought his sisters into the house to watch over me instead. She was supervised at all times when she was with me."

"This sounds like a bad Hollywood movie."

Devi let out a harsh laugh. "Yes. It does. But her life…you just couldn't make it up."

"Why did she marry him in the first place?" asked Vee, still confused as to how an Apsara with such power could end up abused at the hands of a human.

"You have to understand something about the Apsara line. The power is extremely diluted. Wings, the power to fly, the power to read residual auras, fighting strength and skills…there is a list of them, all powers most Apsara have, some in a combination of two of those abilities but that's rare in itself. You are the rarest purist of them all. The only Apsara in history having all of those abilities together.

"Mom had a little bit of the aural reading, and she could read emotions very well. Perhaps that's how she knew he was serious."

"When did you know something was wrong? That she needed help."

Beside her Radhima whispered, "Where exactly are you going with this?" Vee gave a slight shake of her head then stiffened. She probably looked like she had a tic or something.

Devi was speaking, and when Vee looked up, she found her mother staring at her, an odd expression on her face. "In my late teens. I'd been acting out, and we'd had an argument. Not that it could have gotten heated what with my aunts being in the room. To be honest, it was more me being frustrated that I couldn't be with her in private, but I took it out on her.

"I later found her crying in the bathroom. I'd opened the door to see what was happening—perhaps I should have knocked, but stubborn teenagers rarely follow house rules. Ma was tending to a wound on her side, putting some salve onto a bruise where the skin had broken. It was just on her ribs, at her back, a location that made me realize it had to have been inflicted by someone else. I had my suspicions, but I allowed myself to be side-tracked by first investigating my aunts. A sort of self-protection I guess."

"Oh dear. I never knew she saw that," whispered Radhima from my side. I glanced at her, sad for what she'd been through, sad that her daughter had seen her pain in its truest form.

When Vee looked back at Devi, she found her mother giving her that suspicious glance again. Vee threw a question at her quickly, realizing that she was getting too close to having to fess up. "I take it you found out it wasn't them?"

Devi nodded, her brows furrowing as she turned her attention from Vee to her past. "They were almost just as bad to her, but more with words than with physical violence."

"Wait, I thought you told me he didn't hit her physically."

Devi shrugged. "When I finally confronted her she said it was just once. I'd kept a close eye on my aunts and cleared them of the physical abuse, but I saw so clearly what they'd been doing. I guess it helped that I'd taken to eavesdropping. I'd even used a drinking glass against the wall to listen. They gas-lighted her all the time, constant passive aggressive bullshit too. They were also deliberately sabotaging... but that's a whole other conversation. In the end, I narrowed the perpetrator down to one person: my father.

"Little did I know that his cameras were catching me in action. He hauled me up one day, asking why I was spying on his sisters. I lied, because well, how would I have known he had a video feed to prove it? He slapped me, busted my lip, bruised my cheek. Mom went ballistic. After that, we had a long conversation and made a plan to run."

"And you managed to leave without him stopping you?"

Devi nodded. "He couldn't have stopped us even if he'd tried." Her words were cryptic, her tone hard but edged with something else. Vee sighed, feeling the grief her mother was exuding. She was about to tell her mother how sorry she was when Devi spoke. "So are you going to tell me how you know all this? How did you find out something that my mother swore she'd never tell anyone?"

There was a note of what Vee could only describe as fear in Devi's face.

Vee shrugged, entertaining a faint hope that she could get away without telling her mother the truth. "I told you. Radhima told me."

Devi shook her head. "When? She never mentioned that she was going to tell you about her past. She would have come to me first."

Vee sighed. "It was Radhima. She told me. Only…she didn't come to you to tell you about it because she only told me yesterday."

Devi's eyes filled with tears, and she shook her head. "Oh, Vee." She sighed and came toward her daughter, placing her hands on either side of Vee's face. "I'm so sorry, honey. I seem to have forgotten how close the two of you were. In my own grief, I've been selfish, forgetting that you too are dealing with her loss."

Vee shook her head and grabbed her mother's hands. "No, Mom. I'm serious. This isn't in my head. Believe me, I thought it was, but you just confirmed it isn't."

"How did I do that?" whispered Devi, her eyes filled with tears.

"You confirmed what she told me yesterday. Radhima said that when you confirm the truth, then I'll know she's real. I honestly thought it was a figment of my imagination until now. I have to admit it's a relief."

Devi shook her head and held Vee around the shoulders. "Vee, I really think you need to see someone. If you're imagining your grandmother here, now, perhaps you need to talk to someone about it."

Vee shrugged her mother's hand off and turned to stare at her. "I'm not imagining it, and I don't need counseling. I'm telling you. It's her."

Devi inhaled deeply and folded her arms across her chest. Vee knew that stance; her mother was resisting, but she was entertaining Vee only until she could show her daughter how wrong she was.

This time she was in for disappointment.

CHAPTER 19

Vee suppressed the urge to groan out loud.

Instead, she said, "She came to me a few weeks ago. A day or so after the funeral. I thought I was imagining it, and when she kept coming back, I began to get frustrated. But then she warned me that I didn't have all the time in the world to make myself believe her. She told me to come here. She told me to ask you those questions, and now I realize why. Because that proves she's real. How would my imagination have conjured up such a story only to discover that I am right? Those kinds of coincidences only exist in books and movies."

Devi had relaxed slightly, her spine no longer as stiff as a pole. "I don't know what to say, honey."

"So you don't believe me?" asked Vee. She discovered that the feeling curling in the pit of her stomach was hurt.

Devi shook her head and gave Vee a sad smile. "A ghost? I just...I don't—"

"If you're going to say that you don't believe in ghosts, need I remind you that I just killed a couple of demons this morning, a golem broke into my lab a month ago, and I'm an Apsara. I'm not even supposed to exist."

Devi hesitated, then stared around the room as though she couldn't look Vee in the eye. "Okay. You have a point there." Devi sighed and sank onto the sofa. She seemed listless, and reached for her glass, probably just so that her hands were occupied.

Vee glanced at Radhima, who'd remained all too quiet where she stood beside the sofa. She glared at her grandmother then cocked her chin at her mother, silently urging the old woman to show herself.

Then Vee cleared her throat. "She's here. In this room with us." Vee's voice was overly loud, like a bell ringing in a silent room.

Devi straightened, her fingers curled around the glass tightly. "What?" She glanced around the room, then looked back at Vee. "Where?"

Vee looked over and Radhima's ghost. "Help a girl out, would you?" She sent a pleading glance over at her grandmother whose face had suddenly become implacable.

A few moments later, when nothing had happened, Devi looked up at her daughter.

"No, Mom. Just wait a sec. I don't know…maybe she's got her own issues. She'll show you. Just wait."

Still, after a few more minutes, nothing happened. No ghostly granny made an appearance.

Devi put her glass onto the table and got to her feet. Her sigh was filled with sadness as she hurried over to Vee. "You see, honey. It's not real. I don't know what's going on, but this thing about a ghost…I just think…I don't know. Maybe we all just need time to adjust."

Vee swallowed down the tears of frustration that had built within her. She'd stuck her neck out with her mom, and Radhima had failed to confirm her claim. Now her mother believed she was going off the deep end. Vee had taken a risk and look where that had gotten her.

As her disappointment faded, anger filled the vacated space.

Vee nodded slowly and gave Devi a smile. Then, without another word she turned and left the office. As she strode off to the stairwell, her jaw held tight, she wondered if maybe her mother was right and she had just dreamed this whole thing up. She grabbed her security card from her pocket and swiped it through the card reader at the stairwell door.

"You didn't dream it up," said a disembodied voice from beside Vee. The door clicked ajar, and Vee tugged it open, giving the space beside her a dirty look.

"I don't have time for this," Vee mumbled and hurried into the stairwell, heading down the stairs two steps at a time. "Can you leave me alone? I stuck my neck out for you, and now I'm probably going to end up in a psych ward because of it."

"I'm sorry. I can explain."

"No need to explain," Vee said as she reached her floor and swiped her card at the stairwell door. "I know now that I'm just making this shit up."

"Watch your mouth, young lady," said the ghostly voice.

Vee stormed off down the passage and reached her lab which sat at the end of the corridor. "Look, hopefully, I'm not crazy, and you are real, but unless you are prepared to confirm your existence to someone else, I can't help you."

"That's just it, Vee. Nobody else will be able to see me."

Vee froze, card hovering over the reader as she turned to stare at the space beside her, where her grandmother's form was beginning to materialize.

"Now you appear?"

"Nobody else can see me," she repeated.

"Then why did you appear to me in the room just now? You made me think that all you had to do was show yourself for her to believe me."

"I'm sorry, Vee. If I gave you that impression, I'm sorry. It never occurred to me to tell you that. I guess I'm new to this thing too."

Vee took a deep breath. She had gone on an assumption. She should have asked Radhima first, before she'd demanded she materialize for her mother. She only had herself to blame for that, and it wasn't fair to be angry with her grandmother.

She sighed and swiped her card through the reader and headed inside the lab. Lights flickered on as she went, the sensor picking up her presence and turning them all on. No point in wasting solar energy.

At last, she faced the spirit and sighed, "I'm sorry. I shouldn't have put you on the spot like that. And I should have che— What the hell are you wearing?"

Vee stared at her grandmother's clothing.

"What? Why? Is something wrong with it?"

"Ma! Those are jeans. You never wear jeans."

Radhima waved a dismissive hand at Vee. "Since when can't I wear jeans."

Vee folded her arms and lifted an eyebrow. "Firstly, you've never worn jeans in your life. Unless you wore them and danced around in your closet for kicks," Vee huffed.

"And two?"

"Huh?"

"You said one, so I'm assuming there is a two coming along. I'm dead, not senile."

Vee rolled her eyes and rounded the desk, pulling a plas from the in-tray. "Number two was I had no idea that there was such a thing as ghost jeans."

The old woman let out a bark of laughter, which was cut short when Vee's phone pinged with a message from Monroe.

Checked SL house. See report attached.

Vee swiped to open the document and read through it. Her stomach churning.

"What is it?" asked her grandmother.

"It's the report from Monroe. They went to the victim's house. Nothing. No sign of intrusion, everything appears intact. They found more identification though. A social media chat group that the family had set up to keep in touch. The mother and daughter were going away for the weekend." Vee sighed as she stared at the report. "One last hurrah as single women, apparently both of them saw responsibility in their future once the baby was born. The victim was a widowed lawyer, but she'd been disbarred for illegal activity and ended up working as a journalist; disciplinary report on that was classified, happened years ago, so Monroe doesn't see a correlation and neither do I."

Vee glanced up and looked at Radhima. When she'd been alive, Vee used to talk about her cases with the old woman, who would often revert with good points for discussion. Today, she remained silent.

Vee continued to go through the report, giving her grandmother the gist as she went. "It appears she was using the money from her husband's life insurance to assist her daughter with expenses. She'd been frugal though. Plenty left in there for the daughter and the baby." Vee scanned further in the report. "They appeared to be just a normal family, no suspicious connections or activity."

"So you think this attack was random?" asked Radhima.

"I do. If it weren't random, he wouldn't have hesitated when he came across the girl. He would have expected her. Killed her then and there."

"But that depends on what they were after." Radhima was staring off into space, and Vee paused. The old woman was a ghost, and she lived in an in-between world, so how did this world appear to her eyes?

But Vee forced herself to focus. "Which could also mean there is something we are not seeing." Vee sighed. "What could this woman possibly have had that he'd have wanted. He drained her dry. She had no blood left in her veins. She was expendable."

"So why was the pregnant woman not expendable?"

Vee paused and tapped her fingers on the phone's face. "The only difference is that one was pregnant. So if we went on the assumption that they were after the baby, which means I could have misinterpreted the demon's aural language which then begs the question as to why."

A voice echoed through the lab. "Who are you talking to?"

Both Vee and her grandmother turned to the doorway to find Syama standing there with Akil at her side, her fine-boned face all hollows and shadows. She looked emaciated, though her black eyes gleamed with happiness.

Akil's tall and lithe frame seemed somewhat thinner too, as if during his journey he'd been starved of food. His pale hair was lank and oily, and dark shadows circled his almond-shaped eyes. The Sirin—an owl-shifter—looked decidedly filthy too, his usual attire of white pants and white shirt could no longer claim to be any other color but…filthy.

Light shimmered off the pair as they unglamored themselves and walked toward Vee.

Syama stepped closer, squinting at the space beside Vee. "Oh, I see," she said with a wry smile.

"You see what?"

Syama rolled her eyes, one hand on her hip. "I'm not blind," she said to Vee before shifting her gaze to Radhima and saying, "Hello, Ma."

Vee scowled and stared first at Syama and then at her grandmother. "*She* can see you but Mom can't?" Vee wasn't sure if she was furious or just done.

Syama laughed and responded even before Radhima opened her mouth to reply, "Humans can't see ghosts unless that person's spirit is bound to them. So *you* can see Ma but your mom and dad and Mac can't. Supernaturals like Nivaan and Akil can't either, unless they have the sight. I'm neither human nor supernatural." Syama nodded, happy with her explanation.

Vee wasn't. She glowered at Syama. "Do go on."

Syama grinned, not in the least affected by Vee's terrible mood. "I'm a hellhound," she said, her tone implying that it should be obvious. "The role of most hellhounds is almost that of a bounty hunter. We're charged with finding those souls who have either evaded, or escaped, from the underworlds. I, of course, have been given a different role. For which I'm most grateful."

"And what role is that?"

"Watching your back."

CHAPTER 20

After Vee's grandmother had left the lab, disappearing with a promise to return soon, and a warning to 'work on working things out' with Devi, Syama and Akil had given Vee an update on where they'd been.

Syama rubbed her hands together. "I'm sorry. I had no way of contacting you. We've had a bit of a complication," she pointed a decidedly grubby finger at the floor, "down under."

Vee swallowed a snort and motioned for Syama to continue before sharing a questioning glance with Akil. He turned away as soon as he could, and Vee found herself studying the smudges on his cheek, the fading bruise on his right eye and his swollen and bruised lower lip.

He seemed to be favoring one leg too, putting more weight on his right foot and holding onto the nearby counter every few minutes. Vee turned her attention back to Syama, giving her a more thorough once-over.

The hellhound's dull leather trousers were torn at the knees, revealing deep gashes and bruises caked with dirt. Her face too bore the evidence of a beating. Vee's head began to throb with heat as she recognized the signs of older, almost healed, bruises beneath the bruised cheek and jaw as well as Syama's own matching black eye.

Though curious, Vee decided it would be best for them to tell her at their own pace. They certainly looked like they'd both been through an ordeal.

"When I received that call to return home for debriefing after the whole nexus-asura-trishula incident, I believed it was just a standard handover of information."

Vee rounded the counter to where a handful of high stools were scattered. She took a seat and sighed as she touched her own tender bruises. Syama drew closer and sank onto the seat beside Vee, frowning at Vee's wince. Akil followed too, hovering for a moment before grabbing the seat beyond Syama.

Excellent.

Vee hid a smile at her success. She straightened and said, "And I take it that was not the case?"

"Nope."

Syama's face scrunched and then she winced as blood oozed from her cheek, welling into a glistening ruby bead. She lifted her finger to dab at her wound. She studied the blood on her fingertip then wiped it off on her pants, her face inscrutable, her neck stiff.

"Not in the least. My superior was killed," Syama said, her eyes shining with tears. "It was a coup of sorts, details of which I am unable to share. Not right now at any rate. Not until the dust settles." Syama cleared her throat and looked around the room as she blinked away more tears.

Unable to share? Did she mean she wasn't at liberty to? Or that she just wasn't ready? Vee had never seen Syama this emotionally affected by anything. And though Vee felt the urge to wrap the younger girl in her arms, offer her some comfort, her gut told her that Syama wouldn't want such a display of affection.

So Vee stayed where she was. "How did you get out?"

Syama poked a thumb at Akil, who was still strangely silent.

He wasn't usually the talkative type, but this silence...it spoke more of reticence, than of having nothing to say. "You sent him, so I guess I have to thank you."

Vee turned to the sirin, frowning, but he just pointed a slim finger at Syama who'd already continued to speak. Though frustrated, Vee shifted her attention back to the hellhound. "Akil here came looking for me, snooping around when he found no trace. He had to go two levels deeper into the underworld to find me. Very dangerous trip, but he did it."

"He got you out?" Vee asked, leaning closer. For all the worry that she'd had, she found herself so grateful that the pair was back with her, more or less in one piece. And still both breathing. She couldn't handle any more deaths. Or ghosts, for that matter.

Syama shook her head, her short black hair glinting in the white light from above. She usually wore it neatly spiked, but today it was in disarray, longer stands drooping over her forehead, much of it plastered flat to one side of her head as if she'd risen from her bed and forgotten to run a brush through it. Now, she thrust her hair away from her face and smirked. "Nope. He went back up to Patala."

Vee was more than confused and was beginning to feel a bout of fatigue hitting her. Not unusual considering the extensively long days she'd endured recently. "So Akil didn't save you." Vee turned to glare at Akil, but he was looking at Syama as she drew out her retelling of their adventures. He looked tired but was still projecting calm.

"No. He did save me."

"Syama," both Akil and Vee yelled in unison, Akil rolling his eyes and Vee doing more frowning.

"Sorry, Akil couldn't find a way into the dungeon. It was spelled so he couldn't jump me out. That would have been way too easy of course. In the end, he went back up top and brought reinforcements. He was allowed to return but there was a battle, and I was saved, and now I'm here."

"Syama, you do have some concept of a debrief, right?"

Syama grinned. She knew her behavior would be annoying Vee and she was enjoying it far too much. Then she giggled. "Don't worry. I'll send a report to your email. It's too much to run through here and now. Besides, we're both tired and need some rest and food."

Akil grunted, bringing Vee's attention back to him. "Took a vow of silence or something?"

For a moment he looked pained. Then the expression faded, and Vee had to wonder if she'd imagined it. "No. I merely had nothing significant to add. I was certain that Syama would provide a detailed explanation that would suffice."

Vee got the feeling that Akil didn't want to talk about what was bothering him—because Vee knew that there was something he wasn't yet prepared to say. He'd need time, but Vee planned to get him to talk. She only hoped that it hadn't been something traumatic.

Vee was pulled from her introspection by Syama who was waving her hand in front of Vee's face. "Earth to Vee," the hell-hound said loudly.

Vee blinked and batted her hand away. "Shut up. You two better get going. You do look rather tired. And you guys stink." Vee wrinkled her nose at the odor drifting to her from the pair.

At least that brought a grin from Akil. "It is difficult to find a place to bathe in caves and lava fields and battle trenches." With that, he reached for Syama's arm, and the two shimmered for a moment before disintegrating into particles of light.

Vee had taken a few minutes to absorb what had just happened. First Radhima, and then the terrible twins returning from hell? Things were never normal when it came to Vee's life.

Now, under the microscope, Vee was studying the brain matter that her dad had retrieved from her hair. She'd already studied, confirmed, and refrigerated the bhayakara goo.

She'd sent samples of all her forensic evidence off to be tested for DNA, but now she was busy making slides to analyze the brain structure. Over a long period, they'd been documenting the DNA and brain structure of many of the demons Vee had crossed paths with. It was interesting to compare human brain structure to that of the demonic element—in this case the pey.

It turned out they were not that much different to humans in physiology. It had surprised Vee to discover that pey had brain matter. The old horror stories told to her by the older people she'd come into contact with, were more along the line of the pey being a devilish creature, more a spirit than a corporeal entity.

It seemed that the folk tales had evolved in order to decrease the fear, for if humans were to know the truth of the demonic existence, the folk tales would have been filled with a lot more morbid horror.

As it was, the demons' banishment to Naraka millennia ago would have contributed to the lack of realism in the tales from the past. No doubt it had been centuries since humans had come into contact with a pey.

Vee prepared and refrigerated the slides then ordered the tests that she needed done. She would have to process some of the samples herself, but she still had to attend to her FBI tasks.

CHAPTER 21

Vee threw on silky purple lounge pants, a teal singlet, and a multi-colored cardigan. Nothing sedate about relaxing clothes. She twisted her long hair into an untidy bun on the top of her head and rolled her shoulders. Relaxing was serious business, and she sure looked the part.

Right down to her fluffy pink socks.

After checking Syama's and Akil's rooms, she headed downstairs in search of the two shifters. Vee suspected they'd be in the gym and hoped they wouldn't be training. They damned well better not be, given their conditions.

She hurried down the stairs, wrapping her cardigan around herself as she entered the cooler climate of the gym.

Thankfully, neither of the two were working out. Vee felt almost disappointed. She'd been so geared up to tell the two of them off. But all she did was smile when she found them both sitting on the floor, backs to the floor-to-ceiling wall-to-wall mirror.

"You guys having a party without me?"

Syama snorted and pointed at a small bag on the floor in front of her. Vee sank down, smoothly moving into a cross-legged position as she opened the bag. Marshmallows, a paper bag with a donut, and a bar of chocolate.

"Interesting selection," Vee said smiling as she reached inside to withdraw the donut. Things were so crazy in her life that she realized that the small things were the ones she should appreciate.

"No."

Vee looked up, frowning at Syama, only to find the hellhound pointing beside Vee. A pizza box lay at her side, lid open. "You went to Tony's?" Syama nodded. "And you bought my favorite." Vee didn't waste time lifting a slice of margarita with double cheese and garlic onto her palm. The slice was huge, but she ate, enjoying the low conversation of her two sidekicks as they poured cherry cola and passed her a glass.

"You guys were craving New York food, I take it?" Vee asked after chewing and swallowing.

Both nodded. "We didn't get everything we missed. Still time for more," Akil said with a grin. His mouth was covered in powdered sugar from the donut and Vee couldn't decide if she wanted a second slice of pizza or the donut first.

Instead, Vee sipped the cola, swallowing as fast as she could. She didn't have the heart to tell Syama that she hated the drink. It tasted like cough medicine to Vee, but she'd mentioned once that she'd loved it as a kid and Syama had believed that was the case in the present too.

"Now," said Akil. "Is there something you want to tell us?"

Vee took another slice and shoved a bite into her mouth, her aim to avoid the topic for as long as possible. But in the end, the pizza was gone, and she stared at the cola, unsure if she could use the drink as a delaying tactic. That was more like torture.

Syama let out a sigh, and Vee looked up to catch her roll her eyes. "For Yama's sake, I know you don't like the stuff. Here," she grabbed a small bottle of flavored water from the grocery bag at her side and held it out.

Vee's eyes narrowed. "You had this all along?" She opened it and took a long sip, relieved to have been saved from having to drink the cola.

"Yes. I do believe we have reached a point in our relationship where we can be honest with each other." As Syama spoke, Vee found Akil looking over at her, his expression contemplative and concerned. Vee knew there was a conversation in their future. One that didn't include Syama.

"I do believe we are at that point." Vee grinned and said, "So yes, I hate the stuff. Tastes like cough medicine." Vee gave a delicate shudder, sending her two friends into bursts of laughter.

"Good. More for me." Syama smirked, then lifted her chin at Vee. "So, spill. Or someone else will soon enough."

Vee sighed and gave the pair a rundown of bhayakara and pey demons, unknown cigar-smoking voyeurs, deadly cabdrivers, and asshole detectives, not to mention the murder-abduction case. What she didn't talk about was her mother's revelation of what Radhima had been through. That was not her story to tell.

Syama's mouth was agape. "We leave you alone for a few days, and everything goes to crap?"

Vee swallowed the temptation to remind the hellhound that her absence had been way more than a couple of days. Instead, she shrugged. "Never let it be said that a day in the life of Vee Shankar was ever boring."

"You can say that again," the hellhound mumbled before reaching for a donut. "One thing is for certain, though..."

"Which is?" asked Vee.

"You're not going anywhere without us from here on out," Syama said, her eyes glinting.

Vee didn't respond. The pair had been tasked with her protection. She didn't have much of a choice in the matter, but she didn't feel the need to decline their protection either. So she didn't respond and ate marshmallows instead.

A heavy silence fell over the gym, pregnant with so many

questions that Vee decided she couldn't wait any longer. "So. You guys going to tell me what's going on?"

"Nothing. Just that we've been through a very strange experience and we're just in recovery mode. But that does not mean we won't be keeping an eye on you. No shirking of duties here."

"Says the person that was out like a light for three hours solid." Akil's tone was dry.

Vee gave a mock gasp, holding her hand in front of her mouth, eyes wide in horror. "You slept for three whole hours?" She was a little surprised as Syama didn't require much sleep. She tended to pass the time—which Vee spent sleeping—doing other things like reading books to occupy her time. "Are you okay?"

Akil cleared his throat. "Only the fact that she was captured and interrogated, and almost starved to death over a period of two weeks."

Vee lifted her gaze to the owl shifter's face. He seemed to be taking Syama's ordeal very hard, but Vee wasn't surprised. Though the two hadn't hit it off at their first meeting, they'd formed a fast friendship and had vowed to remain at Vee's side no matter what. Syama had disappeared without a word, which had worried Vee enough to have to ask Akil to go and look for her.

Vee opened her mouth to ask what had happened, but Akil got to his feet. "You need to get some rest," he said. Only when Vee looked up did she realize that he was talking to Syama.

The hellhound's eyes widened, flashing with annoyance, but then her irritation faded and she sighed. "Can't argue with that." She got to her feet and dusted her butt off. When she bent to gather the detritus of their late-night picnic, Akil brushed her away.

"Bed," he said, the syllable ringing through the gym.

Vee's eyebrows lifted a little, but she remained silent as Syama wiggled her fingers in a goodnight wave and then shimmered away into nothing.

Akil was busy filling his bag with empty drink cans, and donut and chocolate bar wrappings.

"Are you two okay?" Vee asked softly.

His spine stiffened, and he grabbed the pizza boxes and straightened. Taking a long breath, he turned to Vee. "I'm fine. She'll be fine."

"What is it you are not telling me?" Vee spoke softly, hoping the hurt she felt hadn't filtered through to her question.

Akil's head snapped up, his eyes widened just enough for Vee to know that he had heard. He shook his head. "It's not that we don't want to tell you." He sighed, his eyes casting about as if he was searching out a reason, something that would appease Vee. Then he sighed. "It is a long tale. She has been through a lot. She will tell you. I know it. It is just not my truth to tell."

Vee bit her lip, considering Akil's position. "I understand. I guess I'll just have to wait until she is ready to talk to me about it."

Akil gave a rueful smile. He seemed guarded, as if he wanted to tell Vee, but something held him back.

Vee walked over to him and patted his shoulder. "You're a good man, Akil. Syama should be happy to call you a friend. I know I am." She squeezed his shoulder, then walked over to the stairs. Perhaps it was Syama who had to tell Vee her story herself.

And Vee would just have to wait.

No matter how worried Vee was about her hellhound sidekick, no matter how impatient she was to know the details, she had no choice. Syama would come to Vee when she was ready.

"I wanted to tell you." Akil's voice rang out behind Vee. She paused, one foot on the first riser, and looked over her shoulder. "I want to tell you," he said softly, his face contorted with so many emotions that Vee was unable to put a finger on one that stood out. Frustration, grief, confusion, hurt. The amalgamation of emotional turmoil the kid was experiencing struck Vee deep within her gut.

Vee forced a smile onto her face and shook her head. "It's not for you to tell," Vee said keeping her tone neutral. "She'll come around in her own time."

Akil let out a sigh, the strain on his face and body visibly departing.

Vee shook her head then. "Just make sure you take good care of her," Vee said, then hurried up the stairs.

She heard Akil's voice as she reached the landing.

"I am trying, but she's a pain in the ass."

CHAPTER 22

Vee felt like she had just fallen asleep when her phone buzzed. She groaned as she forced her head off the softness of her pillow—her skull felt too heavy, as if even the muscles in her neck were resisting her efforts to move.

She reached out at the nightstand—narrowly missed knocking her lamp over—and grabbed the phone, muttering curses at the device. Squinting at the brightly-lit screen, Vee swiped the notification to find a text message from Detective Monroe.

Would you be happy to meet?

What an odd text? *Happy* to meet? A frown spread across Vee's forehead as she sat up and pushed her hair out of her face. She sent a reply asking for a location, and within seconds Monroe named The Lucky Clover, a dingy bar over in Hunts Point. It struck Vee as extremely odd that Monroe would hang out at a bar which Vee knew was frequented by a lot of supernaturals. Mostly of the demon persuasion.

It occurred to Vee—only momentarily—that Andrea Monroe

could possibly be a supernatural herself and Vee would not have known it. It made Vee a little uncomfortable to know that she didn't qualify as supernatural on a stupid technicality. Although, being a deific being should be better than just being supernatural.

Vee texted *'On my way'* and then rolled over and groaned into her pillow. Going out at two in the morning wasn't something she wanted to do, but she knew a thing or two about fostering good relationships with other law enforcement officers.

Monroe had always given Vee a hard time—ever since day one—but even now Vee knew it was in her own best interest to meet the detective, if only to find out if everything was okay.

More especially, in case Monroe had news.

What news it could be that would require a dead-of-night meeting, Vee could only speculate.

Rolling out of bed, Vee dragged on her clothing from last night, then tugged her hair into a knot at the base of her skull. She was half-way down the hall when she stopped in her tracks. She couldn't go without Syama. She needed her sidekick back online. Vee also had to admit that she needed to ensure she remained as safe as possible. Which meant she had to avoid lurking on the city streets in the middle of the night without some sort of protection.

Vee knocked on Syama's door, tapping her feet as she waited. A minute passed, and Vee let out a frustrated grunt. She knocked again and glared at the door.

"One knock will do. Did someone lose their patience today?"

Vee flinched at the voice that came from next to her left shoulder, sighed deeply, then turned to glare at the hellhound. "Do you have to shock the living daylights out of me?"

Syama frowned, her nose crinkling. "I never could understand that phrase. What happens if you shock a person in the middle of the night...like now? Is it called living nightlights?"

Vee heaved a second heavy sigh and grabbed Syama's arm. "I'm tired, I'm grumpy, and I'm supposed to be dead like two times over already. Please just take me to the Lucky Clover before I knock the living nightlights out of you."

Syama chuckled, and her form began to shimmer. Vee held tightly to her arm as the hellhound shifted through the planes and reappeared inside the alley across the road from the Lucky Clover.

Light flickered from within the bar, and Vee could make out a few darkened shapes hunched over their tables.

Vee noted, almost absentmindedly, that since the last time she'd been to the bar the owner had seen fit to fix the sign. The C in the fluorescent marquee above the bar had been broken for so long that most people now affectionately referred to the bar as The Lucky Lover.

Glancing at Syama, Vee did a double-take at the sight of Akil, who looked particularly fresh for that time of the morning, bringing new meaning to the phrase 'night owl'.

She opened her mouth to ask him what he was doing there, then thought the better of it. Instead, she threw him a look filled with warning—against what Vee wasn't exactly sure. He *had* surprised her after all.

The trio watched the street for traffic, or anyone who would notice Vee appearing out of thin air. The coast seemed to be clear, and Vee gave Syama the go ahead with a single nod. The hellhound dropped the glamor from over Vee and tugged on her leather jacket. In the time that Syama had become part of Vee's life, she'd transformed herself, loving the goth/biker look.

Today she wore black fishnet gloves, black pinstriped skintight pants, chunky black knee-high boots, a purple shirt—most of it covered by the jacket, though Vee knew it would be emblazoned with the name of some rock band that had been famous decades ago. Vee had to hand it to the hellhound; she looked awesome.

Now, Vee shook a warning finger at Syama, and then glanced at Akil beyond the hellhound's shoulder. "I need to speak to

Monroe. She sounded a little too antsy, so something is bugging her, but I need you two to keep watch. I've had two attempts on my person in the last day, so I can't predict what will happen next."

"Define 'attempts on my person'," Syama asked, folding her arms.

Vee sighed. "One attempted murder, weapon long jagged claws and uber-sharp teeth, perps: two pey demons currently dead. One attempted murder, weapon New York City cab, perp: one demon, evaporated into thin air." Vee eyed the hellhound. "Satisfied?"

Syama groaned. "Man, I really wish profanity didn't taste like marigolds, or I'd be swearing right now."

"Marigolds?" Vee laughed as she stared at Syama.

"Yeah. When I was little, my mother used to shove marigold-leaf paste into my mouth. Burns like hell and the taste is disgusting."

Vee snorted. "I thought that was supposed to be done with soap? Or, worst case scenario with a chili."

Syama smirked. "Nope. Not where I come from. Things are hard down below."

Vee shook her head as she gave the street one last check. "Marigolds are hard?" she asked in disbelief, sharing an amused look with Akil, whose face had appeared impassive until Syama's complaint.

"Marigolds are the most disgusting flower on the planet. Worse than jasmine."

As the trio crossed the street, Vee sent Syama a questioning glance. "I think you may be coming down with something."

Syama snorted, reaching for the red-glazed glass door to the entrance to the Lucky Clover. She and Akil had remained glamored the entire time, and any witnesses to Vee's approach to the bar would have seen only one person. "You can't make me change my mind. No matter how hard you try," said the hellhound as she held the door open for Vee, who winced at the sound of the doorbell as it jangled above their heads.

"Be careful," growled Vee, keeping her voice low, "You're invisible so this door just magically opened for me before I even reached it."

"Shit. Sorry."

Vee didn't answer, more so because they stepped into a churning mess of noise and heat and alcohol fumes. It all hit Vee like a punch to the head, and she wobbled on her feet. Just the tiniest bit, but enough for Akil to place a helping hand to Vee's back in support.

Vee straightened and took a breath, then marched toward the bar—an enormous thing that stuck out in the middle of the floor and ran in a full U-shape, serving customers on both sides of a bar that divided the room in half.

At the far end sat Monroe, nursing a glass that still contained a finger of a golden liquid. Beyond the bar, Vee noticed the establishment was light on supernaturals. "Wonder where all the demons are," whispered Syama from Vee's side.

"Just one more thing to worry about; fewer demons being something only *we* would worry about," Vee muttered as they closed in on Monroe.

The detective barely glanced up as Vee arrived and took the empty seat beside her. "You okay?" Vee asked, having to raise her voice to be heard. The bartender sauntered over, his plaid shirt and orange beard making him look like a lumberjack just home from a day's work. Vee pointed at Monroe's drink, and hoped it was something she'd be able to stomach.

Monroe looked over at her, the detective's eyes unusually clear for someone who looked inebriated. She'd called Vee here, sounding weird. And now she looked neither of those things. Vee's gut tightened as she wondered if this was possibly a setup, and the woman she was talking to was not Monroe.

Then the detective cleared her throat, waved at the bartender for another drink and glanced back at Vee. "Heard about the cab incident." She sounded like she was saying she was sorry, but the words and the tone of her voice didn't jell.

"Gianni told you?"

"Yeah. The shithead came upstairs just as we were rounding things up. Stood in the doorway giving us a rundown of how he saved your pretty ass."

Vee snorted. "As much as I'd have liked to say that he hadn't saved me, he did. Although I'm not ruling out the possibility that he set the whole thing up to put me off balance."

Monroe grunted as she lifted her glass and swirled the amber liquid in the glass. "Yeah. Come swooping in and save the nice FBI agent and then win the jurisdiction battle."

The detective downed the remainder of her drink and slammed the glass onto the bare wood surface of the bar counter.

"I hate to say it, but I wouldn't put it past him. Or his sleazy pretty-boy partner."

Vee sighed as she scanned the area around them again. Syama had remained at Monroe's back, calmly scanning the thin crowd. Akil had drifted to Vee's right-hand side, protecting her from an approach from that direction. If people noticed that they were unconsciously giving the area behind Monroe and Vee a wide berth, they didn't say anything.

"What's up?" Monroe eyed Vee, only half-turning to her. The bartender brought two drinks and deposited one in front of each of the women, then walked off.

"Didn't know you drank." When Vee lifted her glass and threw Monroe a curious glance, the detective replied, "Thought you guys weren't allowed to drink."

Vee chuckled. "Think you got your brown people mixed up." Then she took a sip and enjoyed the warmth of the liquid as it slipped down her throat.

"Must have. Sorry."

Vee glanced over at Monroe—surprised the detective had

apologized—and what she saw was confusion and contrition. Interesting how Vee had worked with the woman for so many months, and the pair had never progressed past their encounters at their crime-scenes and the odd phone-call that amounted to little more than a report or an update of some sort.

Vee had to admit that she herself had been prejudiced, assuming after a couple of meetings that Monroe was one of those women who felt threatened by other women in power and that she'd be more of an opponent than an ally. So, could she really judge Monroe now?

Monroe let out a soft bark of laughter, but the sound was anything but amused. "Those DNA results. That's just bullshit."

"What do you mean?" Vee asked taking another sip before sharing a worried glance with Syama over the detective's shoulder. Did Monroe suspect something was jinky with the results? Vee had told Brent more than once that one day someone was going to figure out something was wrong with those results. She'd suggested they do their own testing in all of the cases, even obtain warrants to force the cops to part with samples for testing at an independent lab. But Rossi had believed they were fine. *As long as we are careful,* he'd said.

Now Vee had to wonder if careful hadn't been enough.

"Monroe?" Vee nudged the detective's arm.

Monroe looked up at Vee, widening her eyes as if she were forcing herself to remain awake. "There wasn't enough tissue under her fingernails to get a conclusive match. And that's bullshit. I saw it myself when they scraped her hands. There was enough. I saw it—I'm not imagining things." She paused and took another sip before slamming her glass onto the bar. "There was enough. So what's this crap?"

"And?" urged Vee. She wasn't sure if Monroe was playing her, holding the knowledge over her. All Vee had to do to clear it up was to message Brent, and she'd have her answer in seconds, but she forced herself to remain calm and patient.

Monroe sipped her drink again and coughed before wiping her mouth off on her sleeve. "And the hair samples? You won't believe it—" Monroe broke off, laughing again, the sound loud enough that Vee noticed a few patrons glancing their way. Monroe hiccupped. "They came back dead. No DNA? You telling me that two full, intact, uncontaminated hair samples that did not belong to the victim just happened to not have sufficient DNA on them to identify at least something about the killer?"

Vee was amazed that the detective had managed to speak such a long sentence in her state of inebriation, but she schooled her features to one of understanding and sympathy.

Monroe shook her head, eyed Vee out of the corner of her eye. Then she pointed at Vee.

"And you? You're suspicious."

Oh shit.

CHAPTER 23

Vee's heart thudded as she waited to hear what else Monroe had to say, waited for the detective to admit that she was onto Vee, that she knew what Vee was, and what she'd been hiding.

Vee took another sip to buy herself some time.

Monroe laughed, the sound gurgling in her throat. "You think one day you'll ever tell me how you do it?" Monroe asked, eyeing Vee out of the corner of her eye.

Swallowing a sigh of relief, Vee responded, "Maybe. I don't know." She shrugged.

Monroe snorted then started to giggle. Vee reached over and patted her shoulder. "You need to get home. Get some rest. I don't think the next few days are going to be easy on any of us. Not until we find that missing woman. Two lives are at stake."

"Did you get the report?"

"That the house gave us nothing?" Vee nodded. "Yeah. If that was a dead end, then we look elsewhere. They went to the hotel for some mother-daughter time. Means they weren't into anything criminal."

"Not that we know of."

Vee nodded. "Anything else we need to know, I'm sure it can wait until tomorrow."

"And if he kills her tonight?"

Vee paused and took a breath. "If that does happen, if we do lose her or the baby or both of them, then we have to accept that there wasn't anything we could have done at the time. We have no clue as to motive. We have no idea where he went or where he is keeping her. At the moment, it's out of our hands. Go home. Rest. Look at it fresh in the morning. You're of no use to anyone, including Lucy and her baby, if you don't take care of yourself. Drunk detectives don't often have a high success rate, you know."

Monroe shrugged Vee's hand off her shoulder. "Think I don't know all this bullshit?"

"Then what's wrong? Why the self-pity?"

"It's not self-pity." Monroe turned to stare at Vee. "Have you ever seen something that you didn't think was possible, but you knew in your gut it was real?"

Vee's own gut tightened in response to the woman's words. Was Monroe suspicious about what Vee was? What she could do? Had she somehow realized that Vee's ability was not necessarily based on plain old human deduction?

Vee felt a poke in her ribs and glanced back in the direction of Akil who'd likely prodded her just to pull Vee out of her worried introspection. The sirin gave her a pointed look and Vee shifted in her seat, then glanced back at Monroe.

The detective was frowning at Vee. Then she turned to look beyond Vee, and stared directly at Akil for a few, painfully long moments. After what seemed like an eternity, Monroe turned back to Vee. "What were you staring at?"

"Nothing. It's just the bar is on the empty side."

Monroe shrugged. "You familiar with this place?"

"Came here once, a while back. Was way busier then."

"Yeah. I think they had some kind of corporate buyout or something. The bar changed hands recently."

That explained the fixed letter C.

Vee pursed her lips and nodded, interested but aware of the late hour—or early depending on the way you look at it—and she was tired, Monroe was drunk, and the ratio of demons to humans in the bar leaned dangerously toward non-human. Vee had no clue as to the allegiance of the new owner, which meant the best thing to do now was to get the hell out of there.

Syama seemed to think so too. She shifted closer to Vee. "Let's get her out of here. Some of these guys are not the kind you want to meet in a dark alley."

"Not to mention that we seem to be drawing a bit too much attention," Akil murmured softly. Vee noticed his hand shift toward his hip, fingers closing around the hilt of his narrow-bladed sword.

Vee frowned and then got to her feet. At some point, she'd drained her glass, but she couldn't recall when. She tossed a few bills onto the bar and stared at Monroe. "Coming? Either I help you out of here, or you can get one of these creeps here to take you home. I'm not sure you'll be happy if that happens."

Monroe let out a soft bark of laughter. "Funny. I'm not the type these guys are looking for. That's more your area."

Vee lifted her eyebrow.

"What I meant to say was—"

"Save it for when I get you home." Vee began to walk off, leaving Monroe to trail behind her looking a little too much like a lost puppy. They left the bar and hurried across the road and back into the darkness of the alley.

A light fixed to a wall above them cast a fluorescent glow on the front end of the alley, and the women headed deeper into the shadows. Syama was already throwing her glamor over them when a shout erupted from the street. A small group of men had left the bar, and one glance over her shoulder confirmed they were after her and Monroe.

"C'mon hellhound, do your thing," Vee muttered giving Syama a glare.

"Don't call me that," Syama replied through gritted teeth. Monroe teetered between the hellhound, and Akil who was rolling his eyes, and began to shimmer away.

Vee hadn't yet had time to coax Monroe's address out of her, but the sound of rushing boots on the sidewalk told her they were out of time.

But, before Vee could tell Syama to hurry, the hellhound had already transported them to the garage at Vee's house. They materialized only to have Monroe pass out in a heap on the floor.

"Crap. Good thinking getting us here. I have no idea where she lives."

"Wallet?" suggested Syama.

Vee was barely paying attention to her as she rifled through the detective's pockets. She found the woman's wallet and flicked through the cards before waving one at Syama. Then she read out an address that straddled Harlem and Morningside Heights. Vee found herself extremely grateful that she didn't need to bother with ordering a ride every time she needed to go places. She'd missed the ease of travel that she'd experienced since Syama had arrived and vowed never to take the hellhound—or the sirin—for granted.

As Syama and Akil lifted Monroe off the floor in preparation for the jump, a piece of paper fluttered to the ground. Vee was about to tell the two to wait, but again the hellhound was too fast. They materialized inside Monroe's front room, and almost collapsed under the dead weight of the woman.

Syama and Akil staggered a few steps and dropped Monroe onto the nearest sofa where the detective sank against the cushions and let out a loud snore.

Vee grinned. "Right. Let's get outta here."

"She's going to be super confused when she wakes up." Syama was smiling as she reached for Vee's hand.

"Let's hope we can get away with telling her we drove her home after she passed out," Vee said.

Syama shimmered, and Vee watched in fascination as her own arm took on the strange, almost liquid, luminescent quality that Syama possessed when she jumped. They left Akil to jump on his own, and Syama transported her and Vee back home, landing in Vee's bedroom.

"Door to bed delivery, any hour of the day."

Vee chuckled as Syama turned on her heel and sauntered out into the hall. Outside the window, morning was beginning to brighten the skies, gray light peeking in at the sides of the drapes.

Vee yawned and kicked off her shoes. She was shrugging out of her jacket when she remembered the piece of paper that had fallen from Monroe's pocket. Curious, Vee left her room and hurried downstairs, locating the paper on the garage floor within seconds. It turned out to be a business card.

On one side was a black and red drawing of a lotus, and on the back were contact details for a person named Howard. Vee frowned. What the heck was the card for? No company name, no address, just a name and a phone numbers.

Interesting.

Vee tucked the business card into her back pocket and headed upstairs. Undressing, she padded to her dresser to grab a pen and a post-it note. She wrote a message on one and stuck it on her room door.

Then she dived under the covers and prayed that anyone who dared to come to her room would heed her warning.

5.05am: I'm going to bed. Disturb me at your peril. Much love, V

CHAPTER 24

Two days had passed since they'd discovered the abduction of Lucy and her unborn baby, and as yet no law enforcement agency in the entire state had managed to uncover a thread of evidence that could even suggest where she'd been taken.

Vee had woken up late, checked her phone to discover no messages from Karan about new demon killers on the loose. She did find an update from Brent confirming that he'd fixed all the tests and autopsy reports and that things were fine.

They weren't.

Vee had rung him back almost instantly and had alerted Brent as well as Rossi that Monroe was suspicious. She warned them again that tampering with the reports was going to tip someone off. She repeated her suggestion that going forward they procure their own portions of samples for independent testing—and strongly suggested they be sent to Shankar Industries so Vee herself could spearhead the forensic investigation of that evidence.

Vee didn't enlighten her boss that she was currently redirecting some evidence to her own lab for testing. That was one of those I'll-deal-with-it-when-the-shit-hits-the-fan things.

She'd previously encouraged Rossi to destroy the evidence the forensic techs picked up and even though Monroe's rant about it last night highlighted the danger, destruction of the evidence prior to testing made better sense than tampering with reports after the fact.

Rossi assured Vee that he'd set something up as soon as possible.

Vee's other message was more along the lines of something she preferred to see. Nivaan's voicemail had advised her to be prepared for a night out on the town, that he'd booked a table at Eduardo's in Manhattan, and that jeans was acceptable but that a little fancy won't hurt.

She smiled as she messaged him back, confirming his request for a date.

Request indeed.

Vee headed over to her lab at Shankar Industries and had immersed herself in studying the samples of pey brain she'd prepared the previous day. She'd paused only when she'd identified the existence of a parasitic virus that seemed to live inside the brain of the pey demon.

After considering various options, she began to suspect that she'd be able to create a bio-weapon based on that virus. Perhaps it would be considered unethical, but Vee believed she'd only ever use such a weapon in defense of the innocent.

As the hours passed, Vee found herself filled with glee. She'd taken a chance creating a virus that would attack the pey's immune system. And with the R&D divisions magic-supported equipment, the wait time until the average virus was ready for testing—anything from six to ten weeks—was vastly decreased. By the end of the day, Vee was particularly thrilled to see that the virus growth rate predicted it would be ready within the next day or so.

Perhaps tomorrow, she'd have something to take to the head of R&D for testing consideration.

When Vee finally grabbed her bag and looked at her watch, she found that the day had gone by faster than she'd thought.

And she had a date with a certain lion shifter.

IN THE MIDST of everything that was happening, everything that had happened to her in the course of the last twenty-four hours, Vee was questioning the wisdom of doing something as mundane as having dinner.

With her boyfriend.

When was there ever time for such a thing as romance at a time like this?

Syama had kept Vee company while she'd dressed, and though the hellhound had insisted that she and Akil go with Vee, she'd eventually relented after Vee reminded her that her boyfriend was a dangerous, powerful lion shifter, capable of ripping a human in half if provoked.

Vee was jogging down the stairs in her bare feet, patting the pockets of her jeans for her phone. "Back pocket," came a low baritone from the lounge as she passed.

"Ugh, thanks, Dad. I swear my brain is like a sieve right now."

Her dad snorted. "That's what you call not having enough sleep."

"Sleep is for the weak," she said as she checked her phone in case Nivaan had bailed on her. Coward that she was, she'd been hoping he would, but she had no messages to that effect.

Dinner plans canceled but I'll be picking you up. Have a surprise for you.

Vee's eyebrows rose, her curiosity piqued.

Pocketing her phone, she hurried to the basement, her Dad's footsteps echoing after her. He loitered on the threshold as she rifled through the shelves in search of a handful of small weapons she could hide on her person.

"Did Mac drop off my daggers?" Vee asked as she slipped a wide leather band around her wrist. The band was filled with needles which —depending on where she inserted them— she could use to either paralyze or kill an attacker. The needles were for close combat only, and she'd only ever used them as a last resort. She had her trishula, which hung over her shoulder, glamored to appear to onlookers as though it were a backpack, not to mention her daggers which she usually slid into her boots.

Only today, she wasn't wearing boots.

Raj cleared his throat. "He dropped by around midday. The package is on that counter over there." He pointed behind her.

Vee headed across the narrow room to the opposite counter, making a beeline for a small box. Mac had promised to have them ready two weeks ago but hadn't communicated with her as to when he'd deliver them. She'd almost given up with patience and had been close to picking up the phone and telling Mac she'd pick them up if he wasn't comfortable coming by. She did understand his reluctance though. She wasn't that selfish.

She retrieved the set of six stiletto blades that Mac had been working on for her. He'd explained how, with their super thin handles, they would easily be mistaken for hair sticks. Alternatively, they could be inserted into narrow hemlines and jacket seams. Today, she slid them into hidden pockets on the inner seams of her jeans.

They were mainly throwing knives, cheaply made and untraceable so that she could leave them behind at a scene without fear of being tracked through the materials used in production. The wood of the handles had been coated with an oil resistant resin ensuring Vee would never leave a fingerprint on them.

All ready, Vee turned to face her dad. "How do I look?" She held out her hands, waiting.

"That pink top looks nice," he said, hesitating on the color.

Vee rolled her eyes. "Cerise, Dad. The color is called cerise. Where have you been in the last decade?" She grinned and went to him to give him a hug.

The reference to where he'd been was one the both of them had begun to use as a means of breaking the tension. Because with him there was always tension.

Ever since he'd been returned to them, it had felt as though there was something holding him away from them, not so much physically but emotionally.

Vee understood that he would be suffering from a serious case of PTSD, but her offer of helping him find a counselor had been met with an emphatic 'No' each time.

"He's been good to you?" Her dad's voice broke into her thoughts, and she glanced over at him.

"Yeah," Vee smiled, thinking of Nivaan and how their relationship had developed over the last few months.

"No. I meant Mac." There was an indefinable note to her father's voice, one that cut deep into Vee's heart. She felt as though her answer would mean she'd betrayed her father but if she lied, if she denied her love for Mac then that would amount to almost the same thing.

"Yes," she said, deciding honesty was the way to go. She gave her dad a wry smile. "I wasn't a very nice teenager. Messed up, angry with the world, with Mom. Mac…calmed me down, gave me direction."

Her dad nodded at that, then turned to leave as if that answer had been entirely satisfactory, only his face revealed something else that she couldn't understand.

She followed him out into the hall. "Dad?" she called out. He paused in the hall and turned to her. "I didn't mean to hurt you. Saying that I loved Mac…it doesn't mean I don't love you."

Her dad smiled and came toward her. "I know that. I wasn't here, and he was. I'm grateful that he took such good care of you for all these years. Even when your mom…." He looked away, as though unsure how to complete the sentence.

Vee patted him on the back. "Mom has her own issues. She never got over you. When Mac came along, she was happy, but only for a time. It was as if her longing for you wouldn't allow her to move on. I want to think it was instinct, that somehow she knew you were still alive, that she was waiting for you to come back home."

Her dad smiled and pinched Vee's cheek. "You always know what to say, huh?" He sighed and held her around the shoulders, leading her upstairs. "Someday soon, your Mom is going to have to talk to me about that herself."

Vee turned and pinched his cheek in retaliation, winking as she said, "Nothing is stopping you from going to her, you know. That company still belongs to you. Your offices and labs are all still there. Get a good night's sleep and head out in the morning. Start fresh and let us know you're okay. And if you're not okay, then that's okay too. Just don't keep it to yourself."

Her dad smiled. "Such wisdom from one so young."

Vee rolled her eyes and hurried to fetch her shoes. She balanced on one foot at a time as she slipped the red stilettos on. Just in time too, as the doorbell began to ring. Her dad was at the door in light seconds, opening it to bestow his usual death glare upon poor Nivaan.

"Come on, Dad!"

Vee offered her dad her own death glare, but he pretended not to notice as he ushered Nivaan inside and shut the door. She waited as the usually awkward silence between the men thawed to almost comfortable, before being unable to take it anymore.

Vee was just opening her mouth to inquire at the change in venue for their dinner when Nivaan lifted a finger, silencing her as he stared downward. She hesitated then followed his gaze to where it was focused: at her feet.

"You can't wear those." His tone was admonishing, and almost parental.

What the what?

Vee's eyes widened. Nivaan had never behaved like the overbearing boyfriend prone to mansplaining, but this instruction hovered on the line. "Err...why not? Pretty sure I'm capable of making shoe choices on my own. Or do you not like red stilettos?" She lifted one eyebrow, her expression icy.

Nivaan grinned mischievously. "I like red stilettos. Actually, I love red stilettos...especially when *you're* wearing them." Vee gave him a harsh glare, and he paused, shared an uncomfortable glance with her dad, then he said, "What I meant to say was that, as perfect as your shoe choice is, they may not be as comfortable to walk in where we're going."

Vee's hands moved to her hips of their own accord, and she had to force them back down. She refused to appear a fishwife. "So where *are* you taking me?"

"I hope you're going to like it. The city is holding a cross-cultural promotional parade tonight. People of all shapes, sizes, and colors all mingling in the streets of New York. It will be glorious." Nivaan ended his oration with such an excited grin that even Vee's dad cracked a smile.

Vee laughed. "If that's the case, red stilettos won't do." She toed off the heels and grabbed them from the floor. As she whirled and scurried up the stairs, she yelled, "Be back in a sec."

Then she paused at the top step to send them each a warning glare.

"I'm hungry, and I need to eat. So, don't kill each other, okay?"

CHAPTER 25

She'd left the two men in the hall alone and all the way to her room she wondered if that had been a mistake. They'd been circling each other for almost a month now, and Vee wondered if it had to do with the fact that Nivaan was a mahabidala.

She knew her dad had been involved in paranormal-related investigations—though more on the magical side than the hunting of them—but knowing that lion shifters exist and accepting when your daughter is dating one were two different things.

Hurrying into her room, Vee snagged her walking boots and a pair of comfy socks. She also changed her jacket for one with a thicker down.

She was about to head out the door when a voice stopped her. "You forgot to take a hat." Radhima stood at Vee's drawer and smiled at her.

Vee paused. "Where have you been?"

"Around. Thinking." The old woman had a sad, far-off look on her face.

"Are you feeling better now?"

Another smile. "Getting there."

Vee nodded. "And I don't need a hat. Stop nagging."

"I'm not nagging. It's going to get cold. You should cover up, especially since you're still healing from your injuries. If it were up to me, I'd have you in bed with a book and a cup of hot chocolate, not gallivanting around town with a boy."

Vee rolled her eyes. "I'm getting nagged by a ghost?"

The ghost snorted. "I know what I'm talking about. Take the hat." Vee grunted and turned on her heel, fully intending to ignore the old woman. "If you don't, I'll come with you. Three's company, right?"

Letting out a low growl, Vee stormed to the chest and grabbed a beanie from the drawer. She shoved it into her pocket, aware of the urge to stamp her feet— she wasn't sure if she should be annoyed or amused at her reaction.

Instead, she looked over at her grandmother. "Happy now?"

"Quite."

Vee turned on her heel and headed out of the room. On the threshold, she paused and looked over her shoulder. "By the way, Nivaan is not a boy. He's a grown-ass man."

As she walked off, she had to suppress a bark of laughter. She could have sworn her grandmother's ghost had mumbled something about Vee having it wrong and that Nivaan was a grown man with a great ass.

The old woman never failed to surprise Vee.

Vee hurried back downstairs and found herself interrupting a somewhat passionate conversation about baseball teams. She grabbed Nivaan by the shoulders and physically turned him around. "Come on you big lunk. I know about you men when you talk about sports. You'll be standing here all night."

Nivaan allowed her to turn him around and spoke over his shoulder as he went, "But you love sports too."

"Yeah, I love sports too. But when men argue about sports, they can go around and around in circles for hours just for the heck of it. I wanted a night in, but *you* wanted to brave the city streets. So, let's go before I make you go yourself."

Nivaan headed outside and huffed. "Have you ever read Taming of the Shrew?"

In response, Vee slapped Nivaan on the side with the back of her hand. Nivaan grabbed his gut and faked a pained 'ouch' before dissolving into laughter. With a long-suffering sigh, Vee muttered, "I'm dating a child," then slammed the door to the sound of her father's chuckles.

Vee was smiling as she descended the stairs. Nivaan had gone silent. He'd reached the sidewalk and was looking up at the house. "How's he doing?" he asked, his expression almost indiscernible in the gathering darkness.

"You heard him laughing." Vee smiled, tucking her fingers into her pockets as she stared at the house too. "I think he's mending. He seems to be getting better each day."

"He's come a long way," Nivaan said as he hurried to his Jeep.

Vee climbed in and fastened the seatbelt. "I think he needs help from a PTSD perspective. He's been through so much, a lot of which we have no idea about because he won't tell us what happened to him when he fell into the vortex."

"Does he appear emotionless or hurt?"

"Lack of emotion, definitely. And there's a sadness in his eyes. Whatever happened to him, he's protecting himself from the pain. And I think he's hurting because of Radhima. I think he feels responsible for her death somehow."

Nivaan smiled as he drove them through the streets. "You should become a therapist."

Vee snorted. "Yeah. Like I need a hole in the head."

The drive over to downtown was peppered with banter and light ribbing, which Vee decided had been good fun.

After parking—Nivaan used a friend's space at a nearby parking garage—they strolled the few blocks to where the parade was in full force. Floats were gliding down the street, and boisterous crowds threw confetti and streamers in no specific direction.

Gilded polystyrene dragons followed garish skulls and women dressed in tall headdresses. Those followed a giant statue of an archangel which trailed a float containing a papier mâché effigy of the god Ganesh with his rounded belly and curling elephant trunk.

It was a hodgepodge of religious and cultural presentations that Vee assumed the city hoped would encourage cohesion amongst the different ethnic groups. For what it was worth, Vee believed the plan could work.

As they weaved through the crowd, the street lamps flickered on, throwing myriad colored lights onto the passing crowds who sent up a cheer.

Vee glanced over at Nivaan and grinned. There was no point in talking with the barrage of sounds around them, from music to chanting to yelling.

As she studied his smiling face, Vee wondered at people's perceptions. Nivaan was a respected doctor, with a reputation of skill that was unparalleled. He was also a lion shifter—a mahabidala—a thing from folk tales and horror stories. How many of the people walking this particular street would shriek in horror or turn on him if they knew what he was? The thought turned her stomach as she stared at him, recognizing his vulnerability. People were not ready to know the truth, to know they shared their streets, their workplaces, and even their governments with supernaturals.

Nivaan's voice in her ear made Vee jump. "Hungry?" he yelled.

She winced and shook her head while sticking a finger in her ear and rubbing it hard. She hated anyone talking in her ear. Touching her ears came a close second.

She took Nivaan's offered hand, and they weaved through the crowd toward the food carts that lined one side of the street. The variety of food was astounding and Vee was spoiled for choice.

"Dim sum or buffalo wings?" he asked as he too scanned the selection.

"Both," Vee replied with a grin.

Nivaan nodded, and they headed down the line to make their choices and wait for their orders.

As they took their snacks and drinks and began to walk away from the food area, Nivaan bent close to Vee, and with a grin on his face he asked, "You do know we're being followed, right?"

Vee blinked. She wanted to say something smart, like 'of course, check your two o'clock and my six' but she had nothing. Even with her FBI training—and her Apsara skills—she was so exhausted that she'd lapsed in her awareness of her surroundings.

When he straightened, Nivaan said, "Don't worry. I'm not sure a non-shifter could have detected them."

Vee had to acknowledge that despite her skills she didn't have the nose to track a stalker the way animal shifters like Nivaan did. Not that it made her feel any better.

"How did you know?" she asked as she chewed dim sum that was now tasteless.

"One of them passed us by a few too many times. Amateur move. I got his scent, so it didn't take me long to figure out what they were doing. They're tag-teaming positions which is quite amusing because all it did was make it easier for me to connect the two scents."

"No doubt they have no clue you are what you are," Vee said, smirking.

"Good thing too, or I wouldn't have made them."

Vee forced herself to focus on her food. Stalkers or not, she'd deal with them soon enough. Crumpling the wrappers, she looked around for a trashcan only to find the papers taken from her by Nivaan, who added them to his pile and tossed them into large trash receptacle a few feet behind him.

When he turned back to her, he said, "Now what? Want to draw them into a dark alley somewhere?"

Vee pursed her lips. “I think I quite like that idea.”

“I didn’t mean *you*.”

Vee’s eyes narrowed as she glared at him.

“Be nice,” he warned before she spoke.

Vee huffed and pasted a sweet smile on her face. “I’m fully capable of taking them down.”

“How about we catch them off guard, but let them believe you don’t know you’re being followed?”

Vee sighed and nodded. It was a good plan and would help bring whoever it was now stalking her out into the open. If they believed a third party was onto them while Vee remained ignorant of their presence, they may relent and leave her alone.

She nodded, grinning as if she was having the time of her life. Then she said, “Selfie time? Could be we could get some well-timed accidental photobombs that Brent can run for an ID.”

Nivaan nodded, and the pair proceeded to take almost a dozen photographs in front of various floats and at a number of different angles. Vee’s stalkers were ignorant of the fact that both of them had been caught on camera, both staring right at Vee at the time.

“Lemme see.” Vee waved at Nivaan to hand over the phone and grinned, this time the smile genuine. “Got you, you bastards.”

Nivaan smiled too in order to keep up the act. Then he linked arms with her and said, “Wanna clue me in on why someone is following you?”

“Oh. Probably because someone wants to kill me.”

CHAPTER 26

"What?" Nivaan's steps slowed, but Vee tightened her grip on his hand and pulled him along.

"Day before yesterday, after I went to a murder scene, I was almost run down by a cab. But the driver magically disappeared. I suspected something was up, but these guys they have tailing me, just make me sure now that someone is after me." Vee felt Nivaan's grip on her hand tighten. She didn't think he realized that his own fear and anger were being transmitted to her through a grip that was close to breaking her fingers.

"Honeybuns?" she said, tilting her head close to him. Nivaan glanced over at her, amusement lifting the corners of his eyes. "Please don't break my fingers," she said with a sweet smile.

"Oh shit. Sorry, Vee." Nivaan let go of her fingers then began to manipulate her bones and joints.

"Nivaan?" Vee's voice rose with the question as the pair reached the edge of the festive crowd.

He looked up. "What?"

"What are you doing?" Vee asked, staring at his hands.

"Checking if I've broken anything."

She rolled her eyes. "Do I have a fragile sticker taped across my forehead? I don't break that easy. And besides, you'd know if you broke my fingers. I wouldn't be walking along with a smile on my face."

Nivaan pursed his lips and appeared to consider her words. Then he shook his head. "I don't believe so. I know you. You'd be all concerned about my feelings, and you'd hide the pain and slink home without telling me. I don't trust you."

Vee studied him for a moment. "Good point."

Nivaan smirked, and they turned the corner onto a quieter street. The noise of music and celebration still echoed toward them and would mask any sounds of an attack. Vee had to remind herself that the attack in question could also be carried out on her.

She put herself on high alert, scanning the street and listening to every step behind her.

There, two sets of footsteps followed about a dozen yards back.

Nivaan leaned closer to Vee. "This alleyway should do."

Vee nodded and followed his lead. "You do your shifter thing, and I'll be bait?" she said softly.

Nivaan opened his mouth, and Vee had a feeling he was about to tell her to stay somewhere safe. But something in his eyes changed as he looked at her, and she wondered if it may have been as a result of the death glare that she'd sent him.

"Fine. Get back in the shadows. Beneath that fire escape."

"Okay. And I'm *human* bait, okay. I don't really want to show them my power. It's better I appear vulnerable, so consider me your damsel in distress."

Nivaan grinned. "Whatever the lady requires," he said dipping his head in a short bow.

Vee snorted and watched as he shimmered into nothing, pulling his glamor over himself within seconds.

Just in time too, as the two men turned the corner. Vee watched them as she stood there at the back of the alley, taking up a position where she'd have plenty of space to work with if she found herself in a life or death situation.

She began to pace, appearing to have not seen the oncoming men. They'd grown bold, following like this. It made Vee wonder if perhaps they didn't know what her powers were. All the more reason to not come out guns—or rather trishula, daggers, and needles—blazing.

They were close now, and she glanced up at them. "What do you want?" she asked, inserting a short quaver of fear into her voice.

The first man, whose mustache appeared to be the size of a small rodent, swaggered closer. "You just making this easy for us, aren't you?" he sneered as he came to a stop to look her up and down. He had a thug feel with his ripped jacket, low-riding jeans and baseball cap on back to front. In his hand, he held a gun, a match to the one his partner now had trained on Vee. Guns? So perhaps these guys were not of the supernatural flavor if they were carrying around human weapons.

"Ed, just remember we need to bring her in. Dead, we don't get no payment." The second guy, similarly dressed though he was portly to his partner's skinny and had a glistening dark head. He glanced over at Rat-stache—or rather, Ed—pointedly staring until he received an agreement. Although Baldy had kept his voice low, Vee had heard every word, having strengthened that power years ago.

"Shut your mouth. She'll hear you."

"Yeah. She's got super-hearing now?"

Ed grunted and met Vee's gaze as she backed away, her eyes widened with what she hoped looked like fear. She'd hate to have come across looking like she was demonic or demented. "Leave me alone. You don't want to mess with me. My guy…he'll kill you two."

"What? You're concerned about our lives now?" Ed asked, his tone mocking.

"I'm telling you. He'll tear you guys apart."

"Yeah, yeah, you bitches will say anything to save your asses—"

"Did it occur to you that perhaps the bitch in question would not want to be accosted by two assholes like you?" said a voice from the darkness above.

A large dark shape moved, flitting from the third level fire-escape on the right-hand wall, almost gliding over to the landing closest to Vee.

Vee's attackers turned their attention to Nivaan, both staring up at his shadowed form.

Ed shifted his gaze for an instant to catch his partner staring too. "Watch her," he yelled then turned his gaze back up. But that second of inattention had been his undoing. Nivaan swooped down on him, wrapped an arm around his neck and lifted him off the ground in a leap for the opposite fire escape.

Ed yelled, and his partner shuffled in place in front of Vee. She wanted to laugh at the sight of his face as he watched her, all the while looking like he desperately wanted to check on his partner.

He shifted his head, so his mouth was angled in Nivaan's direction. "Ed? You okay?"

A muffled grunt emanated from the darkness, and Nivaan landed on the ground beside Baldy. The thug let out a yell, shaking his gun first at Vee and then at Nivaan. "Stay where you are," he shouted, spit flying from his mouth. "What did you do with Ed?"

Nivaan smiled and walked further into the shadows. "Oh, you don't have to worry about Ed. He's just hanging around. But maybe Ed's safety is dependent on what *you* have to tell me?"

"What?" the man stuttered, his gaze going up to the side of the building again, then back at Nivaan. Vee followed the man's gaze and bit back a laugh. Somehow, Nivaan had managed to string Ed up, tying him to one of the corners of the overhanging fire-escape landings. He was fully capable of reaching up for the grilled overhang, but any movement of his hands could loosen him from the rope around his arms.

Vee lifted an eyebrow and stared at Nivaan, impressed.

Baldy turned back to Nivaan. "Let him down, or I'm going to shoot your brains out."

"Can you even see me to aim? And you wouldn't want a bullet to rebound and hit the woman, would you? She's a little too valuable for such reckless behavior, don't you think?"

The woman?

So Nivaan was playing at being someone else who was hunting Vee down. She hid a smile and watched her remaining attacker weigh his options.

Still aiming the gun at the shadows, he said, "What do you want?"

"You know what I want. I want to know who sent you? Who are you working for?"

"I don't know."

"What do you mean you don't know? Someone must have hired you two assholes. Sent you instructions, paid you."

"Oh yeah, yeah that. Ed was in charge of that."

"You better know something, or after Ed falls, you're next."

"Okay, okay man, it was on the dark web. It's a site that puts up bios and photographs of people. It's like a bounty hunter site. You take the job, find and deliver the target, and the money is there for you at the handover location."

"But these people are innocent, and you're just going around and rounding them up? For someone you don't even know?" Nivaan's voice rose.

"Look man, I just do the job. Who knows what these people have done. That's not my business. But her—" he pointed at Vee, "—they said she's a pedophile who preys on kids. Passes herself off as a schoolteacher."

Vee's stomach churned, and she felt like she was about to

throw up. Somewhere out there on the web was a profile that claimed she was a sexual predator?

Beyond Ed's clueless partner, Vee caught sight of a shadow flickering at the entrance of the alley. Nivaan didn't seem to have noticed, but Vee had. She blinked, not sure she'd seen it correctly.

A flurry of darkened feathers whirled in a mist made of gray and silver light. And yet the sight of the form sent a chill deep into Vee's heart. She wasn't sure what she'd seen. Perhaps she'd imagined the tall, hunched form, the narrow scrawny neck. Perhaps she'd imagined the glassy dark eyes staring out at her from a feathered body, black as night.

She shivered, but before she could warn Nivaan, bring his attention to the oncoming threat—one that Vee felt was actually worse than these two dark-web hired thugs—Nivaan said, "Wrong buddy. This woman is a medical researcher. You either have the wrong person, or this is part of a hit or abduction situation."

The man lifted a shoulder, twisting his lips as though he didn't really give a damn. "Whatever. So what do you want with her?"

"My employer wants to have a little chat with her."

"No way. You're not taking my payday from me."

"Not like you have much of a say," Vee said, keeping her eye on the shadowy feathered form who had stepped closer to them. "I'd rather go talk to someone I don't know than go anywhere with the likes of you."

The man growled, rage darkening his cheeks to an almost blue-black. His finger looked dangerously close to the trigger. Too close for Vee's liking. She glanced over at the dark patch of shadow that was Nivaan, hoping he'd get the message to get this thing done and get her out of there. She hated that she was hobbled with using her powers, and for now, all she wanted was to get away before the dark figure came too close, because the sick feeling in her gut told her it would not end well.

Nivaan shifted in the darkness then swooped closer to Vee. He both drew his glamor over her rendering her invisible and launched himself into the air using his shifter power. Shots went wild as Vee's attacker finally let loose. He'd obviously given up and was firing on Nivaan—or what he thought to be Nivaan—in the hopes that he would hit her too. He'd lose his money now for sure. And he'd have to find a way to release Ed safely.

Vee smiled as Nivaan set her onto her feet on a nearby rooftop.

"You would make an excellent bad-guy/good-guy/vigilante...guy."

Nivaan snorted as Vee gave a sigh of annoyance. "You lose a few brain cells over there?" he snickered.

Vee hit him on the bicep, but the man just snorted and grinned. "I'm tired. Long day. And people just keep dropping by, only they want to stab me or kill me or suck me dry of my blood or run me over with their cab, or as you have just witnessed, hand me over to some anonymous person on the dark web."

Nivaan grabbed Vee around the shoulders. "You know what my gran used to always say?"

Vee sighed and walked beside Nivaan as they headed toward the rooftop stairwell entrance to the building. "What did she say?" Vee yawned and felt a little dizzy as her adrenaline began to crash.

"She would waggle her finger and say, 'You know beta, God will never put anything on your plate that you cannot shoulder'." Nivaan chuckled. "For the longest time, I was puzzled as to how the food on my plate and my shoulder had anything to with each other."

Vee snorted. "That's 'cos your mind is always on food."

Then as they entered the stairwell, Nivaan let out a low growl. "Not all the time, woman."

And then he slapped her on the ass.

CHAPTER 27

With morning came the reminder for Vee of the men who'd come so close to abducting her, all because of some stupid dark-web site. The thought that someone out there had gone to such an extent to put a bounty on her head…she wasn't sure how to process that.

Nivaan had insisted on staying over and had taken Radhima's room. Vee had been too tired to protest what had seemed like him being excessively protective.

When she got up and headed downstairs, she found he'd already gone but had left a bag of croissants on the kitchen table for her. Smiling, Vee made coffee and devoured the pastries listening for the sound of her dad's footsteps upstairs. But everything was silent except for Syama and Akil who were in the garage sharpening blades.

She could hear the high ringing of the whetstones as the two worked. Downing the last of her coffee, Vee rinsed the mug and placed it in the sink, then hurried to the garage.

"Hey, you two," she said smiling at the sight of their concentrated scowls. "I'm off to the lab. You should be good to drop me off and come straight back."

Syama snorted and got to her feet. "Yeah, sure. Like your lab is so golem-proofed?" She lifted a brow as she slid her dagger into the sheath at her waist.

Vee was about to argue with the hellhound when her phone began to buzz. She lifted a finger, motioning to Syama to wait. Then, as Vee read the message from Monroe, she sighed. "Guess the lab's off the agenda for now."

"You got a case?" asked Akil, also rising and pocketing his whetstone.

Syama rolled her eyes. "Of course, she has a case. She has that look."

"What look?" Vee asked as she studied the address in Talmadge Hill an expensive residential area just outside the city.

Syama smirked and tilted her head, pretending to study Vee's face, her expression serious. "Oh, I think it falls somewhere between tense and constipated."

Akil coughed and choked back a laugh while Vee just stared at the hellhound, not sure what to say. She shook a finger at Syama. "You better watch it," said Vee, shaking her head, knowing her warning would remain forever unheeded. Then she glanced at her phone. "If you're done with your comedy act, we need to go here," she said, holding her phone out so Syama and Akil could read the address.

Akil nodded and shimmered away, returning within seconds. "I have a good spot that we can arrive at and remain unseen."

Vee walked over to Syama who had grabbed Vee's go-bag from the table behind her and was holding it out to her. Slinging it over her shoulder, Vee felt comforted in the knowledge that the weapons were close at hand. Just in case.

Seconds later they arrived within a stand of trees across the road from the address Monroe had sent Vee. The road was quiet, though lined with police and forensic team vehicles.

Akil shimmered into solidity beside Vee and said, "I'll be in the trees. I will let you know if anything happens." Before Vee could respond, the sirin had disappeared, leaving Vee to share a wry smile with Syama.

Thankfully, the patrols had been set further inside the property and Vee was able to cross the road and walk through the open gates and up the drive before someone stopped her. Syama accompanied her, glamor securely hiding her presence.

The cop guarding the scene waved her past, and Vee was directed through the house—an overly ostentatious mansion, Greek pillars guarding the entrance, floor to ceiling windows, faux stone rock facings, and a gigantic fountain taking pride of place directly in front of a pair of double doors large enough for a semi to pass through.

Though open, the door appeared to be hewn from solid wood and patterned with brass, with a distinct oriental feel to it. Vee ignored the eclectic architecture and headed through the long hallway and out a large back door onto a slate-tiled patio.

A glistening sky-blue pool shimmered like a jewel to Vee's left, the sunlight glancing off the surface so brightly that Vee had to shield her eyes against the glare.

Standing on the edge of the scene, Vee surveyed the frenzied activity. Monroe stood on the other side of the clearing, talking to someone on her cell phone as she paced back and forth, waving her free hand. The woman's brow was furrowed, and her cheeks were ruddy.

All sure signs that Monroe was frustrated and furious. But whatever was going on, Vee wasn't interested. She didn't want to allow herself to get sidetracked by the detective's issues. Right now, Vee needed to assess the scene.

"You should have brought the conch," Syama muttered from Vee's side.

Vee resisted the urge to roll her eyes. She understood Syama's concern, and in fact, she shared that concern. But Vee couldn't just use Lord Narasimha's conch just because it was convenient. She didn't believe the boons of the gods were meant to work that way. It wasn't as if the power to freeze time didn't have its consequences. She still recalled the last time she'd used it.

The day her grandmother had died.

"I'm still here, you know."

"Not really," said Vee softly. Then she shook her head and glared at her grandmother's ghost as she stood beside Vee, arms cross as she too surveyed the scene. "And stop doing that. Someone is going to see me talking to you, and they'll have grounds to toss me off active duty."

The ghost grunted and tightened her folded arms. Today, Radhima wore a fitted jacket in a soft teal, and a pair of black jeans. And teal cowboy boots, patterned in a bright pink thread.

"What are you wearing?"

"Are you going to ask me that question every single time we talk?"

"Yes, if you're going to wear something different every time."

"I think she looks great," Syama chimed in.

"You stay out of this," Vee said, turning to glare at Syama.

Syama grinned. "Stop being so hard on her. She has a right to wear what she wants."

Vee opened her mouth and then shut it. She'd been about to argue the fact that yes, her grandmother had a right to wear whatever she wanted, but jeans and cowboy boots were things Vee had never imagined to be part of her style. It was going to take some getting used to.

Vee sighed and rolled her shoulders. "We have work to do. Let's keep our heads in the game, okay?" Vee said, pretty sure that her words were more for herself than Syama. Or Radhima.

Akil had taken up position in a nearby tree, with a view of the entire clearing. Probably the best place to be at this point. Vee headed down the hillside and avoided stepping into the deep puddles of muddy water that dotted the ground.

"These look rather regular, don't they?" asked the ghost.

Vee started at the sound and glanced to her right, but

Radhima was no longer revealing herself. Vee sighed. "You have a good eye. They seem to follow a pattern similar to what footprints would look like."

"Why would someone make holes like that in the ground? Strange shoes? Stilts? Spoked wheels?" Syama was ticking off options that Vee had already considered but had nothing additional to add. Not yet.

"To be honest I don't have a clue," said Vee, keeping her voice low. "Let's have a look at the crime scene itself before we try to make any deductions."

Syama nodded and kept just behind Vee as she walked. Glamored as she was, Vee had to also be careful of talking to her in front of people. Having invisible sidekicks was turning out to be more of a hazard than she'd expected—not to mention ghostly grandmothers.

Vee crossed the shallow clearing and walked onto the neatly manicured lawn of the estate. Despite the cold, and the intermittent snowfall, the grass was lush and verdant. Had it not been for the strange, slippery substance found scattered across the lawn, the view would have been idyllic.

From where she stood, the pieces of pale detritus resembled the shedded skin of a reptile. Vee shuddered as she closed in on Monroe. "What do we have?"

"Something large and very reptile-like."

Radhima—always a stickler for language—muttered, "Reptilian," as Vee asked, "What makes you think reptile?"

Monroe jerked a chin at the papery thin coils of pale skins that littered the lawn. Vee crouched, withdrawing a pen from her jacket pocket. She lifted a long piece and studied it. "They look like sausage casings."

Monroe snorted. "Couldn't have put it better myself."

Vee shrugged. "I could have been more specific and said porcine intestine?"

Monroe shook her head and mimed a barf. "No thanks." Then

she stared around the lawn. "The place is littered with the stuff. I'm not sure what to make of it."

"What's this place got to do with our missing mom-to-be?"

Monroe crooked a finger, and Vee hurried toward her. By the time Vee had reached her side, the woman was already crouched beside another long stretch of shedded skin. She lifted it away to reveal an oval-shaped locket on a slim gold chain.

Vee's eyebrows rose. "I'm guessing Susie had a similar locket on the gold chain she left in the bathroom?"

"Well, identical, yes. But we know it's not Susie's. *That* we have locked up in evidence." Monroe didn't need to explain, but Vee could tell the detective needed to work through how she felt about one more lead that gave them nothing.

"So this must belong to Lucy." Vee leaned closer.

Monroe was nodding and lifting the chain away from the skin. She dropped it into her gloved palm and held it out to Vee who nodded. "Yep."

A pang of sadness filled Vee at the senseless death of Susie and the growing likelihood that her daughter, Lucy, had met the very same fate.

"But what does Lucy have to do with these…things?" Monroe waved a hand at the remains of shedded skins that littered the lawn. Then she sighed and rested her hands on her hips rocking back and forth on her heels. This was one case that was stumping them all.

"Could be any number of things," said Vee. They were empty words, just filler to help appease the detective.

Monroe snorted. "Well, let's just hope it isn't what it looks like. Because the last thing I need is to find out that there is a giant snake roaming the streets of New York, snacking on pregnant women and shedding its skin as it goes."

Vee adjusted her sight, aware that it may well be impossible to clear the lawn so that she could get a better look at the aural patterns around the place. She wasn't surprised to see a twisting meshwork of ragged aural residue that implied a large group of people had traversed this lawn a few hours ago. Vee paused. Not people.

Demons.

More specifically, pey demons.

"It's not snakeskin," murmured Radhima, drawing Vee's attention from the auras. Vee blinked, surprised she hadn't flinched at the sound of the disembodied voice. Perhaps she was getting used to the ghost's presence.

Vee hunkered down again and studied the skins, this time trying to figure out what the sheddings had to do with pey demons. Syama grunted as she too leaned over Vee. "I'm not sure. I feel like I've seen something like this before, but I can't put my finger on it."

"Well, when your finger finds it, can you let me know? 'Cos I'm stumped." Vee sighed and got back to her feet. She was turning to survey the lawn again when movement in the trees caught her attention.

Vee tried to appear casual as she glanced over Syama's shoulder and watched the figure, hidden by the shadows within the small forest to the north of the property. From this distance, it wasn't possible to identify who the observer was, but there was one thing Vee could tell beyond a shadow of a doubt.

Half-hidden amongst the trees and shadows was a pey demon.

CHAPTER 28

"Syama," Vee said, keeping her voice low.

Her tone must have held sufficient warning, enough that it would make Syama stiffen. The hellhound glanced at Vee. "Where?"

Vee pasted a smile on her face. "Behind you, due north, within the trees. Pey demon. Not totally sure, but I see enough to make me bet on it."

Syama nodded. "Okay, how do you want to do this?"

Vee thought for a moment. "Let's go inside the house, preferably somewhere out of his sight. He needs to think that we haven't seen him, and what better way than to appear to leave the lawn?"

"What excuse you going to make to Monroe over there?" Syama asked, darting her gaze in the detective's direction.

Vee shrugged. "Don't need to explain myself to her." With that, Vee turned on her heel and strode off toward the house. Glancing over her shoulder, Vee saw that Syama was standing there, frozen on the spot. Vee turned and waited for the hellhound who eventually moved and began to hurry toward Vee. "You okay?"

Syama nodded. "Yeah. I just needed a moment to gather my thoughts."

Vee nodded. Though she wondered where her ghost had gotten to, she didn't ask. Radhima had an odd habit of appearing like a thought come alive. She'd come when she was needed.

For now, Vee awaited Syama's arrival as she stepped into the front hall of the mansion to which the expansive lawn belonged. Inside the living room to the left, a woman paced the black carpet, her red kaftan flowing behind her. The pair of cops speaking to the woman wore the body language and expressions one would bear when coaxing a wild animal, spines curved, heads somewhat bowed, voices low.

Vee hid a smile and turned to stand near the tall floor to ceiling windows that sat beside the doorway. Through them she watched the tree line, hoping to catch sight of the demon. Vee was disappointed to find that all she saw were shadows.

"Still there?" asked Syama from beside Vee.

"No idea. I can't see him anymore, but it could just be the angle from here. Or he could have left thinking he was in the clear."

Syama nodded. "Ok. You wait here. I'll go check the place out. Track him a little, see where he is and what he's doing. Be back in a few." Syama disappeared, and Vee disliked the feeling of helplessness.

She knew Syama was safe, hell the hellhound had done far more dangerous jobs before she'd ended up on Vee's detail. Still, Vee worried. Part of caring about people Vee guessed.

She forced herself not to pace as she waited for Syama to return. A shadow on the lawn drew Vee's attention, and she shook her head as she watched a white owl fly close to the entrance than change direction. Seconds later, Akil came up behind her, the heels on his shoes making low thunking sounds on the slate-tiled floor.

Before she could speak, Syama shimmered beside Vee, her

eyes wide. "I found him. And I don't think you're going to like where he went."

Vee shrugged. "Just take me there. I don't want to know now."

Syama nodded and held onto Vee, shimmering into nothingness. They reappeared inside dense tree-cover and sank to the ground instantly. Beyond the thicket was a rectangular clearing and at its center was a manhole.

Nothing else in the clearing appeared disturbed, but Vee knew that if Syama brought them here, it meant only one thing.

She was going to have to enter the sewer.

"Crap," Vee muttered.

Syama grinned. "Exactly. I knew you weren't going to like it." She gave Vee an apologetic smile.

Vee shrugged. "Girl's gotta do what she's gotta do," Vee said just as her cell phone began to vibrate. Good thing she always turned the sound off when she was about to head to a crime scene.

"Monroe's trying to get a hold of me I see." She spoke mostly to herself as she tried to figure out what to tell the cop. In the end, she just messaged Monroe to keep her posted and that she'd had an agency emergency, ending with a request for samples of the snakeskin to be sent to her lab at Shankar Industries. "Let's hope that doesn't piss her off even more."

Vee glared at Syama, knowing she was being unreasonably annoyed with the hellhound. It wasn't her fault that the pey had led them to the entrance to an underground tunnel or bunker, or whatever it was. Vee would bet it was the sewer system though. It was just the way her luck worked.

"It's not so bad," Syama said, her tone soothing.

"Speak for yourself," Vee muttered, staring at the manhole cover.

Akil cleared his throat—sounding oddly human, though he was currently perched in a nearby tree, all feathers, and beak, and great big black eyes. "I'm with Vee on this, sorry Syama. Anything underground and filthy is just not my thing."

Syama raised her eyebrows. "Says the guy who was just way underground, and very very filthy not two days ago?"

Akil snorted. "That experience only serves to compound my dislike for this operation."

Vee sighed and straightened her spine. *Man up, woman,* she said beneath her breath. Out loud, she said, "Either way, we have to do this. If it's possible we can track him to where he's holding Lucy, then we'd better get moving. We don't want to lose him because we were squeamish." Vee looked over at Akil, and then at Syama. "You guys can do the glamor thing and throw it over me as well. I don't think I'm good enough at it to use it under pressure."

Syama nodded and glanced over at the manhole, her expression hardened. "Let me just give the place a scan, see where we can arrive safely. Wouldn't be good to arrive in front of a patrol and get blown to bits."

Vee lifted her eyes at Syama's dramatic scenario. It was more like being ripped to pieces than blown to bits. Vee studied the clearing for aural imprints. After a few moments, she let out a disgusted breath. "There are way too many aural patterns to track anything specific. It's good in a way, in that it confirms the demons' presence here, but I'm not going to be able to pick one out of that tangle, let alone try to find the killer's specific aural pattern."

She raised her eyes to meet Syama's gaze. "We're going to have to rely on you once we get in. At least until we're able to identify specific aural patterns."

Syama nodded, her eyes shifting to dangerous blood-red. "It's what I do," she said, smirking. "I'll be in hellhound form until we get inside. It's just easier to track the smells."

They fell silent as Syama shimmered and her body grew translucent. A cloud of swirling gray and black shadows convulsed and reformed until Syama solidified again, in the form of her hellhound.

The beast stood shoulder high to Vee, two pairs of gleaming black eyes watching Vee with the strangest expression. Vee nodded, and Syama turned and trotted off toward the manhole. As she moved she shimmered away and faded to nothing.

The moment between Syama's disappearance and then reappearance felt ten times as long, with Vee imagining all sorts of awful alternate scenarios.

But, thankfully, Syama returned in what Vee confirmed was three minutes and twenty seconds, and solidified in place in her hellhound form. The large black beast shuddered, shaking her head the way a dog would when about to shake off water from its fur.

The movement dispersed a blast of black and gray shadows which swirled and then converged to form Syama's human shape.

"We're good to arrive in one part of a long stretch of tunnel, but we have to hide quickly because from what I saw the patrols are not spaced out too far apart. I tried to search further in the tunnels, but I didn't want to spend too long apart from you two. It's best we stay together."

"Yeah. Worst case scenario we jump straight home."

Syama nodded, and the two women headed to the manhole. The route meant they would be walking into the bare sunlit clearing, bringing them into unprotected space. As they approached, Vee scanned the surrounding bushes and trees, oddly aware of the incongruous beauty of the forest, the sunlight streaming through the trees, dappling the green carpet of grass that covered the ground.

The scene was idyllic, and yet to Vee, it represented a doorway to a hell she didn't want to imagine. Seemed best to wait until she met her hell face to face instead of spending too much time dreaming up possibilities. In Vee's experience, her imagined possibilities tended to be too tame, with the actual events usually far worse than anything she could have dreamed up.

Both Syama and Vee bent and studied the manhole, the gray metal covered in flecks of rust. It appeared to be a few decades old and yet, apart from a few flecks of rust it was clean.

"This looks like an entrance that has been used a lot in the recent past."

Syama nodded then pointed to the left of the manhole where a small shred of translucent white skin lay pooled on the grass. Vee eyed it with disgust and suppressed a shudder. Syama's face mirrored Vee's discomfort. She took a deep breath and focused on the manhole cover. "Well, then, good thing we can bypass that entrance."

CHAPTER 29

Vee found herself more than ready to get inside. In fact, she felt they'd wasted a little too much time already.

Syama was nodding, her expression grave. "I'll see if the way is clear and come straight back." She glanced up at Akil who'd flown closer to a tall oak that threw a shadow over the pair. "You watch her," she said, her tone hard, as if she thought that the owl shifter would not do his duty.

Vee frowned, then shook the thoughts from her head. She had to concentrate. She'd deal with these two and their strange undercurrent when they were home.

"Well," she said to Syama who was staring up at Akil. Syama met her glance, a question in her eyes. Vee lifted a brow. "Waiting for Kaliyug to be over or what?"

Syama rolled her eyes and disappeared, the air glinting with a thousand tiny pinpoints of light. In Syama's absence, Vee glanced up at Akil, her eyes narrowing. The owl lifted his wings, fluffed them out and then rotated his head around for a full turn.

Vee clicked her tongue silently and faced the hole in the ground, waiting for the hellhound to return.

Seconds later, Syama shimmered into solidity beside Vee and nodded. "We'd better go quick. The way is clear, but we may not have too much time. We'll be glamored, but some high-level demons can see us. No telling what level demon they'll have on security detail here."

Vee nodded and reached for Syama's arm, glancing up at the sirin who'd already taken flight. Within seconds, Akil was beside them as Syama's form shimmered and she jumped Vee inside a darkened tunnel. The air smelled wet and musty, and thankfully didn't stink of a sewer. Although that was no guarantee they wouldn't come across one soon enough.

The tunnel was a round pipe made of brick and mortar, harking back to the days when New York's waste and water was still under construction. This particular pipe had a shallow stream of water at ground level and bore no watermark at all.

"This must be an old or no longer used tunnel."

Akil materialized beside Vee, although she could tell he was still glamored from the faint glint of silver at the edges of his body. "What makes you say that?" he asked, studying the brickwork.

"Regular use of the tunnel, meaning water passing here all the time, would leave a horizontal line along the tunnel wall. We don't see any sign of that which suggests this tunnel has been closed off or had been unused for decades. It takes years for a watermark to dry off enough to fade away. And there is still a chance that this is an entry tunnel only and has never been used to transport water into the sewage or wastewater systems beneath the city."

Syama made a face. "Let's get out of here, okay? There's a patrol up ahead that's coming up to that intersection in a few seconds."

Vee glanced around. "Where?" Syama pointed to a narrow channel behind Vee, just wide enough for her to slide into.

"Get inside, and I will stand here. My glamor is impenetrable.

None of these demons would be able to see me. Not unless they are part hellhound themselves."

"Yeah. Then we'll be shit out of luck."

Syama rolled her eyes, and Vee grinned. This felt like old times, and she decided that she was going to enjoy it for the moment. She winked at the hellhound and shimmied into the narrow channel, holding her breath as Akil took off, flying down the tunnel and disappearing into the darkness.

Syama moved to hide Vee, and just in time too. A pair of giants thundered along the tunnel, sending the narrow trickle of water vibrating so hard that droplets rose off the surface of the stream.

Vee watched over Syama's shoulder, half in awe, half in horror as two rakshasa demons walked toward them. Both appeared high-level, but thankfully not powerful enough to sniff out a hellhound.

Syama stiffened, but Vee could tell from the hellhound's aura that she was not at all afraid. In fact, she was totally devoid of emotion, which concerned Vee more than if Syama had been terrified, her heart racing a mile a minute.

It was odd too. Though Syama had come to Vee hardened and experienced, she'd never been emotionally vacant. Another thing to be worried about.

Vee focused as the two rakshasas drew closer, holding her breath as they slowed their steps to come to a stop right in front of Syama's nose. Vee felt a little ill.

They had to stay put and hope for the best. If Syama so much as vibrated a molecule, the two demons would sense it immediately. That much Vee knew when it came to the use of jumping or transporting. The jump left a signature at the entrance to the other side—whatever that was.

So the two women remained stock still waiting to see what the rakshasas would do next.

They began to speak, the sounds guttural and hitting Vee deep in her stomach. Her eardrums rang with the noise, and she winced, tempted to put her fingers in her ears.

But she didn't move. And found herself trying to shut the sound out. Which oddly enough enhanced the clarity of the syllables.

"How long more of this do you think the team is going to handle?" asked one of the demons.

Vee's eyes widened and her mouth opened in shock. She could understand them? No. She must have been imagining it.

But when the next demon opened his mouth, she knew she hadn't imagined it at all. "As long as it takes. You shut your mouth and do your job until the boss tells you we are ready to move on."

The first demon's brows furrowed, his wide red nostrils flaring. Shaking his head, he snorted. "You're just saying that because the boss likes you. Keeps you at her side. We're the ones who have to sleep in the tank while you eat with the Lord."

"Graig. Probably best if you shut your trap."

"Who's going to hear me? We're in this tunnel, maybe two miles away from central command?"

"Shows how dumb you are. Did you read the schematics? The way the sound works in this place? Everything echoes. Cough here and they'll hear it somewhere else. In the tunnels and that's not a good thing 'cos the next thing you know you'll set off the sound traps and end up with a spike through your dumb skull."

The first demon snorted then fell silent, casting his eyes around the tunnel. For a brief instant, Vee could have sworn he'd looked straight at her, over Syama's shoulder and directly into the channel she stood within.

He did pause then to point at the channel and Vee was certain her heart had exploded within her chest.

"What's that?"

"What's what?" said the more senior rakshasa, shifting so that he could see what his partner was pointing at. Metal clinked as their short daggers clanked against each other's armor— the tunnel not being made for two giant rakshasa demons to walk abreast. The two, standing side by side, would measure the same as four human men standing abreast.

At last, he'd shuffled around enough to stare at the channel, and Vee felt the hairs on the back of her neck rise. Now she was caught—dead. The closer they drew, the closer they would be to Syama too.

Shit.

CHAPTER 30

"Ah, who knows. Probably something to do with expansion and contraction of the tunnels. Makes sense that they'd put them in here and there you know. I could be wrong. I didn't do tunnel systems or subterranean architecture at Harvard you know."

The second demon chuckled, and the sound echoed down the tunnel. Senior thunked the idiot on the back of his head and said, "I suggest you shut up for the rest of the route or I'm going to get our routes changed, so I don't have to see your ugly face again for a while. God knows how we're even related."

The second demon glared at his partner. "Fine. Keep it up, and I'll tell Mom."

The first demon had already walked off, leaving his dumber brother standing in front of Syama, shoulders hunched. He kicked the ground, slapping his boot against the water. Vee was positive the demon was pouting. Wonders never ceased.

Then he huffed and slouched off leaving Vee feeling almost sorry for him.

A few minutes later, Syama shifted and turned her face to Vee, her expression a muddle of amusement and frustration.

Vee grinned as she slid out of the channel. "Poor guy. Gotta live up to pretty high standards."

"Yeah," Syama smiled, staring after the two demons who'd already disappeared around the bend in the tunnel.

Then Vee frowned. "Harvard?" She shook her head, but Syama waved a hand at her.

"It's likely he went there," Syama said, grinning when Vee's eyes widened. "You have no idea how long demons have lived among humans, how many decades, centuries that they've been working toward their freedom."

"And sending a rakshasa to Harvard only for him to be on sentry duty?" asked Vee, shaking her head more firmly. "That makes absolutely no sense."

Syama pursed her lips. "It's likely he's being tested. Or he's turned into an entrepreneur of sorts."

"What? As a mercenary?"

Syama nodded. "Looked like the brutish type to me, don't you think."

Vee let out an impatient breath, her hand running over her satchel. She searched the tunnel again. "Where the hell is Akil?"

"Coming," Syama whispered beside Vee as a swoosh of wings echoed toward her. The sirin landed at her feet and transitioned smoothly into his human form, landing in front of Vee with the same grace as if he'd taken a step toward her.

Before he said a word, Vee said, "They have booby-traps everywhere, and many of them noise generated ones."

Akil sighed. "Yes. I was just about to report the same. We have to be careful."

"Syama, how about you go ahead and check things out. Jump us to a safe place. You and Akil can take turns to check the place out. We need to get to their command center Harvard mentioned."

"Who's Harvard?" asked Akil, his voice rising enough to echo around them.

"Shhh," both Vee and Syama turned to admonish him, glaring at him at the same time.

He raised his hands in apology and scanned the tunnel behind him.

Vee glanced at Syama. "Can we get moving. We've wasted enough time already. I want to get in and out of this hole in the ground as fast as possible."

Syama nodded and jerked her head at Akil. "Glamor. I'll be a second." Then she was gone, and Akil was already drawing his glamor over Vee before the hellhound disappeared.

They both stood there, tense and silent until Syama materialized. "Okay. Next stage in this journey begins now."

Vee nodded and held out her arm. Syama took it and then dissolved, shimmering into an almost liquid state before materializing inside what appeared to be a metal vat. Vee glared at Syama. "What is this?" she mouthed.

Syama merely pointed at a large hole in the vat where a rivet had once been. Vee leaned closer and peered through to stare down at the open space below. She had to clap her hand over her mouth to prevent the gasp that escaped her lips.

"What the hell?" Vee mouthed to Syama, this time her own blood pressure had risen so high she felt like the sound of it was reverberating around the metal vat.

The vat was situated to the left of the room and looked out at a long rectangular hall. Here too the walls and floors, as well as the ceiling had been constructed with brick and mortar, a dull red that had almost faded. Almost but not quite.

The hall seemed to be some sort of confluence point for at least a dozen different tunnels, entering the space at varying heights. Many had small fire escape type metal overhangs that lead to the various catwalks running along the walls, some close to ceiling height.

Vee was curious as to what this place was, but there was no

point in asking the question out loud when she knew that neither one of her accomplices would know either.

But it wasn't the large space, or its construction and dimensions that struck horror into Vee's heart. No. What horrified her, what had shocked Syama into utter silence, was the hundreds and hundreds of sacs that hung from every available surface.

Pale white and translucent in places, they were an oblong shape and about the size that could hold a full-grown person comfortably. The sacs shivered and shifted every few moments as if the contents were moving. Hundreds of the sacs hung from the metal catwalks running along the walls, but the ones suspended from the four-story-high ceiling were even more horrifying. The sacs dangled in varying layers from long, ropy sinewy material.

Vee stared over at Syama, her hand still over her mouth. She pointed a finger at the sacs, jerking her head to indicate to Syama that she wanted to go down and investigate.

Syama shook her head. She pointed her forefinger at Vee, indicating she needed a minute, before disappearing. Seconds later, she materialized again and grabbed a hold of Vee.

The hellhound jumped Vee to a tunnel opening that looked out over at the hall. They ducked within the shadowed interior and hunkered down.

Vee withdrew her phone, and proceeded to take a dozen or so photos, then took a video of the place as well. It seemed like overkill, but she needed to be as accurate as possible when she showed this to Karan and Rossi and whoever the hell needed to know about this...nest.

Vee shifted her gaze to Syama and mouthed, "Akil?"

Syama pointed up at a manhole entrance that sat in the middle of the ceiling. Vee nodded although she was disappointed. Not because she'd come prepared to blow stuff up, but rather that she hadn't found what she'd been looking for: the killer pey.

Then she paused. Well, perhaps she was more than a little disappointed that she hadn't gotten to use her weapons.

She sighed softly and held her hand out to Syama. They disintegrated into darkness and solidified inside Vee's garage. Vee stood still for a moment while Akil materialized before her.

Then she shuddered. "Ugh. That place gave me the major heebie-jeebies."

"You can say that again," said Syama making a face.

"What the hell was that place?" Vee whispered, images of the clusters of sacs filling that enormous room haunting her.

Akil was pale as he answered, "It was a nursery."

"A what? A nurs—" Vee's eyes widened. "Oh shit."

Syama was staring at Akil. "What species?"

"From what I could tell it's pey eggs."

"That's how they breed?"

Akil nodded. "They don't breed often. But when they do, it's in a large volume."

"That's not volume," replied Vee, her voice rising. "That's an infestation!"

Akil frowned.

Vee sighed. "They are amassing an army. It's pretty clear from everything we already know that they are looking to overthrow the Demon Horde Assembly."

Vee was half-way to the entrance to the house when Syama called out, "Stop."

Vee looked over her shoulder at the hellhound. "What?" she asked absently, her mind already focused on the next step which was telling a bunch of people what she'd seen.

"You need to take off all your clothes and stick them in the wash. Just being in the vicinity of the unhatched eggs is enough to have the scent penetrate your skin. We didn't get that close, but it's best we wash everything and get in the shower."

Vee sighed and turned around, stalking over to the shower room Mac had constructed off the garage for just such occasions. "I hate to say it, but Mom's idea of this shower room is paying off."

Syama followed Vee as Akil hovered in the doorway. "I'll wait for you two to get done."

Vee nodded and undressed, leaving her phone on the bench opposite the shower cubicles. She headed into the first of two cubicles. Inside was a shelf on which sat a number of medical grade disinfecting washes. She washed and rinsed, then repeated with what her mom had labeled Step 2. She'd almost stepped out when Syama called out over the dividing wall, "Hair too,"

"What? Are you watching me through the wall or something?" Vee grumbled.

"No. I just know you. You're raring to go, want to go talk to a whole lot of people and make a plan and take an army back down there. You're no longer here, so chances of you forgetting something is really high." Syama sucked in a breath, and Vee imagined she was immersing her head beneath the spray. Then the hellhound took another breath and said, "Akil, while you're there, toss the satchels we took with us and put the shoes into the disinfecting tray. There's a bottle of disinfecting liquid sitting beside the shoe tray."

Akil grunted and then fell silent, and as Vee rinsed her hair out, she wondered how Syama was able to remain so calm. Vee's own heart and mind were racing.

"It's because you're human," said a voice from beside Vee.

CHAPTER 31

"Ma!" Vee yelled, glaring at her grandmother before covering herself up with her hands. "What are you doing?" Vee spluttered, water from the shower falling into her face.

Radhima laughed. "What? You think I haven't seen your lady bits before?"

Vee lifted a brow. "Yeah. When I was in diapers or wearing little girl panties." Vee growled as she reached for her towel, risking flashing her boobs at her grandmother. "Things have grown in the interim, Ma. Now, can I have some privacy if you don't mind." She turned and threw her towel around her body, gritting her teeth as the sound of laughter came over the wall.

"You'd better shut it, or I won't be responsible if I end up ringing your neck," she yelled over the wall.

"Why me? I didn't do anything," Syama said choking on her laughter.

"You're laughing. That's enough of a reason. And I can't wring my grandmother's neck so yours will have to do."

Radhima snorted from outside the shower cubicle. "Suddenly you have respect," she muttered.

Vee stepped from the shower. "It's not respect, Ma. You don't have a physical form. Hard to throttle someone if you can't grab a hold of their neck."

The old woman shook her head and looked like she was having a hard time trying not to laugh. Vee turned her back and grabbed a second towel to rub her hair dry and wind it around her head. She picked her phone up from the bench. The phone smelled of disinfectant, and she smiled.

Akil had gotten to the phone faster than Vee. She'd totally forgotten about cleaning the device. Perhaps Syama was right, and she needed to slow down a little.

"I'm going upstairs to give a few people a call."

"So what's our plan?"

"I have to speak to Karan and then Rossi. But as soon as I'm decent, I'm going to see Mom."

"What for?" asked her grandmother, her tone careful.

"I need to know what we have that can help us fight the pey demons. If they are really amassing an army, we need to be prepared. Our R&D division must have a nice variety of weapons that we could add to our arsenal. And I need to check if Monroe sent over the samples of the 'molted skin' from the estate lawn."

"At least we know what that is now," Radhima said as she tapped her arm with one finger. She stood leaning against the far wall, her arms folded as she looked off into nowhere.

Vee couldn't help but notice Ma's use of the word 'We'. She wondered about that but realized she knew enough about her grandmother to know that the old woman wasn't about to be sidelined. And it wasn't as if Vee could get rid of her.

As she turned and walked off, she called to Akil, "You can get that shower now. I have a few things to do, but you guys get the go-bags ready to leave at any minute. I'm not sure what the next step will be, but I think we'll be stopping off at Mom's for a bit."

She didn't wait for a response, just hurried into the house and past the kitchen. Her stomach growled, but she ignored it as she raced up the stairs.

"You really should eat," said Radhima as Vee walked into her bedroom. Her grandmother was sitting on her bed, rubbing her hands over her jean-clad thighs.

Vee shrieked then threw her hands in the air. "We're going to have to work on some boundaries, Ma."

Her grandmother frowned. "Boundaries?"

"Yeah." Vee hurried to her closet and drew out fresh clothing, including jeans and a polo neck sweater. She ignored her grandmother as she lifted her phone, clothing crumpled in one hand as she began to dial. As she waited for Karan to answer, she headed into the bathroom and closed the door. She wasn't about to get naked again in front of her grandmother, no matter what the old woman said. She was partially dressed and had the phone wedged between her ear and her shoulder and had stuck one leg into her jeans when Karan answered.

"Hi, I thought you might want to know asap," she began, only to be cut off.

"I apologize, Miss Shankar. But…Karan is not available."

"Oh…" Vee hesitated. This she had not expected. She'd even prepared herself for Karan to deny her information or help, or both, but his total absence caught her by surprise. She lost her balance, toppled over and landed on her ass, one leg inside the jeans. She ignored the garment and focused on the phone. "Can you have him call me, please? It's urgent. And I mean it's very, very, very urgent. I can't stress it enough."

The voice on the other end of the line was kind and considerate. "I understand. I will convey the message as soon as Karan returns."

"Do you know when that will be?"

"Unfortunately, he did not say when. I apologize for not being helpful, but I assure you, I understand the urgency. I do believe he'd want to hear from you immediately considering it is urgent. I will convey your message as soon as is possible."

Vee let out a sigh, thanked the man and put the phone on the floor beside her. She was still sitting there in her pink lace French knickers, one leg inside her jeans, the other bare and outstretch as she stared off into space.

"Seriously?" said a voice from beside Vee.

"Go away," Vee snapped at Syama who was standing beside her. "Why is it that people keep barging in on me while I'm undressed?"

"Well, if you could actually dress yourself like a fully functional adult, that wouldn't be a problem now would it?" Syama folded her arms and grinned at Vee. "Need a hand?"

Vee swore at Syama, but the hellhound remained unperturbed at the profanity. "Lucky it's me and not Ma. She'd be washing your mouth out for that."

"With what? Ghost soap?" mumbled Vee as she got to her feet.

Syama chuckled and sat on the lid of the closed toilet. "What did Karan say?"

Vee shook her head. "That's just it. I couldn't get a hold of him. He's unavailable."

"That's new."

"You're telling me."

"That explains the position I found you in."

"Huh?" Vee asked as she buttoned her jeans and dragged the sweater over her head.

"You. On your ass. Karan's absence literally made you fall on your ass." Syama giggled.

"I'm glad I'm able to provide you with some comedic entertainment with which to while away your time." Vee glared at Syama as she rubbed conditioner into her hair and combed it through the length.

"Anyway. Akil is ready. What's the plan?"

Vee nodded. "Let's get going to see Mom first. I need to talk to her and her R&D team first before we bring this up with Rossi." Vee grabbed her hairdryer, then paused. "Is dad around?"

Syama shook her head. "Not that I saw. He could be napping, but the man barely sleeps anyway so that would be odd."

Vee nodded. "Okay. I won't be long."

Syama waggled her fingers and disappeared leaving Vee alone to dry her hair and contemplate her thoughts.

Karan had actually not been available.

Wonders would never cease.

CHAPTER 32

"What in the mother's name is that," whispered Devi as Vee cast the video of the nursery filled with pey eggs onto the plasma screen in her mother's office.

Raj stood beside Vee, staring at the screen with the same look of horror on his face as his wife.

Vee was still in shock about having been informed that her dad had gone back to work that morning, that he'd entered his old office across the hall from her mother's and had been working in his lab—attached to his office no less—all morning. On what she wasn't sure, but at this point, she didn't really care. All she knew was that she was overjoyed that he'd ventured out of the house and was doing something constructive with his time.

It made her hope that he was well on his way to recovery. Now she watched her parents stare at the video with the same horror she'd felt when she'd first seen it.

"I wish I'd just torched the whole place, but I didn't want to let them know that we knew they were there."

"That was a good idea," her dad patted her shoulder absently, and Vee hid a smile.

Devi turned to look at her. "You know what that is?" Her eyes were still wide with shock and more than once she'd run her fingers through her hair forgetting she had it in a tight chignon at the back of her head.

"Pey eggs," Raj replied, shocking Vee enough that she did a double take and stared at him. "It's a pey nursery."

Devi nodded, seemingly oblivious to Vee's shock. "I thought as much." She paced for a few seconds then paused to look over at Vee. "What's the plan? Give me context."

Vee took a breath. "It's a case for the FBI, but at this point, I think secrecy is moot. I tried to get a hold of Karan, but he's incommunicado for some weird reason, so we need to come up with a plan first before I take it to Rossi."

Her unsaid words hung in the air. *If I take it to Rossi.*

"Are you considering moving on without the FBI to back you up?" asked her dad. For the first time, he seemed to be siding with the FBI. Again, wonders never seemed to cease.

Vee shook her head. "There's more to this than just a pey nursery." She sighed and sank into the nearest seat. She waved at the empty seats beside her. "Best you sit. You're probably not going to like what you're about to hear. And I'm warning you two, don't go all Mom and Dad on me."

Devi stared at Vee for a moment, her face darkening, giving Vee the impression that her mom was prepared to blow her top even before she found out the bad news. But her dad reached out and touched her mom's shoulder. Devi glanced up at him and stared at his face, concern in her eyes. For a long moment, neither said a word and yet Vee felt as though the pair had held a long meaningful discussion just with their eyes.

Then her mother inhaled, and her shoulders relaxed as she took a seat and faced Vee.

"The case I've been dealing with for the FBI and also for our 'advisor' aka our snitch, has to do with a rash of pey demon attacks that have occurred within the city over the last few weeks. The agency has been on high alert what with the Demon Horde being shaken up due to political upheaval. The word on the street is that the pey demons have broken away and have created their own faction. Anyway, all of that wasn't something we'd connected to the pey demon murders until now."

"Until now?"

Vee waved her hand. "I'm getting ahead of myself. Let me just go back to two nights ago."

"When you came home with pey demon brains in your hair?"

"Yeah, that night," Vee responded eyebrow rising as she glanced over at her dad who shrugged despite the guilty look on his face. "Anyway, so I'd been sent to track a bhayakara demon and ended up running into a pair of pey demons. Or rather they ran into me. At the time I'd chalked it up to coincidence. Were they after me? No idea.

"Later that day another case came up on our radar, a murder/abduction that led us to believe that the pey demons were up to something. The abduction victim is pregnant, and the pey stopped short of killing her the moment he'd realized she was pregnant."

Vee got to her feet and began to pace. Sitting down while telling this tale to her parents had her feeling supremely uncomfortable. "So, Mom, you know about the crazy killer cab driver that we identified as a demon from the aural patterns in the front seat. So way too much demon activity for us to be convinced that it was all a bunch of coincidences. And then someone tried to abduct me last night."

"What? I thought you went out with Nivaan?"

"Yeah. Street parade, food. Was nice and all, until Nivaan spotted them. We drew them into an alley and Nivaan dressed them down. We maintained the image that I was some innocent human. I wanted to rip them to pieces, but Nivaan had another bright idea."

"I agree with Nivaan."

Vee threw her dad a 'who asked you' glare then cleared her throat. "So apparently there is a hit out on me on the Dark Web. And these two bumbling idiots wanted the bounty and were on my tail. Nivaan pretended to abduct me—without revealing who he was of course—and we escaped."

Vee hesitated, not yet certain that she wanted to reveal the existence of the feathered stalker.

"And today?"

"Today we were called out to an estate outside of the city. The back lawn was covered with what looked like shedded snakeskin. I'd taken it as not connected until we found the locket of the abducted woman. And then I spotted the same pey demon in the forest beyond the estate property."

"And of course, you had to follow him."

"Dad." Vee heaved a long-suffering sigh. "FBI agent here? Apsara? It's my job if not my duty. Anyway, we tracked him to a manhole in the middle of the forest, and we nosed around inside the tunnels. It's a stretch of old water or sewerage tunnels that appears to not have been in use for decades. We followed the tunnels which were both booby-trapped and well patrolled. They were definitely guarding something. We ended up coming upon that," Vee pointed a finger at the still of the pey demon nursery. "Now I'm not sure how all of this ties together, but it's connected."

"And why come to us?" Devi asked, smoothing the front of her suit jacket. Vee recognized that movement. Her mother was dying to get into the thick of figuring it out part but was controlling the urge so that Vee could give her opinion.

"Because I think we have better weaponry, possibly also have projects in R&D that we could use."

"And?"

"And because there is a combined threat to my life mixed up somewhere inside this case. Someone wants me enough to throw my face up on the DW and have dozens—"

"DW?"

"Dark Web, Dad," Vee said, her tone saying 'keep up, Dad. "And have dozens of bounty hunters on my tail. Those two were dealt with, but who knows how many more there are out there. I've been keeping on the DL for now—"

"DL?"

"Down Low, Dad," Vee said raising her eyes, her expression saying stop cutting me off. "And I'm coming to Shankar Industries because I'm personally invested in the case. If I went straight to Rossi, he'd more than likely pull me from the case for being too close. Or he'll throw a shitload of babysitters my way which would just hamper my investigation."

Devi got to her feet and began to pace. Seemed Vee had gotten that particular trait from her mother.

"So we have the pey demons who have been on a killing spree in the city. They've broken away from the Demon Horde Assembly. They're also mass-producing a new generation of demons. Then we have pey demons attempting to kill you, and a bounty on your head which may or may not be linked to the pey demons."

Devi turned to Vee who lifted her own fingers. "We have Karan who is currently MIA, we have the Demon Horde who are amassing their efforts on all fronts, and we also have a possibility that the two pey demons who attacked me after I'd offed that bhayakara, had been out to abduct—not kill—me." Vee got to her feet and tapped the table. "If I have to consider the whole thing from a different angle, it's possible that had the female pey not been killed by Rossi's backup team, that the pair would have merely attempted to abduct me."

"So, assuming they want you, but not because they want you to be the main course at their birthing ceremony party, then we have to accept that they are after you for something important."

Vee sighed and walked over to the plasma screen. "Do pey

demons and the apsaras have anything in common? Some past altercation or historical difference of opinion?"

Devi pursed her lips as she considered the option while Raj shook his head. "No. The texts don't define any negative relationship between the apsaras and their species."

"Then who would want an apsara dead? And second to that, should they be focusing only on me, who would want me in particular dead. Do the texts talk about anyone in particular who had a quarrel—or a bone to pick—with a powerful apsara?"

Devi's face was grim. "If anything, *you'd* be the best person to tell us."

Vee frowned. "Now why did I not expect that as an answer?" Vee asked, her tone a little higher than before. "Wait, I know. Because I have no clue, which is why I came to you two."

Vee sank onto the nearest chair, fatigued all of a sudden. The reality of the whole situation had just hit her like a punch to the gut, and she leaned over and groaned.

When she straightened, she realized two things: one, her father was typing away at a laptop at her mother's desk, and two, her mother was digging inside what appeared to be a secret room hidden behind a wall of books. How original?

Vee shook her head and got to her feet. "What's going on?"

"We need the spell."

"What spell?"

"The one to put you under so that you can share the memories of past powerful apsaras."

"What the what?" Vee stood very still as she watched her parents whose brows were furrowed as they concentrated on their respective tasks. "Wait a second. Why don't you guys look surprised?"

She walked closer to her mother, stepping across the threshold and into the little back room.

"What are you looking for?" Vee asked hovering over her

mom even though she knew the woman hated it when people looked over her shoulder.

"Dad's looking for the Guild's details. I'm looking for something that I'd read a while back that could give us a clue as to who might be after you."

"The Guild? Why them?" Now that some time had passed since Vee had first heard of the Guild, she'd taken the mention of them in stride. Though she still wasn't sure what they had to do with this particular situation.

"They'll be the one to help put you into the trance," said a voice from beside Vee.

Coming so soon after crawling around in creepy tunnels, the sound of a voice in her ear shocked Vee so much that she let out a low shriek and flinched so hard that she twisted on her ankle and toppled onto the ground.

"Ma!" she yelled again. "Can you please stop doing that?" Vee glared at her grandmother, who was now wearing a purple sari, but had tied it in a new, and unusual way. Vee sighed. "Nice sari. You have to teach me how to do that," Vee said, pointing at the way the fabric was draped over Radhima's chest then drawn under her arm only to be looped straight back over the same shoulder.

"I will. Now you deal with her," Radhima pointed over her shoulder.

Vee shifted her gaze to look at her mother who was staring at her, eyes wide, mouth open.

CHAPTER 33

"Who are you talking to?" Devi whispered staring blankly at the space beside Vee.

Vee rolled her eyes. "Okay, Mom. I'm not going to pretend anymore just because you don't believe me. She's here. She's wearing a sari in a strange way, but it's pretty cool. Said she'd teach me how to drape it."

Devi said nothing. She closed her mouth and just stared at Vee.

"Ask her if she remembers the broken bust of Nefertiti."

Vee frowned as she rotated herself and sat cross-legged as she pulled a book from the stack that sat in front of her mother. She opened it and said to Devi, "Ma wants to know about a bust of Nefertiti."

Devi's eyes widened, and her face went red. She let out a soft cry and seemed to sink further against the shelf. "No. How did you find that out?" Devi whispered. "And how can you say that to me so calmly?"

Vee glanced up, frowning. She shrugged then cocked her head over to the ghost at her side. "I'm just repeating what she said. I got no clue what it is about."

"Ask her about staying out of sight of the eye of Nefertiti."

Vee rolled her eyes. "That makes no sense, Ma." Her grandmother glared at her and lifted her eyebrows and pursed her lips. "Okay then."

Vee turned to her mother who looked far too pale to be healthy. She hesitated, wondering if her words would end up making her mother ill.

"Ask her," prompted Radhima.

Inhaling deeply, Vee said, "She said to ask you about staying out of sight of the eye of Nefertiti."

Devi let out another cry, one of deep grief that got Vee to her knees. She ignored the book as it tilted and fell to the ground as she leaned over to her mother. "Mom? What's the matter?"

Devi hiccupped and then cleared her throat. Then she looked at the space at Vee's side. "Is she really there?"

Vee shook her head, earning a glare of suspicion. "No, I meant she's at your side now. Over there," Vee said, pointing to the spot beside her mother.

Devi shifted her gaze. "This is weird." She glanced over at Vee, hesitating and a little afraid.

Vee shrugged. "Just talk to her. I'll answer for her. She can't move things just yet."

Devi's eyebrows shot up, but she contained her surprise and shifted her gaze. "Did you tell her?" Devi asked, surprising Vee to no end. What was it that her mother suspected that Radhima had revealed to Vee? It must have been something incredibly important for it to be the first question she asked her mother's ghost.

Radhima shook her head. "I didn't think you were ready. I won't. Not until you say you are ready."

Vee relayed the message word for word and watched her mother burst into tears. Movement at Vee's back had her turning to see her Dad standing on the threshold staring at Devi whose face was glistening with tears, her mascara smudged and her lipstick blotchy.

He looked at Vee, a question in his eyes. His eyes were shifting away, back to his wife when he said, "Oh," as his gaze settled on the spot beside Devi.

Vee frowned then scrambled to her feet.

"Close your ears, Vee," said the old woman.

"Why?'

"I'm going to swear."

"Go right ahead," Vee said with a smile.

Her grandmother used a word that Vee hadn't expected her to even be capable of saying. Vee's jaw dropped.

"And you swear now?" asked Raj, his brow furrowed.

"After what I've been through? I can swear if I want, when I want." Radhima folded her arms and glared at him.

Raj ignored her words. "How long?"

"A week or three," said Vee as she stared between the two of them. "How can you see her? Syama said that only the person she is haunting can see her."

"Yeah, there are other circumstances in which you can see the ghost of a person," Raj said, his voice devoid of emotion.

Devi got to her feet too, staring at her husband. And then at Vee.

Vee asked, "What are you'll talking about. What circumstances?"

Raj let out a heavy sigh. "This is not the way I expected to reveal the truth."

Radhima shook her head. "Don't. Not now."

"Ma said no. She doesn't want you to talk about it now. Can't you see that?"

"Why not? It's going to come out eventually."

Vee glanced over at her grandmother. "I just want my daughter to accept that I'm here. Don't soil this moment."

Raj sighed again and shifted away until he stood just outside the entrance to the small room. "Okay. But we need to talk about it sooner or later."

Radhima nodded and then focused on her daughter. "Our family has a lot of secrets. But I will keep yours. Just the same as I will keep my son's. When you are ready, you can tell me, and we'll do it together."

Vee repeated her grandmother's words and sat back as her mother nodded. "Thank you. And I'm sorry I didn't believe you, Vee."

Vee shook her head. "I wouldn't have believed me either. In fact, I *didn't* believe me. It took an old man in a taxi who confirmed it." Then Vee frowned and faced her grandmother. "How did *he* see you as well, this is all so confusing."

Radhima laughed. "He's an old man, a priest who's communed with the spirits before. Those who are familiar with the realm of the spirits can see the spirits."

"And what about Dad?"

The old ghost chose that moment to clam up.

Devi sighed. "Your Dad's right. There are a number of reasons you will see the ghost of the dead."

Vee brushed her hair from her face and took a deep breath. "Anyone care to tell me what these circumstances are?"

Devi let out a soft, incredibly sad laugh. "The dead are not able to control who can see them. Syama is able to because she's a spirit of the underworld. You can see Ma because she is linked to you for some reason. The old cab driver was likely a spiritual master or a priest of sorts."

Vee's heart began to beat faster as her mom drew closer to revealing how her dad could see Radhima's ghost. Vee had a suspicion, one that made her stomach hard, one she didn't want to hear right then.

She lifted her hand. "Maybe dad is right. Maybe it's not the best time to talk about this."

Devi's eyes glittered as she smiled sadly at her daughter. "There is no reason to pretend here. And no reason to keep the truth silent." Raj stepped into the room, and Vee looked over at him, her eyes filming with tears, her expression mirrored by her mother's.

Radhima looked upset, shaking her head as if she didn't want the words to be said.

Devi stepped closer to her husband, and Raj stiffened, as if he was preparing himself for an onslaught of grief or violence. Or both.

Devi smiled. "The other reason a person can see the ghost of the dead is if that person had died by their hand." Vee clapped a palm over her mouth as her mother spoke the words that had been resonating inside her own head since she'd understood what was happening.

She glanced over at Radhima who was watching Raj, her eyes filled with such love that for a moment Vee was stunned by the realization.

"You killed her to relieve her of her suffering," Vee said the words, her tone emotionless even though she kind of understood. She shifted her gaze from her mother's face, which was filled with understanding, to her dad whose expression was a picture of grief, yet absent of regret.

He nodded and smiled at Radhima. "Hiranyakasipu stabbed her with a spear dipped in poison. He did it so that I could watch her suffering."

"It was my fault," Radhima said.

Vee frowned. "How was it your fault, Ma?" When Vee had entered the cell where Kasipu had held her father and grandmother, she'd found Radhima already dead.

"I should have remained silent. I was stupid…talking to Raj, telling him not to worry about me, that he was the son I never had and that I trusted him to go back and look after our family. That…demon heard me, and he used it against Raj. He used the love I had for my son against him, forcing him to watch me die just to inflict the most amount of pain upon him."

Devi shook her head and stared at Vee. "What is going on?"

There was a desperation in her mother's voice, and Vee put her out of her misery, relating her grandmother's words as quickly as possible. Devi's face was a study of grief and horror, but oddly contained no blame or anger as she regarded her husband.

"She was going to die?" she whispered the question.

Raj nodded, his face taut with sorrow. "The poison had spread so slowly, eating away at her body, but leaving her in excruciating pain. At one point, it seemed as though the pain was getting worse as time went by. I just…I couldn't stand watching her suffer and then when she asked me to end her torture…I refused." Raj coughed and took a deep breath. Radhima held out a hand, cupping his cheek, her eyes filled with love. "But I couldn't let her suffer. She begged me to do it, insisting she wanted to go out with dignity, and not to let her passing be at the hand of a murderous monster like Kasipu.

"At that point, we'd been released from our chains…a game he played with us, making us think he was relenting, that things would get better for us. He'd brought food in metal bowls…. I sharpened the rim of one of the bowls and used it to slice open her jugular. It was the most painless way that I could think of releasing her from her torture. It took a few minutes, and she was gone.

"When Kasipu returned he laughed and laughed at the son who'd been forced to watch his own mother die. When they moved the body, they saw that she'd been injured. He was furious then. I suspect it fueled his anger against you, Vee. I believe my actions made him more determined to find you and to destroy you so that he could see me suffer properly. Since he'd failed with Ma."

Vee shook her head, but her mother cut her off. "How can you blame yourself? We're all complicit here. Even Ma," she said laughing from behind her tears. "We all acted out of familial love, something Kasipu lost because of his own actions. He just found a way to shift that responsibility to someone else. And we were convenient. Raj. You and Hiranyaksha. You were almost friends, weren't you?" Raj nodded. "And Kasipu hated that. He was possessive beyond imagination, and he used his brother's affection for you against you both. Yaksha died in an awful accident, one we cannot blame on anyone—even you Vee." Devi glanced over at Vee whose mouth hung open in shock. "You may have opened the vortex, but you only sped up the inevitable, which was likely for the best."

"But we lost Dad because of it."

"Because of *his* actions, because of mine and Yaksha's and because of Kasipu's madness. Not because of you at all."

Vee fell silent, staring at the tableau of grief that was her family. Then she let out a laugh. "Right, now that we got that out of the way, can we get onto figuring out a way to save me before I become pey demon lunch?"

CHAPTER 34

He turned to face the two gods who sat on the armchairs around the fire. Karan smiled. It seemed fitting that Agni would be the one closer to the flames. He took a breath and walked toward the two gods who had both just arrived within seconds of each other.

The god of fire still possessed some of his power, and as he sat back in the armchair, his hands open on the armrests, he spun a ball of whirling fire a handbreadth above his palm. "Showing off, or bored, brother?" Karan asked as he took the third armchair that had been arranged around the gigantic marble fireplace.

"A little bit of both," Agni said, smiling. Despite the attempt at cheer, it was clear to Karan that the god's eyes did not reflect that emotion. Agni was not in the least cheered or happy. Neither were any of the other gods. Some more than others, Karan knew. When Agni continued to speak, Karan forced himself to focus. "I am showing off, but more for my own self. Of late, I have felt the desire to remind myself of who I am. As though a part of me is afraid I may be dangerously close to losing myself. And then, of course, I am no longer put to good use as I used to be such a long time ago."

Hanuman was strangely silent during Agni's confession. Perhaps the god agreed, but he'd never been a person who would share his emotions readily. Karan was glad though that the two of them had chosen to come to him.

He leaned closer. "What can I do for you? I know this is far from a social visit."

Hanuman gave a short nod. "It is Parvathi. I fear we may have lost control over her."

Karan shook his head. "You forget, brother. We never did have control over her. She has always been on the volatile side."

"It is not her fault," Agni said, glowering at Karan. "I am here, yes, but I want to make sure that we bear in mind that she is hurting. I do not want her to be hurt in the process."

"I understand." Karan nodded, knowing how Agni felt. The god had held a soft spot in his heart for Parvathi for eons now, a fatherly caring that had always been to the goddess's benefit. "Until recently Parvathi has complied. She understood—perhaps she has been angered at His departure, perhaps because He did not take her with Him. I can understand that. We all felt the pain of his leaving, and I can only imagine the depth of her suffering. But her grief has turned insidious, and that makes her dangerous."

"What are you trying to say? You want her neutralized?" Hanuman stared at Karan, eyes wide with shock at the suggestion.

Karan shook his head. "In a sense, yes. I want no harm to come to her, but we need to take steps to prevent everything from coming crashing down on us. I cannot allow anyone to stand in the path of the future He wants for us. We need to make such preparations that would allow us to observe her activities. We need to ensure she has not crossed the line."

"Crossed the line?" asked Hanuman, his brow furrowing even as his glamor mimicked the movement.

"Think like a general in an army, brother."

Hanuman sat back and stared into the fire. "I see. If I were Parvathi I would take steps to find out more about what He is up to."

Karan shook his head. "Think like a General passionate about his mission, perhaps subverted slightly by anger, fear, desperation."

Hanuman let out a long breath. "I know these emotions. I long for Him to return too. And yes, I see what you mean. Parvathi will not be thinking straight. Yes, she will have a plan, a strategy but not one that will be logically sound."

"So what do you think she will do?" asked Agni, tossing the ball of flame from his hand into the fire. The flames spat and sizzled as it absorbed the god's fire into its midst.

"She will find a way to eliminate the one thing that stands in her path."

Karan stiffened. Even though he had already arrived at that same conclusion, he still found the idea repugnant. "She may well have put things in place to facilitate the demise of the apsara."

"I still do not understand why Parvathi has such a deep-seated hatred for this apsara who, to my knowledge, is meant to be the one who helps us find Him, who will be the key to bringing Him home."

Hanuman turned to Agni. "You are well aware, just as I am, that the mother goddess had not taken kindly to being dismissed as the protector of our Lord. She felt He'd cast her aside when He appointed Tilottama as the head of his personal guard."

"But I am confused. Parvathi was still General of the Army of Mt Kailas. Why would she feel threatened by an apsara as a general? And one that it was widely known was ridiculously in love with her sage." Agni almost rolled his eyes. "Are you implying the mother was jealous? If so, I do not believe that. The Mother is love personified."

"Like life and death, love and hate are the other halves of a perfect whole," Karan said softly. "But I do not believe she acted out of jealousy. There is another element working among us who is intent on subverting His rules, who want to gain control of the heavens, if not install themselves on His throne. A faction like this would easily use underhanded means. No person, human or god, is immune to being emotionally manipulated. I do not believe the Mother ever bore such a thought on her own. What I do know is that she was guided into being suspicious. Which led us here, centuries later, where we are at this junction where the future of humanity, of the universe, hangs in the balance because a faction managed to use love as a means to gain control over Him."

Hanuman sighed and sat back while Agni's eyes darkened. "I see things are more dire than I had expected it to be. Do we have intelligence on her movements? Enough to give us an idea of what she is doing on the earthy plane?"

Karan nodded. "I have someone watching her. I had received a report that she had possibly hired a hit man, but I cannot be sure who or what?"

Hanuman got to his feet and began to pace. "This is not the kind of thing I would have expected of her."

Karan wanted to talk the god out of his disbelief, but he had to hope that everything he'd said so far would be sufficient. He'd laid the groundwork, explained where they stood with the Mother Goddess.

Then Hanuman stopped to face Karan. "I will help, but I will not, no more ever, comply if you expect me to hurt her. We bring her back, we rehabilitate her, we help her deal with her emotional battles so that when He returns she can meet him again, whole and filled with her prior power. We all know what it would do to Him should he know his love has taken his departure so negatively."

Karan smiled grimly. "Then you and I are of the same mind," he said as he got to his feet.

Beside him, Agni too rose, turning his back on the fire. The light threw a soft glow around him, making him look very much like the god he was. "I am of the same mind as you. I will help in whatever way you see fit." Karan nodded. Though relieved, there was nothing in this that he enjoyed. He hoped that one day Parvathi would forgive them.

The two gods began to shimmer, preparing to depart. Karan said, "I will send the details, and we can put together a handful of different teams. I have something planned, but please feel free to fine-tune."

Both gods began to shimmer and fade away.

But just before they fully disappeared he saw both bow before him, low and respectful.

"Thank you, my Lord," said Hanuman. "I will do my best to serve you." Beside him, Agni was nodding and bowing.

In response, Lord Vishnu smiled and raised his palm in blessing.

CHAPTER 35

Vee paced back and forth, casting a nervous eye on the door to the boardroom. Both her parents sat at the end of the table, leaving the seat at the head open for her. She'd declined, they'd insisted and Radhima had said, "Shut up and take it," but in a much nicer way.

"How long before they get here?" Vee asked again, probably for the tenth time.

Devi lifted her gaze, from the notepad before her. When the door opened, she smiled at Kesha who strolled inside, bearing a stack of leather folders. After setting it down beside Devi, Kesha shared a glance with her boss before receiving a short nod. Then the girl rounded Devi and came to stand in front of Vee.

Vee frowned and then smiled, the expression probably looking constipated, but she soon forgot all about how she looked when Kesha sank to her knees and touched the front of Vee's black leather boots.

"Ergh," was all Vee managed to utter before she took a step backward.

Kesha sighed and got to her feet.

Devi sighed and said, "I told you so."

Raj sighed and said, "Are you in the least surprised?"

Radhima sighed and said, "I wanted to laugh but a sigh seemed more appropriate."

Vee stared around the room. "What is going on? Have you all gone mad?"

Raj snickered, and Kesha smiled, apparently unaffected by Vee's weird reaction. The PA stepped forward and bowed, this time using only her head to perform the obeisance. "I am honored to meet you Great mother of the Apsaras. I am you servant. Now and forever."

As the girl bowed again, her spine shimmered, and she glowed. For all of two seconds, but it was enough.

"You're an Apsara?"

Kesha nodded. "Devi took me in when I was a very much troubled teenager. I think there may have been no hope for me, but the guild found me, and Devi welcomed me into the fold."

Vee raised her eyebrows. "You're good at keeping secrets. Great poker face."

Kesha's smile disappeared. "I'm sorry I had to lie to you. I had no choice. It was for your own safety."

Vee nodded and forced a smile onto her face. She didn't feel like smiling. She didn't feel like being nice. In fact, she felt like throwing up.

"You're not pregnant, are you?" asked Radhima appearing at Vee's side.

"Aargh," Vee exclaimed. "No. I'm not pregnant. I thought you said you weren't senile?"

Radhima let out a loud bark of laughter, Raj joined in, and Devi admonished Vee with a, "Have some respect young lady."

Vee wanted to remind her mother that she was twenty-six, and she was pretty sure that she was no longer classified as being a young lady.

"Don't kid yourself. You'll be sixty-seven and still be a young lady to them."

"Thanks. Way to make me feel better," Vee said stalking toward the table. She took a seat and opened the leather folder that had been placed at her seat. She reread the presentation that her mom and Kesha had slaved over, confirming all points, other than her feathered stalker had been covered.

The door opened as she completed her first pass, and three women and a man entered the room.

Devi and Raj rose and went to them to shake their hands. As Vee made to rise as well, a voice beside her said, "You stay put. They must come to you." Vee was surprised to find Syama now stood at her side, with Akil guarding the door.

At her right hand, her grandmother agreed with Syama. "When they come to you, then you stand to receive their greeting. Do not bow or touch them."

This was one of the strangest experiences that Vee had ever had. She obeyed and watched as the tallest of the three women completed her greeting of Vee's mother. The Guild member was tall, her form curvaceous and her eyes sparkling. She exuded an aura of power, but Vee also read humility and serenity in her too.

She wore a pale blue silk skirt and over it a matching pale blue coat which appeared to be handmade and shot with gold. The collar and lapels were bordered with a wide band of gold-threaded patterns that glinted with jewels.

She wore a nose-ring, and giant hooped earrings that touched her shoulders. "Ceremonial dress," supplied Radhima.

Behind her, a second woman followed, her own clothing a similar pale color, this time ice white with the barest hint of green. Vee studied the woman's aura, which appeared as edges in a dark shadow. Her bearing was equally regal, but her expression was cooler, her gaze darting around the room and falling on Vee. Her eyes narrowed just the tiniest bit before she caught herself and pulled calm over her that appeared as a physical veil.

Vee knew before her grandmother spoke in her ear that this guild-member would have to be watched. "Ruvani Ghai. When she gets to you, tell her to drop her glamor. And be pleasant, remain calm as you speak," Radhima whispered in her ear.

The first guild member drew alongside Vee and smiled, the dimple in her cheek deepening as she fell to her knees. Vee got to her feet and waited as the woman completed her obeisance.

"This is Ushara Naga. The High Mistress of the Guild. She's the boss."

Vee smiled as the woman got to her feet. For the shortest moment, Vee was at a loss as to what to say, but her grandmother's voice guided her. "Namaste Mother Ushara. Peace be with you."

Ushara smiled, her dimples deepening as she showed her happiness at the meeting. "Great Mother of Apsaras. It is my great honor to serve you. I am your humble hand, in this life and the next."

Vee forced herself to remain in control of her eyebrows. Ushara stepped aside and drifted down the table to seat herself beside Devi. Vee was partially aware of the two women embracing each other with the emotional equivalent of two teenage girls.

The next guild member stopped before Vee, her spine stiff as she dropped to the floor. She performed the greeting and got to her feet, smiling at Vee. The woman's face was round and bore a hint of a beauty that had been lost to age. She appeared to be in her late forties, dark brown eyes, fair-skinned, and straight hair parted in the center of her head. Her hands jangled with bangles and her garments seemed to hum with an aura that gave Vee the impression of beauty.

Vee smiled and said, "Namaste Mother Ruvani. Peace be with you."

The woman's eyes narrowed as Vee spoke her name, but she smiled and said, "Great Mother of Apsaras. It is my great honor to serve you. I am your humble hand, in this life and the next."

She stepped away, and Vee was aware of Ushara's condemnation.

"She wasn't dismissed by you. Remind her about the glamor now."

"Oh, Mother Ruvani?"

Ruvani paused on her way to take a seat at Raj's left. She looked over her shoulder at Vee and waited.

Smiling, Vee said, "We're holding this meeting with the utmost openness and trust in each other. There will be no need for glamors here."

Ruvani's eyes narrowed and her cheeks grew redder. But she inclined her head. "As you wish, Mother of Apsaras. I apologize for forgetting."

Vee was tempted to tell her that she'd seen the woman draw the glamor over herself after she'd entered the room, but she suspected that would not be very diplomatic.

"You learn well, young grasshopper."

The third woman to greet Vee was a woman named Keiron Armitage. The woman's blonde hair hung in ringlets around her shoulders, the color accepted by the pale pink of her ceremonial garb. She voiced her greetings and Vee returned her blessings. The woman exuded a bouncy energy and Vee felt herself tempted to smile.

The last to greet her was a man named, Rohit Soheil. "He's Keiron's husband. Ushara is widowed, and Ruvani is married but currently estranged from her husband."

Vee got the feeling—from the tone in her grandmother's voice —that she was not a fan of Ruvani. For whatever reason, Vee shared that emotion.

Vee took her seat and Devi cleared her throat. "Ushara would you like to call the meeting to order? Kesha will be recording the meeting."

Ushara nodded and spoke a few lines in Sanskrit that Vee

understood meant she was calling upon the gods to bless their meeting.

Then Ushara looked over at Vee and said, "This is quite a report. I'm shocked that the Demon Horde has made such inroads in so short a space of time." She paused and studied the report again. "May I ask how you know of this?"

Vee smiled. "I'm afraid I can't divulge my source. Even the FBI do not know him other than what I believe is a pseudonym."

Ushara nodded but Ruvani scowled, leaning forward to study Vee's face. "How are we to know that this information is to be trusted if we can't confirm the source?"

Vee pursed her lips. "You're going to have to trust me on that. I'm not in a position to lie and there's too much at stake for political games."

Keiron cleared her throat. "What do you need from us? Considering you're going to be doing much of the heavy lifting, it's all we can do to offer what help we can."

Vee glanced at her mother, her eyes urging Devi to respond. Vee had little idea of what she could expect from the Guild, let alone what she was in a position to demand.

"We'll need tactical support," said Devi.

Now *that* was not what Vee had expected.

Ushara nodded. "I can arrange that. We have a special ops team we can put at your disposal."

"We can offer you an arsenal of pey weaponry with a focus on ammunition," Keiron added.

Raj shifted in his seat, hovering his pen over his notepad. "If you can give me specifics on the ammo, we can cross check our store to confirm what exactly we need. I know we've supplied much of your stock, but we also have a few products in R&D that we could re-evaluate for use—it would be more experimental in this instance, but firepower is firepower."

Ushara nodded and glanced over at Ruvani who picked her phone up off the table and began swiping and tapping. Seconds later she said, “I’ve emailed it to you, Devi.” She spoke to Vee’s mom, deliberately ignoring Raj who scowled at her rudeness.

Devi’s lips lifted in one corner as she studied Ruvani’s tight features for a moment. Then she looked up at Kesha. “Can you forward that email on to Raj please, he’ll check on the stock in the stores and armory for us and tell us what R&D can supply.”

Vee leaned forward. “I have one item I can offer.”

All eyes turned to Vee.

CHAPTER 36

"After my run-in with pey brain, I've been working on a formulation that's virus based. It's based on the use of a natural born virus within the brain of the pey demon. I've formulated a clone virus with a tiny change in molecular structure that will present similar to encephalitis or meningitis. It's not fatal, and I've prepared an antidote, but it's sufficient to incapacitate a pey demon within seconds."

"Are you ready for mass production?"

Vee shifted her gaze to Raj who was already scribbling in his notepad as fast as he was physically capable. "I haven't tested on live subjects yet."

"Perhaps you need to go hunting?" Keiron smiled, her eyes sparkling.

Vee shrugged. "I don't believe I need to, but it will be handy to test the speed of symptom onset. It would help to fine-tune the impact." The thought of testing the virus out on a living breathing species felt a little distasteful to Vee, and it must have shown on her face because Ruvani gave a soft laugh.

"Squeamish, are we?"

Vee frowned. "No. Not squeamish. I'm happy to defend

people against a demon attack, whatever the species, but I don't relish the thought of inflicting harm on some random pey we pick up off the streets. In addition, I'm not keen on alerting the pey leadership that we have a possible weapons solution. And it's bio warfare which I'm not even sure is ethical."

Ushara cleared her throat. "I understand your concern but if it's contained, and a temporary measure.... Are there lasting or physically damaging side-effects of the use of your virus?"

Vee shook her head. "Nothing lasting. Swelling on the brain that will subside, fevers and chills that the body itself will manage. Symptoms will be resolved after three days and the demon will go back to being healthy."

"I don't see the point. Why don't we make it lethal and get rid of them once and for all? Aren't you the deadliest demon-killer this side of the millennia?" Ruvani asked, her tone dripping sarcasm. But her words hit a nerve for Vee.

"I'm not used to warfare at this scale, and my experience thus far is enough to prove it. Yes, I kill demons, but I'm not randomly attacking villages filled with innocent demons. I track demons who are causing havoc and harm, and if I can, I arrest them. Elimination is a last resort."

"But the Demon Horde is spilling into our world. The whole point is to eliminate them."

"Then it's clear *you've* missed the point." Vee got to her feet, noticing for the first time that her skin bore a faint shimmering glow. Not sure what it was, she dismissed it and began to pace along the length of the table, forcing Ruvani to twist around to look at her as Vee passed. "The Demon Horde was banished to Naraka millennia ago, at the end of the previous Yuga, for the safety of humanity and the other non-demonic races. Whatever their crimes were, even *we* do not know. But it's our responsibility to control the influx of the demon element into this plane. It's not our responsibility to terminate every single demon we cross paths with. Not all of them are evil, in case you didn't realize that."

"This is amusing," Ruvani said, smirking as she turned her back to Vee and folded her arms. She leaned back and sighed. "Here we thought you were a great warrior, but instead you're afraid of the demons."

The tension around the table intensified as Ushara and Kerion both glared at the woman. But Vee ignored them and said, "I'm far from amused. You speak as though you are ignorant, and bigoted. We live in this plane with the humans, but they could just as easily turn against us because of our species. How would you like to be on the wrong end of an ethnic cleansing?"

Ushara shook her head. "I admit that I hadn't considered this situation from that angle. But I understand where you are coming from. In the past, all we've done is react, kill the demons who cause terror, and that's expanded to searching them out and killing them before they kill. And I suspect we have crossed the line many times already. What you're suggesting is we work smarter, especially to ensure we don't destroy all chances of coming to a common understanding with the Demon Horde—if that should ever come to pass."

"Now you want to treat with them? Are you people insane?" Ruvani's eyes were wide, her cheeks blotchy with anger.

Vee's eyes narrowed as she studied the woman. Her aural patterns were mayhem, twisting lines of blues and greens that made little sense to Vee.

"That woman has never changed," said Radhima at Vee's shoulder. "Just calm down and move along with the meeting."

Radhima was right though. "We're wasting time trying to deal with your dissent, Mother Ruvani. Let's address your objections at a different time." Vee looked over at her dad. "Let's get moving on production of the virus. I'm confident enough that we don't need a field test. I'm not going to hunt down some innocent to perform the test, and we can't afford to wait for another pey attack."

Raj nodded and scribbled some more before motioning to Kesha and getting to his feet. "I'd better set things in motion. Do you need me for the rest?" he asked Devi and then looked at Vee.

Both women shook their heads, and he left the room with Kesha hurrying after him.

CHAPTER 37

Vee wasn't as amped as she'd expected to be.

They'd made a decision to keep Rossi out of the loop for now. If that came back to bite her in the ass, then she'd deal with that when it happened. Worst case scenario, she'd lose her badge, but something told her Rossi wouldn't arbitrarily set her loose. She'd become too valuable to him. Still, she was well aware that he would be supremely pissed off.

Vee and Raj had spent the last few hours with R&D, going over the virus she'd grown and pushing them through the process to transform it into ammunition that consisted of hair thin, needle-like glass chambers. These vessels would be filled with the virus, which would in turn be filled inside the weapons they'd selected.

Raj had agreed with Vee that the adapted, short-barreled shotgun would be perfect for effectively dispersing the needles. They'd redesigned the barrels to enable the dispersal to cover a wider trajectory, the ammunition exploding from the barrel in a wide pattern that covered a one-yard circumference.

Vee would have preferred a wider, horizontal trajectory but

they had far too little time to work on the adjustment. Syama and Akil were performing recon, keeping an eye on the nest to ensure nothing changed in terms of the location or the security.

Even though Akil had assured Vee that pey demons would never move their nurseries as it posed too much of a risk to the embryos as they matured, Vee insisted they keep a close eye on the place.

They'd agreed to hit the nursery the next night. While Vee had toiled at her Dad's side, napping for ten minutes at a time when exhaustion hit her hard, Vee had considered where Lucy was being kept and if she was still alive. It didn't bear thinking about. And the thought that Monroe would be upset should they not find the mother and child, also twisted deep within Vee's gut. If anything, she wanted to find the mother and child for Monroe's sake.

Guilt too filtered through Vee as she worked. A strangely moved part of her wanted to bring the detective in on their mission, but her gut told her that would be a supremely bad idea.

THE NEXT EVENING, they were using the boardroom as a prep room, the redwood table covered in a leather sheet, was weighed down by weaponry. Syama had dropped off Vee's go-bag, filled with all of Vee's weaponry including the conch. Vee tucked it deeper into her bag and concentrated on the weapons.

She was selecting her ammo and filling the specially modified magazines when the door to the boardroom opened and Devi walked in, half a dozen women in tow.

They were dressed in all black, skin tight Lycra, hugging every curve without so much as a single wrinkle. Empty holsters hung from their waists and were strapped to their thighs and shoulders. Each woman wore a tactical helmet, visors black but shimmering with a red overlay that Vee knew would be showing them IR details.

She raised an eyebrow but said nothing as she grabbed her hair and began to wind it into a low bun.

Then women removed their helmets in one smooth move as Devi turned to Vee. "This is Alpha Team. They will be under your command."

Vee nodded, despite the urge to ask who they were and where they'd come from. As their superior, she didn't want to weaken her position of authority by appearing ignorant of their assignment to her. The look on Devi's face told her she'd taken the right stance.

Vee faced the women and nodded. "Who is Team Leader?" she asked scanning the faces, a redhead, a brunette, a Korean, and three women on Indian stock. Vee approved of the mix and hoped the team would work well with her.

Not that they had much choice.

The shortest of the women stepped forward. Her hair was long, black, and sleek, hanging to just below her waist. Her eyes were dark and she had eyelashes to die for. She nodded at Vee, her expression enigmatic. "Team Leader Shivani Virat, Mother Apsara."

Vee nodded and withheld her smile. She knew she had to be neutral and professional. "Where is Bravo Team based, and who are they reporting to?" she asked, glancing over at her mom.

"Bravo Team reports to your personal security team, Mother," Shivani answered, her neck stiff. "Team Leader Ashnee Pavan is reporting to Syama and they're dispatching out of the basement. Comms will be online in ten."

Vee nodded again. She was saved from a response when her father walked into the boardroom, his brow furrowed, a pair of glasses riding low on his nose. He carried a bright red file, on top of which sat a fat black suitcase.

As he hurried inside, weaving between tactical team members

and chairs, it hit Vee hard that her father was a nerd. A scientist, and a bioweapons engineer. Vee hadn't fallen very far when considering the apple and the tree.

He shoved aside a small stack of guns and opened a space for the box. "Here. You'll want this." He waved a hand at the box, then leaned forward to open it with a flourish.

Inside the black interior were two dozen gleaming golden balls.

"Did someone rob a quidditch match?" Vee asked, eyebrow raised.

Two of the tac team members snorted and two choked on their laughter. When Vee glanced over, she could have sworn Shivani had been one of the culprits.

Sense of humor? Check.

Raj turned to look at Vee. "What?"

Vee lifted a hand. "Quidditch Dad. Harry potter? The Snitch?" Her dad stared blankly. "Never mind." She'd been tempted to respond with her usual retort of where he'd been in the last ten years, but had thought the better of it. He was in a professional standing here, as owner of Shankar Industries no less.

His lip quirked and he replied, "Yeah, I know. What rock have I been living under for the last decade, huh?" Vee's eyes widened at him, and she gave a small shake of her head, glancing quickly at the now-perplexed team. "Oh, never mind them. They know my weird sense of humor."

Huh?

Vee glanced at Shivani, who shook her head and smiled at Raj before schooling her features.

Vee cleared her throat. "Okay, boy who lives under rock, please do enlighten us what your bagful of snitches can do?" Vee had totally given up trying to look professional. Her words earned her a roll of the eyes from her mother who raised her hands in the air and looked up at the ceiling, her signature move when asking the gods why she'd been blessed with such a clueless kid.

Her dad on the other hand smiled widely. "They're grenades. Bombs filled with fire. Once the timer goes off the fire mixes with mercury, bursts into flame and doesn't die off until it's consumed all biological elements around it."

"Fire and mercury?"

He nodded. "Plus, a little something to give it wings," he said, grinning.

Vee did a double take, wondering if he'd meant what she thought with his reference to wings. Beside her she caught Shivani looking at him too.

"So you set the timer, and skedaddle. You can't be nearby as the post detonation pressure will push through the tunnels. I've run some sims using Syama's specs of the tunnel layout and I think you will need to jump out of there immediately. You can't run fast enough to avoid the pressure radius of the blast."

"Here," said Vee to Shivani, handing her two grenades. "Keep these two just in case we need a backup kablooey or three."

Shivani took them and glanced up at Vee, her brow furrowed. "There's only two…"

"What?" asked Vee, her mind already onto considering their next step.

Shivani slid the two bombs into the satchel wound around her torso. Its bulk confirmed the presence of a number of weapons for which Vee was glad. You never knew when they'd come in handy.

"We have blast resistant tactical gear," Shivani offered, her eyes questioning.

Raj shook his head. "Sorry Shivs, you're going to have to get totally gone. Unless you want to be flattened. The mercury doesn't mix well with the fire and if something goes wrong, I'd prefer you all get out alive at least. I don't want to deal with your father if you're incinerated by my weapons."

Shivani grinned. "Yes, sir."

"It's her mother who's going to be harder to deal with you know," said Devi as she began distributing sheets of paper to each of the women. "Grab you weapons and gear, suit up and be ready to move out in ten."

CHAPTER 38

After readying her team, Syama left them with Akil and jumped to Vee's side.

"Are you ready?" she asked softly, nodding at the team as they strapped on the last of their weapons.

"Locked and loaded," Vee murmured, her mind going over the plan.

Syama held out a hand to Vee and one to Shivani. She shimmered away, her form disappearing, followed quickly by the room fading away like an image burned to dust. They arrived inside the tunnel that overlooked the nursery of pey eggs and Syama left Vee and the tac team leader there as she made three more trips to ferry the remainder of the team to Vee's side.

"B Team?" asked Vee softly.

Syama pointed at another tunnel which opened a few yards higher on the opposite wall.

Below them, movement drew their attention to the shadows that flitted between the eggs. A small group of demons, clipboards in arms, walked among the eggs ticking items off their lists. One was taking photographs, the other using a strange device that appeared to be a sonogram of sorts. He drew a long narrow wand over the widest portion of the sac and stared at a screen that rested on his arm. From Vee's vantage point, it appeared to reveal the images of a person within the sac, the shape and feel of the image resembling that of an unborn baby.

Vee suppressed a shudder.

Both teams maintained position until the demon baby doctor completed a circuit of random testing before leaving through a tunnel to the far left of the hall.

With their departure, the lights dimmed and Vee squatted. Shivani taped Vee's helmet and mouthed, "Infrared." Vee nodded and flicked the button to turn the IR sensor on. Immediately an overlay of the room shimmered in patterns of red and purple, not unlike Vee's own aural vision.

Vee glanced at Shivani and nodded. The Team leader made a circling motion with her hand in the air above her head, giving both teams the go ahead. Akil and Syama took turns to jump everyone down to ground level where the team members weaved between the hanging sacs, positioning the bombs and setting the times to give them a ten-minute window.

As Vee set the charge on one bomb, she got to her feet and studied the sacs around her. One of the eggs undulated as though the embryo within was moving or turning over. The pale skin of the sac shifted and a face pressed against it, perfectly outlined and almost visible through the thin, near transparent sac.

Vee swallowed a shriek and waved at Syama for a ride out of there. The moment she'd seen the face, she realized that all those eggs contained a living breathing demon. Were they about to commit mass murder?

As she watched from the tunnel above, she softened her breathing and studied the aural patterns from below. As soon as she opened her senses, her mind was flooded with the sound of heartbeats, thrumming loud around her as if they echoed within her head.

But she didn't have a choice anymore. This was a nest of

demons who were hell bent on the destruction of humanity. From what she knew, one of the main dangers of the demonic horde was the individual's ability to transfer their spirits from body to body.

Below them were hundreds of eggs that were more than likely going to be hosts for demonic spirits just waiting in line for a flesh-suit.

Vee had to stop thinking of them as if they were mortal. Destroying this nursery would eliminate this wave of demons from finding a way to physical existence but that didn't mean they wouldn't wait their turn for the next body they could create.

All Vee and her team were doing was hampering their progress.

"Get the teams out. Team Leaders wait to ensure nothing goes wrong."

Shivani nodded and Syama disappeared as she worked on jumping the team out of harm's way. In the end, only Vee, Shivani, and Syama remained, waiting until almost the last moment to jump.

Syama grabbed a hold of Vee and Shivani just as the timers ticked off the last two seconds. When they arrived inside the boardroom it was as if they'd brought part of the blast with them. The three women tumbled out of empty nothing and flew through the air, Syama hitting the glass cabinet, Vee slamming into the table, and Shivani hitting the window before sliding to the ground as a rippling of cracks appeared in the glass.

"Shit," Vee cried out as she rolled off the table and rushed to the Alpha Team leader.

"It's okay. It's triple glazed so you'd need to break all three panes to get out," Devi said as she rushed into the room.

Vee fell to the ground, taking a deep breath. "How long before we can go back?"

"Two minutes until the fire clears and the overheated fumes die away."

Vee nodded and straightened, watching Syama and Shivani as they also rose and dusted themselves off. Shivani glanced over her shoulder at the window and grimaced. "That was close," she said grinning.

Vee didn't answer, her mind too focused on the fact that she hadn't considered the danger they all faced when they'd taken this mission on.

"Ready to go back in T minus thirty seconds," Shivani said nodding at Syama who strode over to Vee.

The Alpha Team leader also followed suit and hurried over to stand beside Vee.

Syama transported them back over to the tunnel and Vee's mouth dropped open. Not only was the tunnel brickwork now blackened, there were chunks gouged out of the walls as if some huge creature had made its way through the rounded corridor scraping gigantic claws into the walls.

Vee steadied herself as her feet hit ground, then shifted forward slowly until she reached the tunnel edge. Down below, destruction awaited as remnants of embryos and burned egg sacs fluttered around on invisible eddies.

The bombs had detonated in sync and the fields of the explosions had spread out and overlapped each other. That along with the devastating fire had turned the embryos into a pool of unrecognizable sludge coating the bottom of the hall.

Vee felt bile rise in her throat and she shifted her gaze away and studied the tunnel around her. As she stepped away from the hall, she found herself pausing to listen.

"What's wrong?" asked Shivani, her voice low even on the comms link.

"Not sure. Just something doesn't feel—"

Something slammed into Vee and Shivani sending them sprawling on the floor of the narrow tunnel. The wall where Vee had just been standing exploded, shavings of splintered brick flew in every direction and Vee felt them stabbing into her protective gear as her helmeted head bounced off the wall. For a moment, she lay there, brain buzzing and then she sucked in a breath and rolled over, blinking the stars from her eyes.

A groan from her side brought her upright and she searched the dusty space for Shivani and Syama. Syama was lying on the floor holding her head. "Thanks dude," Vee murmured as she helped the hellhound up. "Saved my life there."

Syama grunted. "It's what I do," she muttered then coughed.

Shivani was already crouched staring out in the direction from which the bullet had originated. "Sorry, Syama. Know you're a bit shaken up, but let's get out of here before the next one turns us to dust."

Syama nodded and rolled over into a crouch. Vee and Shivani reached out to grab her hand. They shimmered away just in time. Two more missiles plunged into the wall beside the women and exploded.

Again, the three women solidified inside the boardroom, bringing dust and dirt with them.

"Man, the cleaning crew ain't gonna like us after today," muttered Vee as she surveyed the deep dark pile that covered the boardroom floor. Around them the air shimmered with dust, and debris covered the floor.

"Those were live weapons, Vee," said Syama as she dusted herself off.

"They thought we were human." Shivani put her hands on her hips as she tapped her foot.

Just as Vee was about to reply the air beside them boiled and three demons solidified, weapons held high as they surveyed the boardroom and its occupants.

Shit.

Vee surged forward, grabbing her trishula and taking a swing at the tallest demon. His face was bare, and a bright red earring shimmered in his ear. He hit back with his sword, the metal clanging against the trishula. The impact set off a loud ringing that was so bad Vee was tempted to protect her ears with her hands.

Instead, she ignored the sound and focused on throwing her knives at her opponent. Each of the girls battled their own demon—literally. Bullets rang out, slamming into the walls and the window, daggers went wide plunging into chairs and equipment.

"Syama," Vee yelled. "Get us back before we destroy this place."

Without a word, Syama transported them back to the tunnel. Vee knew the effort would drain her, jumping five people would take its toll, but the hellhound didn't seem to miss a stride.

The confined space of the tunnel forced Vee to put the trishula away and reach for her chakra. The sudden appearance of the weapon as Vee whipped it out of her belt loop caught the demon by surprise, and he wasn't fast enough to avoid Vee's wide swipe.

His throat split open and dark blood spurted out of the gash. The demon emitted a gurgling sound, his hands going to the wound as if to stop the blood flow. Then he fell forward, landing on his face and stopped moving.

Shivani despatched her demon with a dagger to the side of the neck while Syama dropped her opponent over the edge of the tunnel into the murky dead-demon embryo sludge.

Just as they thought they were safe, another explosion rocked the tunnel and Vee raised her hands, instinct bringing on her force field. She'd barely practiced using the power and was glad it still worked, especially considering the three of them would have been incinerated had she not raised the protective barrier in time.

Inside the bubble, Vee glanced over at Syama. "Where's B Team? Akil?"

Both Shivani and Syama shook their heads "Comms appears to be down."

"Not good enough. We need to find them and get them to safety."

Shivani put her hand to her ear. "Balance of the squad is reporting they're safe in the basement. Akil went back for Ashnee—she'd remained to guard their flank. They haven't returned yet."

No!

CHAPTER 39

"How long?"

"A few minutes."

"Possibly a few minutes too long, especially in this place." Vee frowned as she spoke, the odd sound echoing in her ears again. She shook her head, even though she knew how incongruous the movement was—it wasn't as if she could shake away a sound that rang *inside* her head.

Vee looked up at Syama, but the hellhound was already shimmering away.

When she returned a few moments later, her eyes were wide, her skin pale. Shaking her head, she said, "I couldn't find him."

"And?" asked Vee, already reading the hellhound's consternation.

"And we have a problem. This isn't the only nursery."

Vee was a little stunned for a moment as she processed Syama's words.

More nurseries meant their mission was far from over. It also meant they'd shown their hand by bombing the nursery in the tunnel.

"We need to check it out. Move fast." Both women nodded.

"Syama, you drop us near the next nursery and we'll check it out, then go tell Dad we need more bombs. Let's hope he made extra. Otherwise we're SOL."

Syama nodded then jumped Vee and Shivani to a wider tunnel, only this one was a space to run electrical conduits and ended in a dead end. Vee's eyes widened as she shuffled along the concrete wall, avoiding the fat ropy electrical wiring that ran down the center of the pipe.

"This isn't good." Syama pointed at the mouth of the pipeline and Vee crawled forward. This time there was no direct access to the nursery. It was barred by a metal grate with spacings no larger than Vee's thumb. It did have a hole in the center, but it was only large enough for the electrical wiring and didn't have space enough for even a Bobby pin to pass through.

And it happened to be the only access point onto the nursery other than two metal doors on the opposite wall.

"It's much smaller than the first one." Vee eyed the collection of eggs through the grating, watching a small groups of white-coated demons do an inspection, very similar to the one they'd performed at the last nursery.

"I'm going to speak to Raj. Be back in a sec."

Below them, the space was smaller, and felt more closed in. "What is this place?"

"It appears to be a basement to some sort of industrial firm. These conduits are for backup power, likely to a computer mainframe."

Syama returned, her face grim. "He'll have it ready in twenty. We need to scope out the rest of the nurseries because if there's this one, you can bet there's more."

Vee nodded. Syama was only saying exactly what she was already thinking.

"This whole thing is way bigger than we expected. And I'm still not entirely sure what Lucy and her baby have to do with this," Vee said softly. Then she pulled herself free from the thoughts. No point in focusing on that for now. There'd be time enough later for that.

"Syama? Can we rely on you to locate the rest of the nurseries?"

The hellhound nodded. "I can locate them, but it would be easier if I had help."

"You worried about Akil?

Syama didn't respond.

"I am too. And you looked for him, but right now we can't do anything other than keep going on with the mission."

"I have a bad feeling about this."

"You and me both, girl. You and me both."

Syama sighed. "I'll get those locations and send them on to you and the team," Syama said then shimmered away.

"I'll coordinate the locations and we'll formulate a plan of attack," said Shivani.

"Yeah. It needs to be coordinated and we have to move—"

Vee was cut off by the sound of shouts from below. Peering through the grate she and Shivani watched as the contingent of demons turned and raced from the room. Vee heard mention of a nursery and explosions, and of someone being captured. They disappeared through the door and Vee heard the clanging of locks on the other side of the doors.

"They secured the location well," Shivani murmured.

"Making it perfect for our attack." Vee paused, considering where the demons had gone. "Surely they aren't going to the nursery we just destroyed. So, I'd guess they must be going to look for whoever they captured."

Vee looked at Shivani and froze as the other girl's eyes widened.

"Akil!"

CHAPTER 40

Vee and Shivani waited impatiently until Syama returned ten minutes later. They were enclosed in the pipe with no possible way out other than to blow the thing to pieces. That was an option they didn't want to consider.

Syama materialized beside them, her face pinched and dark with tension.

"We have to follow the guards. They left here a while ago, and we couldn't follow them," Vee said speaking as fast as possible and motioning for Syama to take them now.

But the hellhound shook her head. "I know."

Vee frowned and looked over at Shivani, then said, "Know what?"

"That they have Akil."

Vee shook her head, wanting it to not be true, but from the look on Syama's face, she knew that was impossible.

Then Vee sighed. "Okay. What can you tell us about where they are holding him?"

"Some kind of magical field. It's next to one of the nurseries which is probably the only reason I found him." Syama swallowed hard then looked up at the top of the shaft, avoiding Vee's eyes. "I should have known something was wrong."

"Don't beat yourself up. We should have all known something was wrong. For now, let's get those charges set at all the nursery location and let's get in and retrieve Akil before the timers go off."

Syama's mouth tightened, forming a thin line and Vee knew she'd best get the hellhound focusing on something other than blaming herself.

Vee looked over at the Alpha Team leader who took her cue and tapped her comms. "We have a green light to set those charges. All teams proceed to each of your locations. Syama will assist to distribute you all."

Syama barely blinked before disappearing, and Vee shook her head. "We really need to get another team member who can help out with the transportation."

"Hopefully one that doesn't get captured," said Shivani with a smile.

Vee grinned and counted the minutes until Syama arrived. She'd barely solidified before saying, "All charges are set. We have twenty minutes to get in, get Akil and get far away."

Vee nodded and reached for Syama's hand as the hellhound said, "He's in some kind of force field, so we're going to have to figure out how to release him first."

"How many guards? Firepower?"

"Six guards, all armed. Looked like handguns to me. Nothing semiautomatic which is odd. They can't be that complacent."

Vee had no idea what to expect from the demons. She'd imagine a more well-organized system with their upper echelon considering their political aims, of which Vee had to admit she knew all too little.

I supposed we'll find out soon enough.

~

THEY ARRIVED under cover of Syama's glamor, and this time there was no safe place to hide. Vee knew all too well that Syama's glamor hid them from the demons, but if Akil had gotten caught, who knew what methods the demons had to detect even a hell-hound glamor.

As they solidified in the furthest corner of the small room, Vee swallowed the urge to cry out in horror.

In the middle of the room, a ball of energy pulsed and spun, its clear skin revealing the prisoner inside. Akil. He hung within the ball, held in place by crackling sparks of mini lightning bolts.

Akil's gaze flitted to the trio the moment they arrived, and he sent them a pointed glance. Vee looked over at what he was indicating, and she gasped at the sight of Lucy lying at the bottom of a similar ball of energy, only this one absent of the lightning.

Good thing too, as the sparks would not have been healthy for the unborn child. Vee studied the young woman, relieved to see that she appeared to be in good health. She lay at the bottom curve of the ball, arms wrapped around her stomach as she curled on her side. Her hair was oily and un-brushed, and her clothing appeared soiled, as if she'd not been allowed to have a change of clothes during the last four days.

Despite the lack of care, Vee was glad the girl was still alive.

When Vee glanced back at Akil, she found him glaring at her. Then he looked away and shook his head. She knew what he was doing. He was trying to tell her something without bringing her presence to the attention of the demons that milled around the room.

The space wasn't overly big; about the size of a large school gymnasium, it contained a trio of large chairs at one end, a long table filled with a medley of food, fruits, and files. And two long dining tables that sat parallel to each other on either side of the hall.

Had they walked into a dining hall?

Vee looked at Syama, but the hellhound's attention was focused on a pair of demons who seemed to be watching her. Vee looked at Shivani who shook her head, her eyes wide with concern.

Up at the end of the hall, one of the larger demons began to laugh, the sound raucous and echoing around the room.

"Your glamor won't work here, hellhound." He snickered as he stared at Syama, his eyes shifting to red and then black, and back again.

Syama had frozen in place in the center aisle and Vee could tell the hellhound wanted to turn around and look at Vee. Instead, she concentrated on the two demons who swaggered to her.

Vee recognized the larger of the two. "Harvard," she muttered, gritting her teeth.

"What?" whispered Shivani from Vee's side. But Vee didn't have time to respond as a sound at her back had the pair spinning around to face another set of demons.

"Ah, the entertainment has arrived. And what better entertainment than to watch an apsara be smashed to death, right?" Cheers rose from the floor as dozens of demons turned to watch the three women face down their demon opponents.

Shivani raised her gun and fired, the blast of her weapon setting the battle in motion. The bullet spread apart and hit wide, slamming into both the demons advancing on them. Though all the glass slivers failed to hit their skin, enough passed through seams and areas where skin was visible.

The two fell and began writing on the floor. Not that it mattered that they'd downed two with one shot. Another pair of demons replaced them and surged forward, not waiting to see what Vee and Shivani would do.

As the Alpha leader fired again, Vee glanced over her shoulder to see a third demon advancing on Syama who was currently fighting two full-grown demons who happened to be almost twice her size.

These guys had no clue as to what a fair fight was.

CHAPTER 41

Vee drew a throwing dagger from her thigh and let it fly, then turned to attack one of the demons who had run full tilt at her. The satisfying thwack as the dagger embedded itself within the demon's eye gave Vee only brief enjoyment.

Before she took the next breath, she was ducking to avoid a double-sided ax, barely escaping with her neck intact.

Shivani struggled to keep up. As they dispatched each opponent, new demons replaced them, onlookers helping to clear away the dead.

A loud growl of anger emanated from the front of the hall. "Three women, you useless pieces of shit. Three women for Yama's sake. Kill them!" he yelled.

"Don't think Yama will be too happy with you using his name," Vee muttered under her breath as she sidestepped a broadsword, then drew a needle from her wrist to plunge into the back of the demon's neck. He went down like a rock and Vee twisted around and delivered the same treatment to his partner who'd backed Shivani into a corner.

"Thanks," Shivani called out. "We need to preserve our ammo."

Vee nodded and glanced over at Syama. Though she'd kept a few demons at bay, Harvard still stalked her, giving her a wide berth.

The demon in charge, who stood up on the dais, relayed instructions to his underlings but remained safely out of reach.

Vee grabbed her trishula and waited only long enough for the spear handle to extend before letting it fly. Golden lightning flashed from the weapon as it streaked through the air, so fast that the demon up front had no time to evade the weapon. It hit him in the throat slamming him into the concrete wall behind him.

Vee spun on her heel and drew her chakra, enjoying the hum it emitted as she let it fly in a wide arc.

She would have felt a little bad that the weapon was so destructive had she and Shivani not been outnumbered and nearly overpowered.

As she fought them off, she noted a mixed bag of demons who appeared to be part of the security squad attached to the pey demon's population initiative.

With their boss eliminated, Vee had expected at least a partial retreat, but nothing seemed to sway the demons from their path.

Vee gritted her teeth. "We don't have the time for this bullshit. How are we doing for time?" she asked Shivani.

The apsara blinked and then said, "T minus ten minutes, thirty-eight seconds and counting."

"Crap, we need to get a move on."

"Syama?"

"I heard," she called without looking in their direction.

Akil was still whiling away his time in the energy ball above their heads, and Vee looked over at the trishula still impaled in the demon's neck up on the dais. Vee didn't wait to apprise Shivani of her intention. She spun on her heel and raced toward the front of the hall. Her speed had quickly transitioned to super-fast, and within a few moments, she was plucking the trishula from the demon's neck.

She didn't wait to see him crumple to the ground. Vee turned and aimed at the energy ball, using all the power in her upper body, she flung the trishula at Akil's prison. The weapon flew through the air, the long handle whipping back and forth as it sped toward the energy ball.

Vee had used the trishula on a hunch, without thinking what would happen when the trishula hit the ball of energy full-force. Almost too late, she understood the ramifications and grabbed for Shivani.

"Syama! Down," she yelled and outstretched to the hellhound.

As soon as Syama complied, Vee threw her hands out and summoned the ball of energy that she knew would protect her and her team from harm in case Akil's energy ball turned violent.

Everything seemed to happen at once.

The trishula's triple pointed spear hit Akil's energy ball. Vee's protective ward spread and grew around her, Syama, and Shivani. The energy ball shattered and Akil flung his arms out in shock.

The blast flew into the hall, the shockwave spreading out like a tsunami, toppling everyone in its path. Except for Vee and her team. And the demon group who were walking into the hall.

The higher up on the Demon Horde ladder a demon was, the more powerful they happened to be. So as Vee squatted within the protection of her bubble of protective magic, she watched in cold horror as the demons strode through the moaning mass that was their security team.

In Vee's peripheral vision she saw Akil fall, speeding up as he closed in on the bare concrete floor. But thankfully, when only half a yard off the ground, he shifted into owl form and swooped to safety along a ledge on the far wall.

As the shockwave, and the accompanying mayhem subsided, Vee straightened and let her protective ward evaporate. She was relieved it had worked when she'd needed it most. She glanced to her left to where the trishula lay on the concrete, two demons eyeing the golden spear, their expressions filled with a strange hunger.

One of them lunged forward, and Vee yelled, "Don't touch it."

But the demon merely sneered and grabbed hold of the handle. The moment his fingers gripped the trishula the demon began to glow, a golden halo forming around his body,

Then Vee ducked the instant before he exploded into ash and dust.

The trishula dropped to the ground, and Vee lunged for it. "I warned you," she said, scooping the weapon up and backing away from the remaining demon who was looking at the remnants of his buddy as the cloud of ash floated around him and drifted to the floor.

"Enough!" a voice rang out around the hall, this one distinctly female despite the guttural growl.

Vee glanced up at the dais to see a pey demon female standing there, arms akimbo, her armor a dull red color that gave the impression that she'd bathed in blood before she'd arrived.

Which was also entirely possible given her species.

The demon lifted her hand, and a high pitched shriek echoed around the room. Vee's gaze snapped toward the origin of the cry, and she sucked back a gasp of horror. The ball in which Lucy sat had begun to disintegrate.

"If you don't call off the bombings, I will kill the girl."

Vee's eyes widened, and she shared a look of concern with Shivani. A few feet ahead, Syama stood with her dagger at the neck of one demon, and another in the gut of another.

Vee hesitated then glanced up at the owl who'd drawn his glamor over him. He was currently perched on a light fixture halfway up the wall to Vee's right.

Another demon hurried inside and went straight to their leader. Harvard again? Hadn't he just been there? He'd likely left to summon his demon boss and had remained to investigate the bombs.

"Queen Ishanie, I have news," he said as he rushed to her.

After the two spoke, they turned to stare at the three women. The demon who Syama had stabbed in the gut began to tilt backward, slowly falling until he hit the ground so hard that the sound of his skull cracking reverberated through the room.

"I've been told we have no more than five minutes left," the queen called out. "Perhaps now would be a good time to send word to cancel the detonations."

"Can't do that. We set the timers manually." Vee shrugged in apology although her face was far from sorry.

Ishanie lifted her hand again and the bubble holding Lucy shivered and thinned again. Vee was about to protest, hoping Akil was ready to jump the girl away when the time was right, when footsteps clattered on the concrete, announcing the arrival of someone who was very large, but who ran like a little child.

One of the demons who'd entered with Ishanie stepped forward, shoulders hunched as he called out, "No you promised you wouldn't hurt her." His voice was whiny, and so unlike Vee's impression of him as a hardened killer.

Vee's jaw dropped as it hit her who this demon was.

The killer Monroe was after. The pey demon who'd killed Susie.

CHAPTER 42

The queen laughed softly. "I'm sorry, Rishi, my son. She will have to die if these nasty people here don't turn off the bombs."

The demon—Rishi—faced Vee and her team and began to cry. "Do what Mother asks. I don't want her to die," he said pointing at Lucy who let out a soft whimper.

The queen clicked her tongue. "There, there, Rishi, you must know we don't need her."

"But I got her for you. Because I heard you say you want to make children. You wanted babies, and I brought you one of your very own."

"And I'm so happy about that my boy," Ishanie replied, her tone clearly revealing her disdain for the human girl, and her impatience with her son.

Vee was floored by the revelation. Had they all been chasing a killer who just happened to be mentally incapacitated? Had their hunt for Lucy and her unborn baby led them to the demon nurseries by accident?

Still, it didn't explain Vee's stalkers-slash-abductors-slash-assassins. For now, she had to concentrate on the queen though. And what she was about to do to Lucy.

"What do you want?" yelled Vee, trying to distract the queen. "Why are you lying to your poor son?"

Rishi glanced at his mother, confused, and Vee grabbed the opportunity.

"Sorry, Rishi. Mommy dearest plans on killing the girl and her baby," Vee said, raising her voice. Around them, the demons gathered were smiling and talking amongst themselves, and Vee heard snippets of conversation filter through to her.

"He's pathetic..."

"She should have gotten rid of him when it happened..."

"The mother goddess won't like this..."

"Her soft spot for him will be her downfall..."

"This crap is just delaying our timeframe..."

Up on the dais, the killer demon stamped his foot and pouted. "But she was a present," Rishi said, tears filling his eyes. "Why you want to kill her? You wanted babies to conquer the city, and I brought you a baby, but now you want to kill it even before it's born." Rishi rambled on, and Vee shook her head.

Time was running out.

Vee glanced at Akil hoping he'd understand what she wanted him to do.

"The goddess won't be happy with you, Mother. She's the goddess of life and creation. You can't kill in her name." Rishi whimpered, shaking his head. He began to chew his nails, his eyes darting left to right.

The queen hushed him. "The mother goddess is very happy with us. She's going to bless us with a boon just like the ones *that* girl has." The demon pointed at Vee.

As all eyes turned to Vee, she felt her stomach go hard. Did this demon queen know about Vee, about who she was? From the look in Queen Ishanie's eyes, Vee was certain she did. Yet she'd referred to Vee as a 'girl' and not an apsara. Was she hiding something from her security team?

"T minus 1 minute and counting," whispered Shivani.

Vee stiffened, preparing herself for what was about to happen. "You got any of the kablooeys left?"

"Yep. All two of them."

"Match the timers and be ready to drop them here."

Shivani didn't answer, but Vee sensed movement as the team leader slid her hand into her satchel and set the timers.

Even though Vee and her team had killed so many of their teammates, none of the demons appeared to be concerned. It made sense that they would not be grieving, especially considering they could come back soon enough, but their complacency was a concern.

Ishanie pointed at Harvard, who'd been standing at attention beside the dais, serving the team. "The mother has assured us that we will prevail. These humans have attempted to overthrow us but have failed outright."

"That's what you think," muttered Vee.

"T minus thirty," whispered Shivani. Syama's spine tensed, and Vee flicked a glance up at Akil. The owl gave a single nod.

"I think you are mistaken. Whoever this mother is that's helping you, she's misleading you into thinking you can take over the Demon Horde Assembly." Vee blurted the words out, hoping to distract the queen.

But Ishanie's face darkened, taking on a bluish hue as she glanced over at Harvard. The look on her face was priceless, revealing her shock at how Vee could have known.

"So that was your plan. You need to work on your poker face, your majesty."

"The mother of creation will not lie to her believers. Our faith is her power," Ishanie ground the words out. "She warned me about you. Told me to ensure we either terminated you, or at least ensured you don't find out about our plans."

Vee shrugged. "You can thank your baby boy over there. His crazy killing spree across the city is what brought me here. All I did was to track his activity and here I am. Don't suppose I can take him into custody?"

Rishi shrieked and scurried over to his mother's side, but Ishanie brushed him off. "Be quiet, or I'll send you back to Naraka."

The demon fell silent although he hid his body—or whatever of it that he could, considering he was twice the size of his mother.

"You can't touch him," Ishanie said taking a step forward. "And neither will I allow you to endanger my plans. Kill her!" she screamed, thrusting her finger at Vee. "Kill them all!"

Too many things happened at once.

"Five seconds," Shivani said, while Syama scurried backward toward the pair. Vee pulled the conch from her own satchel and raised it to her lips. Akil took flight and aimed himself at the ball of energy containing Lucy. Vee flung her chakra at the oncoming demons and sent the trishula flying through the air.

Vee took a breath and blew on the conch, the sound flooding around the room and bringing everything to a standstill. Ishani's eyes were blood-red and filled with rage and Vee registered that the demon hadn't been entirely incapacitated by the power of the conch. It was clear she did have some sort of deific protection, but Vee wasn't sure which of the gods would stand with demons against humanity.

Not humanity, just you, said a voice in Vee's head.

Vee's weapons continued on their paths, and she raced toward the ball as it disintegrated. Lucy was frozen in position inside the sphere and hung there suspended by time. Vee surged into the air, snapping her wings out behind her. Though they'd never been able to allow her to fly through the sky, they were powerful enough to allow Vee to rise at least two stories to grab hold of the pregnant woman. Vee descended and laid the girl on the floor.

Then she turned to Akil who'd been frozen mid-flight, his wings spread.

Vee flew to him then drew him down to stand beside Lucy.

Then Vee grabbed her trishula and faced the destruction caused by the chakra as it flew around the room, slicing into skin and causing untold physical damage to more demons than Vee could count.

She raised her hand, and the chakra returned to her palm with a flat thunk.

Time began to right itself as eyelids shifted and fingers moved.

And just like that, the power of the conch faded.

"3…," said Shivani.

Akil flapped his wings and shifted into human form, wrapping his arms around Lucy.

Syama reached Vee's side as three demons fell to the ground around them.

"2…" Shivani murmured as she pulled the two bombs from the satchel and threw them flying toward Ishanie and her royal retinue and the others in the midst of the remaining demons behind Vee's team.

Akil disappeared with Lucy. Rishi let out a shriek of horror, putting his hands to his head and then screaming as he stared at the empty space where Lucy had been only moments before.

Ishanie raised her hands and sent a bolt of lightning straight at Vee.

"1," Shivani called out as Syama turned and grabbed onto the two of them yelling, "Vee, watch out."

As they disintegrated, Vee watched the lightning bolt fly closer, her nerves making her feel nauseous as she realized that it was going to hit even if they managed to get out of there in time.

Then the bombs went off, spreading fire and brimstone around the small room, the shockwave throwing Vee and her team off their feet.

As she flew through the air, Syama jumped them to the basement of Shankar Industries, but Vee and Shivani continued to fly through the air. The remnants of the shockwave had jumped with them and flooded the basement sending the gathered members of Alpha and Bravo teams flying. They'd all been in the process of running to Vee and Shivani's aid when the shockwave caught them and threw them backward.

Vee hit a large concrete pillar so hard when she heard the crunch of bone she knew she'd broken something.

But broken bones were the last things on her mind as she watched the lightning bolt streak toward her. Stunned as she was, she couldn't move, could just watch as Syama shimmered to nothing, likely intending to jump to Vee's aid.

But it was too late.

The lightning shifted color turning from bright white to pale blue and then it split in two, the large bolt kept coming at Vee, the second one moving off at a shallow angle. The bolt seemed intelligent, as if it knew that it had to cause the maximum amount of damage possible.

The two lightning bolts hit at the same time. One high on Vee's chest just below her collarbone. And the other through Shivani's abdomen. The power of the bolts cut through their armor and impaled both girls before embedding themselves into the concrete at their backs.

Wracked with pain, Vee barely managed to shift her gaze toward Shivani, only to see the Alpha team leader slip forward, unconscious.

Then reality slipped away, and Vee was most grateful for the reprieve from the most excruciating pain she'd ever felt.

CHAPTER 43

When Vee opened her eyes, she saw a face that she had least expect to.

"Mac," she croaked, her throat raw as she swallowed against the pain.

"Shh," he said, leaning forward and putting a straw into her mouth. "Drink. You need the water."

Vee sipped and then fell back drained after only the small movement. Her body ached, and her chest was on fire. "How long have I been out? Is Shivani okay? Did we get all the nurseries? Is the demon queen dead?"

Mac let out a bark of laughter, his skin crinkling at the corners of his eyes. He cupped her cheek. "You be quiet. Too many questions aren't good for you."

"You'll have to answer them at some point," Vee grunted.

Mac nodded and deposited the water onto the nightstand. He took a seat on the mattress beside Vee and patted her hand. "To answer those questions...You've been unconscious for two days. Your body is still fighting the lightning bolt's effects. I hate to say I told you so but you should have taken my offer of bulletproof clothing." Mac chuckled.

"That bad, eh?" Vee smiled.

"Worse. It was potent. Old earth magic embedded within the electric bolt. There's worse news though."

"Hit me with it," Vee said then laughed. The vibrations sent sharp stabs of pain into her chest, and she coughed. "Ow, that bloody hurts."

Mac shook his head. "That's what I'm trying to tell you. The bolt split inside you. It left a shard embedded inside your collarbone. The docs don't think they can take it out without completely removing your collarbone."

Vee stared at Mac, eyes wide. "Shit. I'm stuck with this?" she asked in a whisper. The fire flared again within her chest, and Vee's breath caught in her throat. She was going to have to live with this agony?

Mac nodded. "But it gets worse," he said and then fell silent as if struggling to get the words out.

Vee nodded for him to continue and when he didn't, she reached for his hand. Though the blood was rushing through her ears, she knew she could take whatever he was going to say. She could handle it.

Mac cleared his throat. "To answer your second question, no she's not okay. The bolt that entered her abdomen broke off into multiple shards. The surgeons removed as many as they could, but they had to stop before they caused more harm than good."

Vee's ears were ringing with the revelation. Shivani was injured far worse than Vee. "Is she conscious?"

Mac shook his head. "They've placed her in an induced coma. Your mom's using her advanced statis program to put her deeper under than a normal human. The guild thinks that she'll be fine. Shivs is strong, has always been. But we'll only know when she is awakened."

"How long will it take?"

"Devi has spoken with the medical team. They feel two weeks, to begin with, will be a good place to start. They'll run an MRI scan then to look for changes."

Vee nodded. "And her family? Have they been told?"

Mac smiled. "Shivani was an orphan. The Guild and...all of us, we're her family."

Mac's words brought tears to Vee's eyes, but she blinked them away. "Syama? Akil?"

"They're both fine, working on clean-up with Raj and Devi. Which brings up to question three." Mac grinned. "You succeeded. All the nurseries that we know of were obliterated."

"That we know of?"

Mac shrugged. "Syama insists she got all, but you know me, Vee. I don't work in absolutes."

Vee grunted. "Probably means the answer to question four is also a non-absolute."

"Well, you learn, my young padawan." Mac smirked.

Vee rolled her eyes. "Thanks for your wisdom, Yoda."

Mac laughed, but his response was cut off by Devi as she glided into the room, Raj following close behind. "The pey queen is dead, but we all know with pey demons they can return. Whatever contingencies she had in place, she'd have been stupid not to plan for such an event. We've had word from our sources within the Demon Horde Assembly—"

"We have sources in the DH Assembly," Vee asked.

Devi gave her a harsh glare, "—and they've confirmed the pey demons have been banned from the assembly until they elect a different leader. All those who participated in the attempt to undermine the assembly have been rounded up and 'taken care of'." Devi used air quotes to emphasize what she thought of the phrase. "Alpha and Bravo teams have coordinated the clean-up, and it seems the Assembly are leaving us to it. Rumor has it they would prefer a peaceful transition but—"

"That ain't happening," Vee finished for her.

Devi smiled and then shook her head. "We still don't know the identity of the goddess the pey demons mentioned."

"How many goddesses of creation and life are there?" Vee asked wryly. She had her mind on one particular goddess, but it seems blasphemous to even mention her name out loud in conjunction with such an accusation.

Devi nodded, her face dark with worry. "I've reached the same conclusion. Which is why I have a suggestion, a way for us to identify her once and for all."

Raj raised his eyebrows, and Vee saw Mac frown. The two men shared a glance of concern, but neither said a word.

Vee cleared her throat. "We'll do with me what you wish. We need to know for sure, or I'll be dodging killers every day."

Raj cleared his throat appearing of the mind to change the subject. "You've had messages from Rossi, Monroe, Brent, and a Doctor Feldman. I counted sixteen."

"Did you guys not tell them what happened to me?"

Devi shook her head. "We messaged saying you were taken ill, but we didn't give them any further details. They are probably messaging to wish you well. It's not a surprise they are concerned."

"More likely they are looking for answers," Vee said wryly. "Rossi will be easy, but Monroe might be a different story altogether."

Devi cleared her throat, then glanced at Mac and then at Raj. There was an odd expression in her eyes and Vee had to suppress a grin. She'd had an image of her mother as a queen of a great kingdom living in a lap of luxury, with a harem of handsome, intelligent men at her beck and call. The ultimate reverse harem story.

Vee schooled her features and straightened as a knock on the door opened a floodgate of visitors. Syama entered bearing a box of chocolates and what looked like bath bombs. Akil held a fat bouquet of helium balloons. And Nivaan entered with a bouquet of flowers in one hand and a squirming kid in the other.

"Sorry," he said as he twisted his niece around and secured her on his hip with one hand. "I'm babysitter today." He leaned over and kissed Vee hard on the lips, not caring in the least that both her dads were watching him.

When Nivaan straightened, he passed Sona over to Syama who grabbed the child and swung her around in the air, eliciting a chorus of high-pitched giggles from her. Vee shook her head. Apparently, a lot happened when a person was unconscious.

The door opened again, and a few new faces appeared with Syama calling out informal intros to some of the guild agents. Though they all appeared in good spirits, Vee could see the underlying worry in their eyes.

With her hospital room filled with people, she realized that whatever happened she was surrounded by people who loved her.

The only person missing was Radhima.

"I'm right here, dear," the old woman said from the other side of the bed. Today she wore a cerise peasant top, a long denim skirt, and a pair of brown leather cowboy boots.

"Snazzy, Ma," Vee murmured under her breath.

"Nice pink top, Ma," whispered Raj as he grinned over at the ghost.

Two voices hissed at him. "It's cerise!"

CHAPTER 44

Lord Agni strode into the large boardroom. His heart was heavy at having to perform a task which Vishnu would do with such ease.

The members of the council shuffled around as they greeted each other and took their seats. Two places were significantly empty.

That of Lord Shiva, whose absence was still deeply painful. And that of Lord Vishnu, whose disappearance was going to damage the solidarity he'd fashioned from this eclectic team of gods.

When Agni took Lord Vishnu's position at the head of the table, he heard the rumble of confusion and discontent among the gods.

"What's going on, brother Agni. Where is Lord Vishnu?"

Agni swallowed and took the seat, feeling the fire well up inside him, fueled by worry and grief and uncertainty.

He cast a glance around the room, ensuring that when he reached one particular set of eyes that he didn't flinch, didn't give any indication of his suspicions.

Agni cleared his throat. "I am afraid I have bad news, brothers, and sisters. I sit here today in the position rightfully belonging to my brother Vishnu. He left instructions a while ago that should he be incapacitated in any way, that I take over the reins for him." Agni waved a hand at Hanuman. "With the help of a handful of other gods that he elected. I am not solely responsible here and neither would I want to be, as this is a burden for one much stronger than I."

The gods spoke soft assurances that he was underestimating his abilities and Agni nodded his thanks before clearing his throat.

"Now, our first issue on the agenda is to find out what happened to Vishnu. Brother Hanuman and I spoke to him not two nights ago. And even then, he had expressed concerns that there was one amongst us that sought to divide us, who wished to cause dissent among our family."

All eyes remained on Agni as he stared around the room. Vishnu had singled out Parvathi, but oddly the mother goddess did not display any form of guilt or concern that she may have been found out. Agni filed that observation away, wondering if it meant something important.

Then he cleared his throat. "In addition, we have heard from various sources including the Guild of the Apsaras that there was an attempted uprising within one of the sub-cults of the Demon Horde. The pey demons, under the governance of Queen Ishanie, broke away and attempted to establish their own assembly in order to challenge the Demon Horde Assembly over territorial rights to New York. We are still unclear on the details, but as far as we know, Ishanie and her enclave have all been destroyed."

Agni glanced over the faces who all stared at him, expressions ranging from shock to distaste. Parvathi's expression reflected those of the other gods at the meeting. Again, Agni made a note that her reaction didn't match that of a guilty party. Either that or Parvathi was an accomplished liar. Something he didn't want to believe.

"What is our next move," Hanuman asked leaning forward.

"We ought to gather an army, build a defense against the next uprising. Because I can guarantee there will be one. Everything Vishnu warned us of has come to pass. Our main aim is to control the Horde, to ensure they do not break the final chains that hold them at bay."

"How long before that happens?" asked Yama, his brows furrowed. "I am doing all I can to bolster the gate from my end, but they've managed to overthrow Naraka already. I am of the mind to retreat in order to save my people. But I will not do that. If you think we can hold them back long enough…just until He returns…"

Agni nodded. "Vishnu was certain. He did everything in his power to ensure it, going to extents which I did not believe we were even capable of."

"What does that mean?" asked Kali. "What extents?"

Agni smiled. "Nothing bad. It is just that Vishnu visited the human plane, lived there for a time in order to infiltrate, to uncover information, to help those he believed would be of help to us."

Kali nodded, her expression determined. Agni was certain that after this board meeting he would be receiving a visit from the goddess. She had that look on her face that said she wasn't done, but she was happy to wait.

Agni looked at the faces of the gods around the table. "In our brother's absence, we must continue his work. I know we have all had our doubts that He still watches over us—or even that He will return to us—but it is time we stood together. The dangers multiply in untold powers if we ignore Vishnu's words."

"Did you know that Vishnu has been speaking with Him?" asked Parvathi, her voice ringing out across the room, eyes flashing.

Agni shook his head then sighed. "I suspect we all believed that to be the case. He knew too much. But I am glad for it. He was our conduit to our Lord. Now, I am uncertain as to how we will survive being totally away from Him."

Hanuman got to his feet, then placed his weapon on the table in front of him. The rounded head of the weapon gleamed, shedding a golden glow onto the many faces that watched him. "You have my weapons, my might, and my heart. I will do anything that it takes."

One by one the gods rose and presented their weapons. And Agni watched them smiling. At last, they were joining together to work as one. He stared at the weapons on the table from Yama's sword to Surya's gleaming scythe to Parvathi's fragile red lotus, and he felt a surge of power run through him, and he believed now.

The gods were ascending.

~ TO BE CONTINUED ~

***The APSARA CHRONICLES will continue with* DOMINION FALLING**

FREE STARTER LIBRARY - JOIN MY NEWSLETTER

Get the following titles FREE when you subscribe to my newsletter.

Tee's Newsletter

http://smarturl.it/TeesMailingList

ABOUT THE AUTHOR

I have been a writer from the time I was old enough to recognize that reading was a doorway into my imagination. Poetry was my first foray into the art of the written word. Books were my best friends, my escape, my haven. I am essentially a recluse but this part of my personality is impossible to practice given I have two teenage daughters, who are actually my friends, my tea-makers, my confidantes… I am blessed with a husband who has left me for golf. It's a fair trade as I have left him for writing. We are both passionate supporters of each other's loves – it works wonderfully…

My heart is currently broken in two. One half resides in South Africa where my old roots still remain, and my heart still longs for the endless beaches and the smell of moist soil after a summer downpour. My love for Ma Afrika will never fade. The other half of me has been transplanted to the Land of the Long White Cloud. The land of the Taniwha, beautiful Maraes, and volcanoes. The land of green, pure beauty that truly inspires. And because I am so torn between these two lands – I shall forever remain cross-eyed.

Stalk Tee here:

www.tgayer.com

tee@tgayer.com

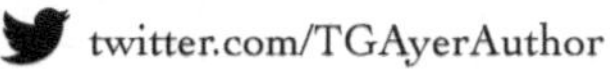

www.ingramcontent.com/pod-product-compliance
Lightning Source LLC
Chambersburg PA
CBHW020946120726
47905CB00008B/2705

* 9 7 8 0 9 9 5 1 1 2 6 3 6 *